CRUEL WINTER
OF THE
MOUNTAIN MAN

**Look for these exciting Western series
from bestselling authors
William W. Johnstone and J.A. Johnstone**

The Mountain Man

Luke Jensen: Bounty Hunter

Brannigan's Land

The Jensen Brand

Preacher and MacCallister

The Red Ryan Westerns

Perley Gates

Have Brides, Will Travel

Guns of the Vigilantes

Shotgun Johnny

The Chuckwagon Trail

The Jackals

The Slash and Pecos Westerns

The Texas Moonshiners

Stoneface Finnegan Westerns

Ben Savage: Saloon Ranger

The Buck Trammel Westerns

The Death and Texas Westerns

The Hunter Buchanon Westerns

Tinhorn

Will Tanner, U.S. Deputy Marshal

CRUEL WINTER
OF THE
MOUNTAIN MAN

WILLIAM W.
JOHNSTONE
AND J.A. JOHNSTONE

PINNACLE BOOKS
Kensington Publishing Corp.
www.kensingtonbooks.com

First printing: December 2022

ISBN-13: 978-0-7860-4894-6
ISBN-13: 978-0-7860-4895-3 (eBook)

10 9 8 7 6 5 4 3 2 1

Printed in the United States of America

CHAPTER 1

Smoke Jensen was riding into a trap. He knew it. He could have gone back the way he came from, but that would have meant turning his back on trouble.

Smoke wasn't in the habit of doing that.

So he reined in, pausing atop a slight rise for a moment to reach behind him and get the sheepskin jacket that was rolled up and lashed behind the saddle. He unrolled the jacket and shrugged into it. Nothing unusual about that, since the air had a definite chill to it today.

But the brief delay gave him a chance to look over the layout in front of him without seeming like he suspected anything was wrong.

Ahead of him, the terrain sloped gently down to a broad, level stretch of mostly sandy ground dotted with clumps of hardy grass and the occasional scrubby mesquite tree. Typical for the Texas Panhandle.

To the left of that open ground rose a rocky ridge that ran for several hundred yards, looking like the spiky backbone of some giant creature mostly buried in the earth.

To the right, the land fell away in a sweep of rugged badlands dominated by red sandstone upthrusts and riven by gullies. It was picturesque, a smaller version of the more impressive Palo Duro Canyon a good ways south of here.

Smoke had been there several years earlier, visiting the famous rancher Charles Goodnight.

Out here in the middle of nowhere, border lines didn't mean much. Smoke was pretty sure he had crossed from New Mexico Territory into Texas earlier that day, but he couldn't have said exactly where.

All he knew was that he was headed for the town of Salt Lick, and if he kept going in this direction, he ought to find it.

Assuming he escaped the trap he was riding into, he reminded himself.

He wondered just who had laid that trap. As far as he knew, he didn't have any enemies in these parts, but like it or not, given the adventurous life he had led, hombres who wanted his scalp could pop up almost anywhere.

That could literally be true in this case. Although the back of the Comanche resistance had been broken with their defeat at the Battle of Palo Duro Canyon several years earlier, along with the destruction of their horse herd in that same clash, small bands of warriors had been able to find enough mounts that they were still waging a sporadic war against the white settlers. They raided isolated ranches and preyed on lone pilgrims traveling across the Staked Plains.

Smoke didn't know if the men waiting up ahead for him were red or white, and he didn't care. They were in his way and might try to stop him. That was all that mattered.

He clucked to the big gray stallion and nudged it into motion with his knees. He'd been stopped for less than a minute to get the jacket out and put it on, but that had been plenty of time for him to take in the scene.

A few minutes earlier, his keen eyes had picked up something that most men would have missed: a tendril of gray smoke rising against the gray sky, which he now knew had been coming from that ridge to the north even though it had disappeared.

When he had topped the little rise where he had paused, he had seen a thin haze of dust settling to the right, just in front of those badlands. That had been enough to tell him immediately what had happened.

Somebody who had made camp on that ridge had spotted him approaching. Quickly, they had put out the fire, unaware that he'd already noticed the smoke. Some of them had galloped across the flat and hurried into those breaks to the south.

Had all of them abandoned the camp and fled into the badlands? Were they just trying to get away?

Smoke had no way of knowing. But his gut told him that the group had split up, some remaining hidden on the ridge, the rest taking cover in the rugged terrain to the south. That was an ambush in the making. Smoke trusted his instincts.

He also knew he was being a little foolish, riding right into a trap this way. They might outnumber him fifty to one. He had battled some pretty high odds before and come out alive and triumphant, but maybe not any quite that overwhelming.

Pretending he had no idea he was being watched, he rode forward, descending the gentle slope and starting out onto the flat.

How far would they allow him to go? He had to get far enough away from the rise behind him that he couldn't whirl his mount around, race back up there, and go to ground in a defensive position. They would want him out in the open, with nowhere to run.

Smoke obliged them, riding steadily until the rise was at least half a mile behind him.

That was when the two groups finally broke from cover, three of them coming down the ridge at such a reckless pace that their ponies' hooves slipped and slid on the rocky slope, four more surging up from one of the gullies at the edge of the badlands. They raced toward him, yipping and howling, Comanche warriors bent on at least a small measure of revenge on the hated whites who had usurped them as lords of the plains.

Smoke reined in sharply and hauled his Winchester from its saddle scabbard. Gunfire already boomed from the on-rushing raiders to his right. Powder smoke spurted from rifle barrels.

The bullets were falling short, though. The Comanche warriors were shooting from galloping ponies and aiming too low. It would have been a miracle if any of their bullets had found the target.

Smoke didn't intend to make that same mistake.

The gray stallion was accustomed to the racket of a gun battle and the sharp tang of powder smoke. He stood still as Smoke considered the distance and wind and drew a bead on one of the men racing toward him from the badlands. They were a little closer than the ones coming from the ridge, so they were a more immediate threat. Smoke elevated the rifle's barrel a little more and settled the Winchester's sights where he wanted them, then he stroked the trigger.

The rifle cracked and kicked against his shoulder. A split second later, he saw the man he had aimed at fling his arms wide and go backward off his mount as if he'd been swatted off the running pony by a giant hand.

The other three warriors slowed a little, clearly surprised that one of their little band had been shot at such a range.

They kept coming on, though, which brought them even closer. Smoke shifted his aim and fired again. One of the remaining three jerked, swayed, and would have toppled off his pony if the man riding beside him hadn't reached out quickly and caught hold of his arm.

The shrill yips didn't sound quite as enthusiastic now as the two unwounded warriors swung in a wide turn and headed back toward the badlands, taking the wounded man with them.

That left the three who'd been hidden on the ridge. They were still charging toward Smoke. He twisted in the saddle and aimed the Winchester. One of the Comanche peeled off before Smoke even pressed the trigger, unwilling to ride right into the face of that deadly accurate fire. The other two came on stubbornly.

The Winchester cracked again. Smoke's shot was off the mark, but only slightly. It struck one of the ponies instead of the rider, and judging by the way the animal went down, its front legs collapsing underneath it, the bullet killed the pony instantly.

The warrior flew over the pony's head, crashed to the ground, rolled over several times, and then lay still.

Smoke worked the rifle's lever. It looked like the one man still attacking him wasn't going to give up. That warrior was close now, bending forward over his pony's neck, using the animal for cover as he fired at Smoke with a handgun. Smoke wasn't too surprised the man was using a Colt. The Indians had picked up plenty of revolvers during raids, and some of them had gotten pretty good with the irons.

This one was good enough that one of the slugs creased Smoke's stallion, burning along the big horse's hip. No matter how well-trained a horse was, it was going to react to a sudden, sharp pain like that. The stallion let out a shrill whinny and reared up on its hind legs. Smoke stayed in the saddle, but he wasn't able to fire any more shots before the attacking warrior reached him.

The two horses almost collided. The Comanche skillfully veered his mount aside at the last instant and leaped from the pony's back as he flashed past Smoke. The warrior's shoulder rammed into Smoke's chest and drove him off the stallion. Both men plunged to the ground and landed hard.

The impact knocked the breath out of Smoke and jolted the rifle from his hand. He rolled over and came up on a knee, bracing himself with his left hand on the ground while he tried to drag air back into his lungs.

A few yards away, the Comanche warrior looked equally shaken as he pushed himself up from the ground. He was young, Smoke saw. Probably hadn't seen more than twenty summers yet.

But that didn't make him any less dangerous. He had dropped the gun, but with a savage cry he jerked a knife from a loop at the waist of his buckskin trousers and flung himself at Smoke. The knife flashed up and then down.

Smoke surged to his feet and caught the warrior's knife wrist as the blade descended. Smoke's powerful arm and shoulder muscles stopped that potential killing stroke before it could land.

At the same time, he hooked his right fist into the warrior's midsection with such force that the man doubled over with a pained grunt. Smoke's left hand clamped shut hard enough to make the bones in the warrior's right wrist grind together. A quick twist forced him to drop the knife.

Smoke tugged down and at the same time brought up his right knee. It smashed into the Indian's face with bone-shattering power. Blood spurted from the warrior's flattened nose. When Smoke let go of him and stepped back, the Comanche collapsed. Crimson worms crawled from his eyes and ears, too.

He wouldn't be getting up again, Smoke knew. The blow to the face had fractured his skull and probably driven shards of bone up into his brain, killing him.

Smoke felt a twinge of regret that one so young had to die simply because he couldn't let go of the hate he felt.

Most of the older warriors had realized by now that they couldn't win in the long run, and they had gone to the reservations over in Indian Territory.

It was only these young firebrands who still ran wild, causing innocent folks on both sides to die.

Smoke's hat had flown off when the warrior tackled him. He looked around now, spotted the gray Stetson lying on the ground, and picked it up.

Before he could put it on his head, another war cry rang over the plains.

Smoke dropped the hat and turned swiftly to see another young Comanche warrior rushing toward him on foot and brandishing a tomahawk. This had to be the one whose horse he had shot out from under him, Smoke realized. The fall had knocked him out momentarily, but now he had recovered enough to continue the attack.

Smoke ducked under the tomahawk as it slashed at his head. He got a shoulder in the warrior's belly, grabbed him around the thighs, and heaved him up and over. The young man let out a startled cry as he found himself wheeling through the air. That yell was cut short as he landed hard on his back.

Smoke had already pivoted around. The warrior had managed to hang on to the tomahawk, but a well-aimed kick from Smoke sent it flying away.

Smoke stepped back as his hand dropped to the holster on his right hip. The Colt that rested there had stayed in its holster, despite all the ruckus. He palmed out the gun as the Comanche rolled over and started to scramble to his feet.

The metallic ratcheting sound as Smoke eared back the Colt's hammer made the young man freeze.

"I don't particularly want to kill you, son," Smoke said, "but I will if I have to. Why don't you take your friend's pony and light a shuck on out of here?"

He didn't know if the warrior spoke English, but he thought he saw understanding in the young man's eyes . . . along with burning hate. For a second, Smoke thought the Comanche was going to charge him again, but then the man started backing off.

"That's right," Smoke told him. "Go home, or better yet, go join the others at the reservation. I know it's not what you're used to, or what you want, but it's better than dying, isn't it?"

The thing of it was, if Smoke had been in this young man's position, he wasn't sure how he would have answered that question. Some things *were* worse than dying, and some things were worth risking your life for.

But not today, apparently. The warrior turned abruptly and ran to the pony that stood a few yards away. He grabbed the rope hackamore, vaulted onto the pony's back, and jerked it around. With a strident shout directed at Smoke, he kicked the pony into a run and galloped back toward the ridge where he and his friends had lurked to start with.

Smoke understood some of the Comanche tongue, but he couldn't make out the words the young warrior had yelled at him. He was pretty sure it wasn't anything complimentary, though.

He waited until the warrior vanished over the ridge; then, with a rueful smile, he slid the Colt back into leather.

This time when he picked up his hat, he was able to put it on without being interrupted. He found the Winchester he had dropped, checked to make sure the barrel wasn't fouled, and replaced the cartridges he had fired before snugging it back in the saddle boot.

With that taken care of, he examined the stallion's wound. The hide was red and sore-looking where the bullet had burned, but the injury hadn't bled much. Smoke took a can of medicinal ointment from one of his saddlebags and daubed some of the black, smelly stuff on the wound.

"Sorry, old son," Smoke said when the stallion tossed his head. "This'll help it heal up."

Once that was tended to and the medication put away, Smoke scanned the landscape around him. It wasn't beyond the realm of possibility that the warriors who had survived could double back and launch another attack on him.

He didn't think it was likely, though. They had already lost two out of the seven members of their party, and another was wounded; Smoke didn't know how badly. But Indians, more than most, considered the potential risk versus the potential reward when deciding whether or not to attack. After what had happened, they probably considered Smoke too big a chunk to bite off again.

Sure enough, he saw no signs of them. He swung up into the saddle and heeled the stallion into motion again. With any luck, he would reach Salt Lick today.

He hoped the man he was going to see would still be alive when he got there.

CHAPTER 2

Big Rock, Colorado, one week earlier

"So there I was, surrounded by twenty of the mangiest, surliest, bloodthirstiest gun-wolves you'd ever hope to see . . . or hope *not* to see, I reckon I ought to say . . . and ever' one of 'em filled his hand at the same time. Them guns made such a racket when they went off that it was like a thunderstorm there in that saloon, and the bullets was flyin' around me so close I couldn't even blink without one o' those slugs cuttin' off an eyelash."

"Good Lord! How'd you ever survive such a thing as that, Pearlie?"

"I didn't. Those varmints shot me plumb to doll rags. There wasn't a piece o' me left that was big enough to bother buryin'."

Wes "Pearlie" Fontaine sipped his coffee and leaned back in his chair with a big grin on his rugged face.

Calvin Woods stared at his best friend in confusion for a moment, then scowled.

"You were just funnin' me," he accused. "You made up the whole blamed thing. I thought you were gonna tell me you shot your way out of there, like . . . like Smoke would've!"

"Smoke might've done something like that, all right,"

Pearlie allowed. "I'm a fair hand with a gun, I won't deny it, but when Smoke goes to shootin', sometimes it seems plumb supernatural-like."

Both men were sitting at a table in Louis Longmont's restaurant and saloon, one of the best places to eat and certainly the best place to drink in Big Rock. At another table in the rear of the room, their employer, Smoke Jensen, sat with his wife Sally and Louis Longmont himself, the gambler and former gunman who owned this establishment.

Pearlie was the foreman on the Sugarloaf, the Jensen ranch located seven miles west of the settlement. A man who had made his living by hiring out his gun, a few years earlier he had found himself on the wrong side of a clash with Smoke. It hadn't taken Pearlie long to realize that he was on the wrong side in more ways than one. He had thrown in with Smoke to help defeat that threat to peace in this beautiful valley, and they had been staunch friends ever since.

Cal had come along a few years later, just a kid, and, as he freely admitted now, a pretty dumb one at that. Broke, starving, and desperate, he had tried to rob Sally Jensen. It had been a stroke of luck for Cal that he hadn't wound up dead. It was even more fortunate for him that Sally had extended her sympathy to him and gotten him a job on the Sugarloaf.

Given the opportunity, Cal had turned into a top hand and was second only to Pearlie among the Sugarloaf crew these days. Pearlie had let it be known that he was already preparing Cal to take over as foreman one of these days . . . although that would still be a long time in the future.

They had ridden into Big Rock with Smoke this morning, the three of them following the buckboard being driven by Sally. At the moment, the buckboard was parked in front of Goldstein's Mercantile, where the supplies Sally had ordered would be loaded as soon as they were ready.

In the meantime, Smoke and Sally had walked up the street to Longmont's to get some coffee and visit with their friend. Cal and Pearlie had headed for the Brown Dirt Cowboy Saloon, which most of the punchers in the area patronized when they were in town. The Brown Dirt Cowboy wasn't fancy, but the beer was cold.

Today, however, when they got there, they found the place closed. That was almost unheard of. Emmett Brown, the owner, wasn't the sort of man to pass up any chance to make a profit.

A man passing by in the street had noticed the two cowboys from the Sugarloaf standing in front of the saloon, looking confused. He had chuckled and said, "I reckon you boys haven't heard."

"Heard what?" Pearlie asked. Then, with a look of alarm on his face, he added, "Ol' Brown ain't closed the place down for good, has he?"

"No, no," the townsman replied. "There was a big brawl in there last night. Place got busted up so bad that Emmett decided to just go ahead and close while repairs are being done. The carpenters are supposed to get started later today, from what I've heard."

"Well, that's a relief, I suppose."

Cal said, "I don't know that I'd care that much, one way or the other. Longmont's is a lot nicer place."

"That's just it. Longmont's *is* nice, so a fella's got to be on his best behavior there. Even proper, respectable ladies like Miss Sally go there. Sometimes you want to go somewhere you can just cut loose your wolf, you know what I mean?"

"I suppose. But I'm not an old lobo like you, Pearlie."

That had put a grin on Pearlie's face. He clapped a hand on Cal's shoulder and said, "Come on. We'll go get some of that Cajun coffee Louis serves."

Now as they sat in Longmont's, where Pearlie had spun

the yarn about being cornered by twenty of his enemies at once, both men were sort of glad the Brown Dirt Cowboy had been closed. This was nice.

Which meant, Pearlie reflected later, that something—or some*body*—was bound to come along and ruin it.

Sally was laughing at something Longmont had said, when the double front doors swung open and three men walked in. Most of the customers didn't pay any attention to them, since folks came in and went out of Longmont's all the time and, at first glance, there was nothing unusual about these three.

Smoke sat up a little straighter in his chair, though, and Louis did the same thing. The instincts of both men, honed to sharp edges by the dangerous lives they'd led, had warned them that the newcomers might be trouble on the hoof.

Then Louis muttered something in French under his breath and added, "My apologies, Sally. I forgot momentarily that you speak the language."

"That's all right, Louis," she said. "I assume something must be wrong, or you wouldn't have reacted like that."

"You know those fellas?" Smoke drawled.

Louis nodded. "One of them. And the other two appear to be cut from the same cloth."

One of the men was slightly ahead of the other two. He was whipcord lean, with a hawkish face, dark eyes, and a narrow mustache. His gaze reached across the room and landed on Louis. He stiffened, and even though a tiny smile tugged at the corners of the mouth, the expression didn't reach his eyes or do anything to relieve the grim cast of his face.

He started toward the table where Smoke, Sally, and Louis sat. The other two were close behind him.

"Sally, honey," Smoke said, "why don't you go sit with Pearlie and Cal?"

She didn't move. "If there's a chance of trouble, don't you think it'll be less likely to break out if I stay? I mean, nobody's going to start anything with a woman sitting here, right?"

Louis said, "Normally, I might agree with you, Sally, but in this case, I concur with Smoke. I'd very much appreciate it if you'd move over there."

Sally looked back and forth between her husband and their friend and then said, "All right." She got to her feet and, without hurrying, walked over to the table where Pearlie and Cal sat.

The two cowboys stood up hurriedly but respectfully, and Cal held one of the empty chairs for Sally as she sat down. Pearlie leaned forward and said something to her. Smoke figured he was asking her what it was all about. Sally's eloquent shrug was all the answer she could give.

The three men came to a stop not far from the table where Smoke and Louis sat. Louis regarded the leader coolly and said, "Hello, Stockard."

"Longmont," the man returned, his tone equally chilly. "I'll wager you never thought you'd see me again."

"To be honest, I never even gave the question any thought." The words held a not-so-subtle undertone of contempt.

The eyes of the man called Stockard cut over to Smoke for a second. "Who's your friend?"

"You got that right," Smoke said. "Just a friend. Nobody important."

Stockard's lips curled in a sneer under the mustache. "Then you should stand up and move away from here . . . *friend*. Carefully. My business is with Longmont, nobody else."

"I don't believe we actually have any business," Louis said.

"Damn right we do. I'm here to talk about the way you ran out on me up in the Dakota Territory, eight years ago."

"No one ran out on you," Louis responded sharply. "It was your own choice to turn back. You knew Crowder's men weren't far behind us and you might be caught."

The sneer on Stockard's face turned into a snarl. "I had to turn back. I had to go back for Jill. Wouldn't you have risked getting caught for a woman you loved?"

"First of all, that woman was married and wanted nothing to do with you. *You* were the one obsessed with *her*. She'd made it plain she wanted you to leave her alone."

Stockard slashed the air with his left hand. "That was just an act! She just wanted to get me more interested. You know how women are."

"Indeed, I do," Longmont murmured. "That's why I've never had to force myself on one. After word got around of what happened with Jill, you didn't have a friend west of the Mississippi, Stockard. No one cared whether or not Crowder's men strung you up." His shoulders, elegant in the expensive suit coat, rose and fell slightly. "I certainly didn't, when I heard that's what took place. That's why, as I said, I never bothered thinking about you again."

"They came close to hanging me," Stockard rasped. "I reckon plenty hoped that they had. But not quite. You're wrong, Longmont. I still had a few friends. They helped me get away at the last minute. We lit out for California, and that's where I've been ever since."

Longmont sighed. "Why couldn't you have stayed there?"

"Because it's been eating away at me, gnawing on my insides, the way you betrayed me. We rode together, Longmont. You should have sided me."

"We took money from the same employer and the job was over. That's all. We were never partners."

"Maybe not." Stockard moved his coat back a little on the

right side, exposing the walnut butt of the holstered Colt he wore on that hip. "But I still have a score to settle with you."

The hubbub of talk and laughter inside the restaurant and saloon had died away gradually as more and more people took notice of the confrontation at the table in the rear corner. Now a tense silence hung over the whole room.

One of Longmont's regular bartenders, a man called Poke, dropped his right hand out of sight behind the bar. Smoke knew there was a sawed-off shotgun on a shelf under there. Smoke caught Poke's eye and gave a tiny shake of his head. The bartender didn't need to cut loose with that gut-shredder. Too many innocent folks might get in the way of the buckshot if he did.

"You know," Smoke said, "holding a grudge like that is bad for your health, mister. It sours the stomach and angrifies the blood. Makes a man prone to apoplexy."

Stockard didn't take his eyes off Longmont as he growled, "Are you still here, you damned fool?"

"Yeah, I'm here." Smoke's voice hardened. "And you should know, if you push this much farther, I'll have to kill those two hombres you brought along with you, while Louis is busy killing you."

For the first time, one of the other men spoke. "Just who the hell do you think you are, mister?"

"Name's Jensen."

"Smoke Jensen," Louis added.

Each of the men with Stockard took a step back.

"Jensen," one of them repeated nervously. "You never said nothin' about any damned Smoke Jensen, Stockard."

"What does it matter?" Stockard snapped. "There are two of you, aren't there?"

"Yeah," the other man said, "but he's Smoke Jensen. I heard tell that he killed twenty men in one fight up in Idaho a while back!"

"If I'm remembering right, it was only nineteen," Smoke said. He paused, then added, "Details like that tend to slip a man's mind after a while."

"Don't listen to him," Stockard said. "He's just trying to spook you!"

"Forget it, Stockard," the second man said. "We're out."

"I paid you—"

"Not enough."

The two men looked at each other, angled their heads toward the doors, and then turned and headed in that direction, their spurs jingling in the silence as they crossed the room.

Stockard glanced briefly after them, then returned his hate-filled glare to Louis Longmont.

"Let those filthy cowards run out on me," he said. "That doesn't make any difference. Just like when *you* ran out on me, Longmont. You were a filthy coward, too."

Longmont rose slowly to his feet. "I'll not be talked to like that in my own establishment," he said. "Nor anywhere else, for that matter. I hoped to avoid this, but you leave me no choice."

"What about you, Jensen?" Stockard snapped. "Are you taking cards in this hand?"

"This is Louis's game," Smoke said. "I wouldn't think about horning in."

"All right, then. I guess we'll just—"

Stockard's hand flashed to his gun. If he'd hoped to take Longmont by surprise by making his move in mid-sentence like that, he was sadly disappointed. Longmont's gun came out of its holster in a blur.

Stockard was fairly fast, but no match for Louis Longmont. He cleared leather, but his gun hadn't come level when Longmont's Colt roared. Flame lanced from the barrel. Stockard rocked back, put his left hand to his chest, and struggled to raise his arm so he could get one shot off, at least.

At that moment, the doors crashed open and the two men who had come with Stockard to Big Rock charged through the entrance with guns in their fists. They opened fire on the table in the back corner of the room.

Smoke rose smoothly to his feet. He had drawn his Colt too swiftly for the eye to follow. The gun appeared in his hand as if by magic. It blasted twice, both slugs pounding into the chest of the attacker on the left, who went over backward.

Longmont turned slightly and triggered his gun. The bullet ripped into the other man and turned him half around. His legs got tangled with each other and he lost his balance, falling onto a table where a poker game had been going on. Cards, chips, and money flew wildly in the air as the table legs gave way and collapsed under the impact.

Stockard finally fired while Louis was distracted. Louis took a step back as the bullet struck him, but he stayed on his feet, swung his Colt back toward Stockard, and slammed another bullet into the vengeful gunman.

Smoke threw a shot at Stockard at the same time. The two reports came so close together that they sounded like one. Stockard went down, his gun slipping from nerveless fingers. His bloody chest rose and fell several times, raggedly, and then stilled forever.

"How bad are you hit?" Smoke said to Louis.

The gambler was a little pale but composed. He opened his coat and vest and looked at the bloodstain spreading on the left side of his white shirt.

"I've cut myself worse shaving," he said dismissively.

Smoke grinned. He looked over at the other table and saw that Pearlie and Cal were both on their feet, guns in hands if needed, standing so that their bodies completely shielded Sally. Either of them would have gladly taken a bullet for her.

"You'd better sit down," Smoke said to Louis. "I know you're not hurt bad, but you're bleeding. You might get dizzy."

Longmont made a scoffing sound at that, but he lowered himself onto one of the chairs.

"Somebody go fetch the doc," Smoke said to the room at large as he walked over to the two men who had tried to launch a sneak attack. He kicked their fallen guns out of reach before checking to make sure both were dead. They were.

From where he was sitting, Longmont said, "They thought they would make their try while you were distracted by Stockard's fight with me. If they succeeded, they would have been known far and wide as the men who killed Smoke Jensen." Louis let out a contemptuous snort. "That mistake cost them their lives." He made a face. "Stockard never would have winged me if I hadn't been busy shooting one of those other scoundrels."

"That was the last bit of luck he had, though," Smoke said, "or ever will again."

Several of the customers hurried out of the saloon. Smoke figured at least one of them would run down the street to the doctor's office. The others were probably looking for friends so they could boast about witnessing the shootout in Longmont's.

A man coming in from the boardwalk outside had to wait until the rush let up. He holstered the gun he held in his right hand. An envelope of some sort was in his left. A badge pinned to his vest showed under the lapel of his coat.

With his now-free right hand, the newcomer thumbed back his hat and shook his head as he looked at the trio of sprawled, bloody bodies.

"When I heard shooting, I figured you'd be mixed up in this, Smoke," Sheriff Monte Carson said. "I saw you and Sally coming in here earlier."

Smoke chuckled. "Don't blame me for this one, Monte. This was one of Louis's old enemies who decided to look him up and say howdy with a bullet. I was just sort of along for the ride, you might say."

"Louis, are you all right?" Monte asked with a worried frown. "You look a mite peaked, the way you're just sitting there like that."

"I'm fine. It's just a crease."

"Doctor should be on his way by now," Smoke added.

"All right, then. Since everything appears to be under control, I reckon I'll go ahead and give you this."

Monte held out the envelope.

"What is it?" Smoke asked.

"Letter for you. I happened to be in the post office a few minutes ago, and when I said something about seeing you come into town, the postmaster asked me to tell you he had a special delivery for you and that you should come by to pick it up. Since I knew where you were, I offered to bring it to you." Monte smiled. "Special delivery, just like the man said."

Sally came over to join them as Smoke opened the envelope and took out a folded sheet of paper. He unfolded the paper, read the words printed on it in a blocky hand, and the look that appeared on his face prompted Sally to ask with a worried frown, "What is it, Smoke?"

"News from an old friend," he said. "And it's not good."

CHAPTER 3

The letter came from Salt Lick, Texas, Smoke explained a few minutes later as he and Sally sat again at Louis's usual table. Pearlie, Cal, and Monte Carson had joined them. The doctor had arrived and gone into Louis's office with the gambler to see about patching up that wound.

Tom Nunnley, who did double duty in Big Rock as the undertaker as well as owning one of the hardware stores, had already been and gone with his wagon and a couple of assistants. By now, Stockard and his two allies, names as yet unknown, reposed in the back room of Nunnley's undertaking parlor . . . the room with the drain built into the floor so it could be washed easily with buckets of water.

"Seems like maybe I've heard of Salt Lick," Pearlie said, "but I couldn't tell you right where it is."

"And Texas is a mighty big place," Cal put in. The two cowboys had been to the Lone Star State several times with Smoke on Sugarloaf business. "When we went to that big ol' ranch down there in far South Texas, it seemed like it took forever and a day to get there."

Smoke smiled at that comment and said, "Salt Lick is all the way up at the other end of the state from Captain King's ranch. It's in the Panhandle, not far from the border with

New Mexico Territory on the west and Indian Territory on the north. In other words, it's a lot closer to us here in Colorado than it is to most other places in Texas."

"You say that letter's from the fella who's the marshal there?" Monte asked.

"The former marshal, Jonas Madigan. He says he's retired and has taken off the badge. Passed it on to somebody else. That's the problem."

"How do you figure that?"

"Because Jonas is the sort of man who doesn't have any quit in him," Smoke said. "I thought he'd wear that badge until he crossed the divide, and even then he'd probably want to be buried with it pinned on him."

Monte shrugged and said, "Sometimes when a man gets older, he gets tired. Even if he loves what he's doing and it's what he always wanted to do, he just doesn't have it in him anymore. Or maybe he wants to keep going but his body won't let him."

Smoke nodded. "Jonas admits that he's been feeling poorly. That's not at all like him, either. I never knew him to complain." Smoke tapped a fingertip on the sheet of paper lying on the table in front of him. "For him to write a letter like this, asking me to come and see him, he must be in pretty bad shape."

"Like he wants to see you one more time while he's still around," Pearlie suggested.

"Exactly."

Sally said, "I recognize Marshal Madigan's name because I know you've traded a few letters with him over the years, Smoke, but I had no idea the two of you were close. You've never talked much about him."

"It was a long time ago that I met him," Smoke said. "Before you and I knew each other."

A solemn look came over Smoke's face as his thoughts

went back to those days. It had been a hard time in his life. His father was dead, murdered by evil men, and he had believed that his brother Luke and his old friend Preacher had been sent over the divide by those same greedy, gold-lusting double-crossers. He had lost his first wife and their child, or rather, had them taken away from him by killers. It had seemed like everything that could go wrong in the life of one Kirby "Smoke" Jensen was bound and determined to do so, and there wasn't a blasted thing he could do to stop it.

Sally knew more about those days than anyone else at the table. She and Smoke had met toward the end of that violent period in his life. But he hadn't told even her everything that had gone on then.

He'd talked about it some with Pearlie and Louis and Monte but hadn't spilled the whole story to them, either. It had been a busy time in Smoke's life. Busy . . . and bloody . . . and heart-breaking . . .

Smoke pushed those memories out of his thoughts. The present had its roots in the past, of course, but nothing that had happened back then could be changed. The smart man kept his eyes on the here and now.

So when Sally asked him, "What are you going to do about this letter, Smoke?" he didn't hesitate in giving his answer.

"I'll take a ride down to Salt Lick and pay Jonas a visit," he said. "That's what he wants, even if he's too blasted proud and stubborn to come right out and say why. It won't take but about a week to get there, and I reckon you can spare me at the ranch right now."

"You want some company, Smoke?" Pearlie and Cal asked in unison, as if they'd practiced it. Then they glared at each other across the table.

"Don't go hornin' in, youngster," Pearlie said.

"I've got just as much right to go along with Smoke as you do," Cal said.

Smoke laughed. "Neither of you are going. With winter coming on, there's still a lot of work to do around the ranch. I'll be counting on my two top hands to take care of everything that needs to be done, as well as any new problems that might come up."

"What about me?" Sally asked.

Smoke shook his head. "I'll need to travel fast and light. I looked up Salt Lick on the map, back when Jonas first took the marshal's job there. As I recall, there's no railroad, no telegraph office. Just a stagecoach that runs up from Amarillo once a week. I can make better time by riding down through Raton Pass and then cutting southeast from there."

"I'll be worried about you, traveling alone like that."

"No offense, Sally," Monte said, "but you *are* talking about Smoke Jensen. If there's anybody in this world who can take care of himself out on the plains, it's Smoke."

"Oh, I know that." She turned to Smoke. "But won't you get lonely?"

"Sure, I will," he admitted. "I always get lonely when I'm away from home. But I feel like I owe it to Jonas to pay him one last visit, if I can get there in time."

While they were talking, Louis Longmont emerged from his office, followed by the doctor, who was closing his black medical bag. Louis's tie was undone and his vest was unbuttoned, but other than that, he was his usual dapper self, despite getting shot a short time earlier. The right side of his shirt bulged a little from the bandage the doctor had placed there.

"Jonas?" Louis repeated, having overheard the tail end

of the conversation. "Are you talking about Jonas Madigan, Smoke?"

"That's right," Smoke said. "Do you know him, too?"

Louis laughed and said, "We've met. He put me in jail one time, up in Montana."

"Jail!" Sally exclaimed. "For gambling?"

"Suspicion of murder," Louis said blandly. "Madigan was a U.S. deputy marshal at the time and had it in his head that I was a regulator. He thought I was working for one of the local cattle barons and had shot and killed some settlers from ambush."

Smoke said, "I never heard about that. They must've found you not guilty."

"Oh, it never came to trial. I had a pretty good idea who was really responsible for those killings, and after I talked it over with Madigan, he rounded up the men who were behind the trouble. They confessed in hopes of avoiding the gallows." Louis shook his head. "Unfortunately for them, that didn't work. But it got me out from behind bars."

He pulled out a chair and winced a little. The effort must have pained him slightly. The doctor said, "I'll come by later and change the dressing on that wound, Louis. You'll be fine, just don't get in any more fandangos until you heal up."

"I'll make every effort," Longmont promised. "I'm a peaceable man these days."

"Yeah, I keep saying the same thing," Smoke put in dryly. "We've all seen how that works out."

Louis asked, "Now, what's this about Jonas Madigan?"

Smoke showed Louis the letter and explained the situation. Louis nodded and said, "You're going down to Texas, of course?"

"Figured I would."

"I'd offer to come with you, but I'm afraid our friend the doctor would veto that idea."

"I've already had some volunteers," Smoke said, "but I reckon I'll take this little *pasear* by myself."

"A ride of several hundred miles is hardly a little *pasear*. And although I hate to say it, if you're right about Madigan being ill, there's a chance he will have passed on before you can get there."

"I know it," Smoke said. "That's why I'm not going to waste any time. I'll ride out today . . . and hope that Jonas is still alive when I reach Salt Lick."

CHAPTER 4

Salt Lick, Texas

The sky was cloudless but seemed to be a deeper blue than usual. Even though the wind blew from the south, the air was cool enough that it had a bite to it.

The wind wasn't the only thing that blew in from the south. Two strangers rode into town from that direction. One of them kept glancing at the sky and saying something under his breath.

"What's that you keep mutterin' about, Rome?" the other man asked. He sounded annoyed.

"I don't like it, that's all," the man called Rome answered. "There's a change in the weather comin'."

"Well, when you stop and think about it, there's *always* a change in the weather comin', ain't there? I mean, it don't stay the same all the time. It's just that sometimes it takes longer for the change to get here."

"That ain't what I meant, and you know it, Atkins."

"Well, it's what you *said.*"

"Just shut up," Rome snapped. "We came here to have a look around, not to argue about the damn weather."

Atkins nodded ahead of them. "Well, then, take a look."

To be honest, there wasn't that much to see. Salt Lick

wasn't a big town. Maybe three hundred souls lived here. The main street was three blocks long and lined with the sort of businesses you'd expect to find in a settlement that was the supply center for the ranches, big and small, in the area: a couple of general mercantiles, a hardware store, a greengrocer's, a blacksmith with an adjoining saddle shop.

Salt Lick also boasted a doctor's office, two lawyers (and that was two too many, in the opinion of some folks), a weekly newspaper, and even a ladies' millinery, because there were women in town and some ranch wives and daughters who wanted a nice new dress now and then without having to go all the way to Amarillo for it.

Salt Lick also had four saloons, more than any other sort of establishment, because cowboys could be counted on to ride into town every payday and blow their wages. To help with that, in addition to the saloons, there were a couple of houses on the northernmost side street that burned red lamps in their windows at night.

By way of contrast, on the southernmost side street were two churches, Baptist and Methodist, and a Catholic mission, as well as the schoolhouse. The town cemetery was at the far eastern end of that street, with a wrought iron fence around it and two cottonwood trees that the caretaker nursed through the frigid winters and blazing summers.

The most impressive building in Salt Lick, though, was the two-story, redbrick bank. It even had a clock tower that was taller than either of the church steeples.

"Would you look at that," Atkins said softly as he and his companion rode past the bank.

"I'm lookin', I'm lookin'," Rome said. He lifted a hand and dragged the back of it across his mouth. "But what I could really use is a drink."

Atkins pointed ahead of them, on the other side of the

street. "There's a saloon right up yonder. And it's top-notch. The sign says so."

Indeed it did. APPLE JACK'S TOP NOTCH SALOON, the sign nailed to the awning over the boardwalk announced. Atkins and Rome turned their horses in that direction.

They swung down from the saddles, tied the horses to the hitch rail in front of the saloon, and had just stepped up onto the boardwalk when one of the double doors leading into the saloon opened from the inside. The weather was cool enough today that the batwings were fastened back and the doors closed. A young man stepped out, almost running into the newcomers.

Everybody stopped where they were. The young man looked the strangers up and down with a thoroughness that bordered on insulting. Atkins and Rome stood there and took it, though.

Because there was a badge pinned to the man's shirt under his coat, and they didn't want any trouble.

"You fellas are new in town, aren't you?" Marshal Ted Cardwell asked. He hooked his thumbs in his gunbelt so his right hand wouldn't be far from the Colt on his right hip . . . and, to be honest, because he liked the way that stance looked as he stood there rocking slightly back and forth on the balls of his feet.

The man on Cardwell's right was stocky and barrel-chested, with a lock of lank, fair hair falling over his forehead from under his battered, thumbed-back hat. The man on the left was slimmer and taller, with dark hair and a nervous look on a face that reminded the local lawman of a rabbit. Both were dressed in range clothes that weren't exactly ragged but showed plenty of wear. Their horses and saddles were nothing special, either.

And neither were the holsters they wore or the guns that rode in those holsters. Nothing fancy, just functional.

The stocky, fair-haired stranger summoned up a grin. "We're brand-new, in fact, Marshal," he said. "Just rode into town not three minutes ago. I'm Sid Atkins, and my partner here is Bart Rome. You wouldn't happen to know of any ridin' jobs around here, would you?"

"Cowboys on the drift, are you?"

"Yes, sir, that's us." As if he sensed what Cardwell was about to say, Atkins went on, "Oh, we know it ain't a good time of year to be lookin' for work. Most spreads have already pared down their crews for the winter. Fact of the matter is, that's what happened to us. We were ridin' for an outfit down south of here, but since we were the last to sign on, we got let go first."

"What outfit would that be?" Cardwell asked. "And how far south?"

"Triple J, down around Lubbock."

Cardwell nodded. He had heard, vaguely, of the Triple J. He didn't have any reason to disbelieve what Atkins was telling him, but he'd made it a habit not to take any stranger's story at face value. A good lawman was suspicious of everyone if he didn't know for a fact that they were harmless.

"You're looking for work, but you have enough money for a drink?"

"Well, you know how it is, Marshal. Got to save back a little for necessities."

Cardwell looked at Bart Rome. "Don't you have anything to say for yourself?"

Rome leaned his head toward the other man. "Sid's said it all, I reckon."

Cardwell reached a decision. He jerked a thumb over his shoulder and said, "All right, go on in. And to answer your question, no, I don't know of any spreads around here that are hiring. So you don't have any reason to stay in Salt Lick for very long. You understand what I'm saying?"

"Sure do, Marshal," Atkins said with a nod. "We'll have that drink, let our horses rest for a spell, and then move on later today."

"That'd be best," Cardwell said, returning the nod. With his thumbs still hooked in his gunbelt, he turned and headed east along the boardwalk, not looking back to see what the two saddle tramps did next. In the past, he had overheard a few people whispering about how he had a swagger in his walk, but he preferred to think of it as a firm, confident stride.

Just the sort of walk a good lawman ought to have.

"I know what you're thinkin'," Atkins said quietly to Rome, "but we can't afford to plug no badge-toter in the back, no matter how big a stuffed shirt he is."

Rome blew out his breath in a disgusted sound. "You're right, you're right," he admitted. "Let's go on in and get that drink, before I forget why we're here."

Atkins opened the door and went in first. Out of habit, he looked around, checking for any potential threats.

He didn't see any. Apple Jack's Top-Notch Saloon looked just like hundreds, maybe thousands, of other saloons in small cowtowns. The hardwood bar was to the right, ten or twelve tables to the left. A piano against the back wall, and a pot-bellied stove tucked in a rear corner. Wagon wheel chandeliers hung from the ceiling. Atkins didn't see any roulette wheels or other gambling equipment. Poker and blackjack would be the order of the day in a place like this.

In fact, a poker game was going on at one of the tables. Four men sat around it, looking at the cards in their hands. Three looked like cowboys; the fourth had a bushy black beard and a wild thatch of black hair. He wore a canvas apron with numerous scorched spots on it over a rough work shirt with the sleeves rolled up to reveal hairy forearms thick with muscle. He would be the local blacksmith, Atkins decided.

Three more men stood at the bar nursing mugs of beer. There weren't any other customers in the place at this time of day.

The man behind the bar was big, but most of his size appeared to run to fat. He wore a white shirt with sleeve garters, a black vest with gold brocade on it, and a red string tie. Curly hair topped a face as red and round as an apple, and Atkins had a hunch he knew how the man had gotten his nickname.

The bartender waved a hand with fingers as thick and blunt as sausages. "Come on, boys, belly on up to the bar," he called in a high-pitched voice to the newcomers. "Welcome to Salt Lick! First drink's on the house."

Atkins and Rome stepped up to the bar. Atkins gave the other drinkers a friendly nod. Rome ignored them, as usual.

"Beer for us, thanks," Atkins told the bartender. "It's been a long, dusty trail, so we're much obliged to you."

"Always happy to see new folks in town. This here is Apple Jack's, and I'm Apple Jack." He filled two mugs from a tap and placed them in front of Atkins and Rome. "What brings you fellas to Salt Lick?"

Atkins took a swallow of the beer and licked foam from his upper lip. "Lookin' for work."

Apple Jack pursed his lips and shook his head. "Bad time of year for it."

"Yeah, that's what your marshal said when we talked to him outside."

"You met Marshal Cardwell, did you?" The jovial tone went out of Apple Jack's voice, and his deep-set eyes got more solemn. It didn't seem he was all that fond of the local law.

"That's right. But just in passing."

"I reckon he told you to keep on passin'. Passin' through, that is."

"Well, he might have mentioned something like that," Atkins allowed.

"Ted Cardwell doesn't care much for strangers, which, seein' as he's responsible for keepin' the peace, I reckon I can understand." Apple Jack grinned, making his cheeks even rosier. "But everybody was a stranger when he first got where he is, wasn't he? Unless, I suppose, he was born there."

One of the other men at the bar said, "Jack, you just don't like the marshal runnin' off potential customers."

"Well, I sure can't make a livin' off you fellas who take three hours to drink a single beer!"

"That there's a full house!" the blacksmith at the poker table rumbled as he slapped his cards down and claimed a pot.

Atkins said, "I wouldn't think you'd have much trouble here, a sleepy little settlement like this."

"Oh, don't let Salt Lick fool ya," Apple Jack said. "It can get busy around here, especially durin' round-up time and on paydays. Lots of folks in town then. They come in from all the ranches hereabouts."

"And money in the bank, I expect, if it's payday. Got to have that before all those wages can wind up in your till, am I right, Apple Jack?"

That prompted a booming laugh from the bartender. "That's my best day of the month, for sure!"

"Bart and me been driftin' for a while, so we've kind of lost track of what day it is. It ain't the first of the month, is it?"

"Shoot, no. If it was, there's be a whole bunch more folks in here. That's not for another five days."

"Well, it's too bad we won't see it. I don't reckon your Marshal Cardwell would want us hangin' around for that long."

Rome spoke up for the first time in a while, saying, "I thought the marshal here was an hombre named Madigan."

Apple Jack's head bobbed up and down. "Yes, sir, Jonas Madigan used to be our law. One of the finest men you'd ever want to meet."

"Something happen to him?" Atkins asked.

Apple Jack lowered his voice a little as he said, "He took sick a while back. Had to retire. Plumb shame, too. I don't think he was ready to hang it up, but he just wasn't in good enough shape to keep up with the job. Ted Cardwell was his deputy, so he got the marshal's badge. I reckon he'll grow into the job."

The saloonkeeper didn't sound entirely convinced of that statement, however.

"Who replaced Cardwell as deputy?"

"Nobody, yet. Town council says the marshal can handle things by himself for now, and they'll see about hirin' a deputy later."

Atkins and Rome had been sipping their beers while they talked. Now Atkins picked up his mug and drained what was left in it. Rome followed suit. They pushed the empties across the bar and Atkins said, "We'll have another round." He grinned and added, "Wouldn't really be fittin' to have a drink on the house and not buy at least one more, now would it?"

Apple Jack glanced at the other drinkers and said, "I wish more people thought like you, friend."

Atkins didn't want to push his luck, so he stopped talking about the local law and money in the bank and made idle conversation about the ranches in the area, instead, while he and Rome drank that second beer. The other men at the bar were friendly enough and provided the names of several spreads and owners, while echoing what the strangers had been told already, that nobody in these parts was hiring right now.

"Well, it's good to know what's around here, anyway," Atkins commented. "Who knows, Bart and me might drift back through here someday, when things are lookin' up a mite."

They stopped after the second beer. Atkins slid a silver dollar across the bar to Apple Jack, who said, "You got some change comin'."

"Keep it," Atkins told him. "We got our money's worth in pleasant conversation, didn't we, Bart?"

Rome just grunted. He didn't speak until they had left the saloon and were outside again, with the doors closed.

"I reckon we got our money's worth, all right," he said. "And we'll be back, no doubt about that."

Atkins stroked his fingertips over his chin, frowned in thought, and said, "Maybe sooner than you think."

Rome glanced at him. "What do you mean?"

"I mean, I'm not sure we ought to wait for the others. We can hit that bank tonight, just you and me, and be well over the line in New Mexico by mornin'."

Rome's eyes widened. "You mean double-cross the rest of the bunch . . . and *him?*" He shook his head. "Anyway, it's not payday yet. There ought to be more money coming in later."

"Yeah, but however much is in there, it'd be divided two ways, instead of split up a whole heap more."

"I don't know . . ."

"Just think about it, Bart, that's all I'm askin' you."

"All right, I don't suppose it would hurt anything to do that."

"That's the spirit. Now, let's mount up and move on.

That little pissant of a lawman's liable to be lurkin' around somewhere watchin' us, and we might as well let him think he's got us buffaloed." Atkins chuckled. "He'll find out how wrong he is, soon enough, I reckon."

They turned their horses and rode out of town, heading back south, the direction they had come from.

Because of that, neither of them noticed the man riding into Salt Lick from the north.

CHAPTER 5

Smoke had never been in Salt Lick, but Jonas Madigan had described the settlement in his letters. So Smoke knew he was in the right place, even before he saw the gilt letters on the front window of a small building that read SALT LICK TRIBUNE. That would be the newspaper office, Smoke mused.

Might be as good a place as any to find the information he needed, he decided. He reined the stallion over to the hitch rail in front of the building and dismounted.

The front half of the room had a couple of desks in it, with nobody sitting at them. The printing press was in the back half of the room, behind a short wooden railing with a gate in it. There were also a couple of composing tables back there, shelves holding various pieces of equipment, and several waist-high cabinets that Smoke knew would contain trays of type.

The press made a clattering racket as a man in an ink-smeared canvas apron operated it. A boy who looked to be about twelve years old picked up one of the sheets that came off it, being careful to hold the paper by the edges so he wouldn't smear the freshly printed ink.

"Looks good, Pa," the boy called over the noise of the printing press. He had as deep a voice as Smoke had ever heard coming out of a youngster's mouth, sort of a cross between a bullfrog's croak and a foghorn.

The boy set the sheet aside, hitched up his trousers, and plucked a half-smoked cigar from an ashtray sitting atop one of the cabinets. He puffed on the cigar like an experienced smoker.

"Blast it, Ralph," the man said. "Get that stogie out of your mouth. Your ma will kick my hind end to Fort Worth and back if she catches you smoking."

"Ma ain't comin' in here and you know it." Ralph had brown hair and freckles on his pugnacious face. "She hates the sound of the press and the smell o' ink. Good thing we don't, ain't it?"

"Isn't it," the man corrected halfheartedly, as if he knew it wouldn't do any good, the same way he'd sounded when he told the boy to stop smoking the cigar. He inclined his head toward the front of the room and went on, "Anyway, we've got a customer. You don't want to make a bad impression."

Ralph glanced at Smoke and said, "Oh. Sorry." He set the cigar back in the ashtray and strode over to the railing. He thrust his hand out and went on, "Put 'er there, mister. Welcome to the *Salt Lick Tribune*."

"Howdy," Smoke said as he shook hands with the boy. For a second, given the cigar, Ralph's deep voice, and his general demeanor, Smoke wondered if he was actually dealing with a little fella like Preacher's old friend Audie, the former professor who had survived a hazardous life as a mountain man for many, many years, despite being only three feet tall.

No, Ralph was an actual child, Smoke decided, just an unusual one.

"What can we do you for?" Ralph went on, as if he ran

the business here. He sounded hopeful as he added, "Need to take out an ad?"

"No, I'm afraid not," Smoke said. "But I'm looking for someone, and when I saw your office, I figured a newspaper would be a good place to ask."

"We're in the business of chargin' folks to tell 'em what they want to know."

The printing press had fallen silent. The man who had been operating it walked toward the railing as he wiped his ink-stained hands on a rag.

"Don't be so mercenary, Ralph," he said. "There are other things in life besides making money."

"Yeah, things that waste your time when you could be turnin' a profit," Ralph responded.

The man held out his hand to Smoke. "Edward Warren," he introduced himself. "It's a pleasure to meet you."

"Likewise," Smoke said as he clasped the man's hand. "I'm Smoke Jensen."

While Warren and Smoke were introducing themselves, Ralph had turned discreetly and reached back to sneak the cigar out of the ashtray. He had just put it in his mouth and taken a puff on it when Smoke said his name. Ralph's jaw dropped, and the cigar fell to the floor at his feet. The way he gaped at Smoke showed that he had completely forgotten about the stogie.

"Smoke Jensen!" he exclaimed after a few seconds of stunned silence. "*The* Smoke Jensen?"

Warren turned to look curiously at his son. "You've heard of Mr. Jensen, Ralph?"

"Heard of him? Shucks, Pa, *everybody's* heard of Smoke Jensen! There's not a more famous gunfighter anywhere on the frontier!"

"Well, I don't know about that, son," Smoke said with a smile.

Warren frowned. "You're not looking for trouble, are you, Mr. Jensen?"

Smoke held up both hands, palms out. "No, sir. Just information, like I said. Do you happen to know Jonas Madigan? Used to be the marshal here in Salt Lick?"

The newspaperman's frown became more one of confusion than worry. "Marshal Madigan? Of course, I know him. Everybody in Salt Lick does." He caught his breath. "Wait a minute. You haven't come here to *shoot* Marshal Madigan, have you?"

"Shucks, Pa!" Ralph said, his voice booming like a bass drum. "Smoke Jensen ain't the sort of gunfighter who goes around shootin' lawmen. He just shoots bank robbers and rustlers and owlhoots like that."

"I don't plan on shooting anybody," Smoke said. "Jonas is an old friend of mine, and I'm just here to pay him a visit, that's all."

Warren blew out a relieved breath. "Oh. That's all right, I suppose. A good thing, actually. A visit from an old friend might lift his spirits. In case you haven't heard, he's been doing rather . . . poorly."

Smoke nodded and said, "Yes, I know. I had a letter from him, up in Colorado where I live, and although he didn't go into detail, he mentioned that his health wasn't good and he'd like to see me again." Smoke paused, then added, "He *is* still alive?"

"As far as I know. And I think I would have heard if there had been any bad news."

"He's at home?"

"That's right. And before you ask, I'll be happy to tell you where to find it. When you leave here, go on to the corner and turn left onto Crosby Avenue. The marshal's home will be the eighth house on your right, close to the edge of town."

Smoke nodded. "I'm obliged to you, Mr. Warren. It's good to meet you. And you, too, Ralph. You might want to take a look down at the floor, though. That stogie's leaving a burned spot."

"Oh, shoot!" Ralph yelped as he bent over quickly to pick up the cigar. The front door of the newspaper office opened as he straightened, and when he looked in that direction, his eyes widened in alarm. His father snatched the cigar butt away from him and stuck it in his mouth.

Smoke glanced over his shoulder and saw a young, pretty woman with upswept blond hair entering the office.

"Howdy, Ma," Ralph said. "I, uh, I didn't expect to see you here."

She smiled, but then her expression turned frosty when she looked at her husband. "Edward, I thought we talked about you smoking around Ralph. It's a bad influence on him. If you keep doing it, he might want to pick up the filthy habit himself someday."

Warren took the cigar out of his mouth and stubbed it out in the ashtray as he said, "Yes, of course, you're right, Evelyn. We were just busy getting the paper out, and I forgot what I was doing. Old habits, you know. They sometimes come back without you even realizing."

"Well, it's your job to realize such things where our son is concerned."

Smoke figured it was time for him to withdraw from this situation, so he nodded to Warren and Ralph, said, "Thanks for the information, fellas," and pinched the brim of his hat to Mrs. Warren as he went by. "Ma'am."

He heard Evelyn Warren saying something else as he closed the door, but he couldn't make it out. He grinned as he went to his horse. Seemed like Edward Warren had his hands full with both his wife and his son.

Smoke continued looking around Salt Lick as he rode toward the next intersection. He noticed the bank on the corner to his right. Up ahead on the left, two doors past the intersection, was a sturdy-looking building with a sign hanging from the awning out front that read MARSHAL'S OFFICE. A man stood on the boardwalk in front of the office door, his back straight and his thumbs hooked in his gunbelt.

The man's head swiveled toward Smoke. He stiffened even more. He turned and strode toward the intersection, lifting his left hand as he did so.

"Hold it right there, mister," he called.

Smoke didn't care for the man's tone. For a second, he was tempted to just ignore the command and keep riding.

Then, with a sigh, he pulled back gently on the stallion's reins and turned the horse toward the man who had hailed him. He had spotted the afternoon sun reflecting off the badge pinned to the man's shirt.

This would be the hombre who had replaced Jonas Madigan as Salt Lick's marshal.

Smoke brought the stallion to a stop in front of a hitch rail. The lawman stood on the boardwalk on the other side of the rail, giving Smoke an intent stare.

"Something I can do for you, Marshal?"

"This seems to be Salt Lick's day for visitors."

Smoke didn't know what that meant, but he didn't care enough to ask.

"You can start by telling me who you are and what you're doing here," the marshal said.

He rubbed Smoke the wrong way just enough to be annoying. Smoke said, "What I'm doing is riding down a public street. As for who I am, I'm not sure you've got any call to be asking that."

The marshal's face darkened with anger. "An attitude like that is enough to get you thrown behind bars, mister," he snapped. "I would've just run you out of town, like those last two saddle tramps, but if you want to get mouthy about it, I'll be glad to oblige."

The man was young, probably not even thirty yet, and clearly full of himself, puffed up by the badge he wore. Smoke would have enjoyed sticking a pin in him and letting out some of that hot air, but he didn't want to take the time and trouble. Also, he usually cooperated with representatives of the law . . . when they would let him.

"Take it easy, Marshal," he said. "I meant no offense. It's just that I'm on my way to visit a sick friend, and I'd like to go ahead and get there."

"What sick friend?"

"Jonas Madigan." Smoke nodded toward the badge on the marshal's chest. "The man who used to pack that star."

The marshal glared. "You look like a gunman to me. If you've got a score to settle with Marshal Madigan and heard that he was sick, you'll have to go through me first."

Well, that was an admirable attitude, Smoke thought, even though the marshal was still a stiff-necked pain in the rear end. He shook his head and said, "No settling scores. Jonas and I are old friends, and that's the truth. You can come along to his house with me just to make sure, if you want to." Smoke paused. "By the way, since you asked me, my name is Smoke Jensen."

A woman passing by on the boardwalk on the other side of the street stopped and called across, "Excuse me, sir. Did I just hear you say that your name is Jensen?"

Smoke looked around as she stepped down from the low boardwalk and started toward them. She was middle-aged, wearing a brown dress and hat, and was still rather attractive. The thick, dark brown hair under the hat had a few strands of gray in it, and a few wrinkles were visible on her face, but overall, those things just gave her character instead of detracting from her looks.

The marshal held up his left hand toward her and said, "Now, Mrs. Dollinger, you'd better stay back. This saddle tramp might be dangerous—"

"If his name is Smoke Jensen, he's no saddle tramp," the woman said crisply. "In fact, he's one of the most successful ranchers in Colorado, and he's a well-known adventurer and pistoleer. More importantly, he's one of Jonas's friends!"

"I tried to tell you, Marshal," Smoke drawled.

The young lawman looked both angry and embarrassed. He said, "He could be lying about who he is—"

"I don't think so. I've seen pictures of Smoke Jensen in the illustrated magazines, and I'm certain that's who this gentleman is."

Smoke swung down from the saddle and took off his hat. "Thank you for stepping in, ma'am," he said. "I didn't want to get off on the wrong foot with the marshal."

She held out a graceful, gloved hand. "I'm Mrs. Miriam Dollinger, Mr. Jensen."

"It's a pleasure and an honor, Mrs. Dollinger," Smoke said as he took her hand.

"I was just on my way to Jonas's house right now. Would you care to accompany me?"

"I'd like that just fine, ma'am."

Clearly bothered by being ignored, the marshal said, "Wait just a minute. I'm not finished with you, Jensen."

"I think you are, Ted," Mrs. Dollinger said. "I'm sorry. Marshal Cardwell, I meant to say."

Smoke saw the amusement in her eyes and had a hard time not grinning himself. She had slipped a barb into the stuffed-shirt lawman better than he could have. She offered Smoke her right arm, and he linked his left with it. They started along the street, with him leading the stallion.

"Just wait . . . I didn't . . ." Marshal Cardwell sputtered behind them. With a frustrated sigh, he gave up and called after them, "Just watch your step while you're in Salt Lick, Jensen!"

Smoke turned his head and threw back over his shoulder, "I'll do that, Marshal, thanks."

He and Mrs. Dollinger walked on. After they had gone a short distance, she said quietly, "Ted can be an absolute popinjay at times, but he's really not a bad sort once you get to know him, Mr. Jensen. He's awfully young for the responsibility that's been thrust upon him."

"Taking over for Jonas, you mean?"

"That's right." Her expression and demeanor grew more solemn. "Ted was a perfectly competent deputy, as long as he had Jonas telling him what to do. Once the decisions were his and his alone, I think he started to doubt himself. And in order to make up for that, he acts like he does."

"I expect Jonas left some mighty big footprints to follow."

"He certainly did. Salt Lick was quite a wild place at one time, you know. Jonas tamed it down until it's a fine place for decent folks to live."

"He was always good about things like that," Smoke agreed.

"This town owes him a great debt. More than we can ever repay, in fact, even if . . . if we had longer to do so."

The slight catch in her voice made Smoke look over at her. Her face was drawn with emotion now.

"How long does he have left?"

"Oh, I don't know. I'm not a doctor, Mr. Jensen, and even Dr. Stannard would admit that whatever he told you, it would only be a guess. But not long, surely." She hugged his arm a little tighter. "I'm glad you got here in time. I was hoping you would."

"You knew I was coming?"

"Jonas and I are friends, too. I knew he had written to you. In fact, I mailed the letter for him."

Smoke wondered briefly if there was still a Mr. Dollinger. For a moment, he thought he had heard something in the woman's voice that spoke of a deeper connection than mere friendship.

But that was none of his business, and just then Miriam Dollinger went on, "Here we are. This is Jonas's house."

CHAPTER 6

It was a neat little one-story cottage with a front porch on the left half facing the street. The walls were white-washed, and the trim was painted green. A wisteria grew in front of the porch, next to the steps. The branches twined around the posts holding up the porch roof. To the right was a redbud tree, and over the top of the house, Smoke saw several oaks growing in the back. All the trees were bare at this time of year, but he thought it would be a really pretty place in the summer.

Of course, by the next summer Jonas Madigan probably wouldn't be here anymore.

"The town provided the house, in addition to Jonas's salary," Mrs. Dollinger went on, breaking into that grim thought, "and when his health forced him to give up the marshal's job, the council voted unanimously not to take the house away from him."

"That was considerate of them, I reckon," Smoke said.

"Well"—and now a bleak note entered her voice as she unknowingly echoed Smoke's thought from a moment earlier—"no one expects him to need it for all that much longer."

Before they could go up the steps to the porch, a man

bustled around the corner of the house by the redbud and lifted an age-gnarled hand in greeting.

"Howdy there, Miz Dollinger," he said. "I was just checkin' on the supply o' firewood in the back. Looks like the marshal could use a mite more. I'll drop some off later in the day. Don't want to run outta wood for the stove, seein' as how we got a mighty chilly cold snap on the way."

"And how would you know that, Windy?" Mrs. Dollinger asked with a smile.

"'Cause these ol' bones o' mine tell me so! My knee and my hip and my elbow are all sayin' there's a heap o' cold weather comin', and some snow, too, more'n likely. They ain't never lied to me in all these years."

"Well, if you trust them, Windy, then so do I." She nodded toward Smoke and went on, "This is an old friend of Jonas's who has come to visit, Smoke Jensen. Mr. Jensen, this is George Whittaker, our local handyman."

"Smoke Jensen?" Whittaker repeated as his eyes widened. "Sure enough? I've heard the marshal talk about knowin' you, but I wasn't sure it was true."

"Plenty true," Smoke responded with a grin. He put out his hand. "I'm glad to meet you, Mr. Whittaker."

"Oh, tarnation, don't call me mister. Folks around here just call me Windy, on account of I talk a mite and like to tell stories." He pumped Smoke's hand. "It's a plumb honor to meet you, Mr. Jensen."

"Make it Smoke . . . Windy."

Smoke felt an instant liking for this old-timer. Windy Whittaker was a little below medium height. He would have been a little taller if his legs hadn't been so bowed from many years obviously spent in a saddle. His denim trousers were tucked into high-topped boots, and he wore a buckskin vest over an old flannel shirt with holes in the sleeves at the elbows. His hat had seen better days, too. A white beard bristled from his jaws, and the deep, permanent tan on his weathered face made him resemble a pecan with whiskers.

"You've been helping take care of Jonas?" Smoke went on.

Windy's head bobbed up and down. "That's right. He's always been good to me, so it's the least I can do. Now and again, I worked for him as a part-time jailer, back when he was still wearin' the marshal's badge."

"You don't help out Marshal Cardwell?"

Windy's forehead creased at that question. "You know Marshal Cardwell?"

"Mr. Jensen made his acquaintance a short time ago, while he was on his way here," Mrs. Dollinger said.

"Lemme guess. He tried to run you outta town."

"I believe the thought crossed his mind," Smoke allowed. "How did you know that?"

"Because he likes to run off any strangers who ride into Salt Lick. I reckon he's afraid they might start some trouble, so he tries to move 'em on before they get a chance to."

That was exactly how Smoke had sized up Marshal Ted Cardwell.

"I figure he'd try to run me out, too, if he thought he could get away with it," Windy continued. "He considers me just some shiftless ol' rapscallion."

"No one's ever going to run you out of town, Windy," Mrs. Dollinger assured him with a smile. "Why, rapscallion or not, you're as much of a fixture around here as the town well."

Smoke had spotted that well at the south end of town, with a waist-high stone wall around it and a wooden awning that had a windlass with a bucket attached to it. It looked like it had been there a long time . . . and so did Windy Whittaker.

"Maybe so, but that wet-behind-the-ears so-called marshal made it plumb clear that he wouldn't be needin' my help once he pinned on that badge." Windy sniffed. "I know when I ain't wanted. I ain't one to bull my way in."

"Well, Jonas wants and appreciates your help, and I do, too," Mrs. Dollinger told him. "You say you'll bring more firewood over later?"

Windy tugged at the brim of his old hat and said, "Yes'm, I sure will."

"Thank you." She smiled at Smoke. "We had better go on in. Jonas may have heard us talking, and he'll wonder who's out here."

"He can still hear that well?" Smoke asked.

"His eyes and ears are almost as good as they ever were." The woman's smile took on a sad tinge. "It's just the rest of his body that's betrayed him."

She and Smoke climbed the three steps to the porch. She opened the front door without knocking, displaying an easy familiarity that once again made Smoke wonder if there was something more than friendship between her and Jonas Madigan. The door opened directly into a parlor. Mrs. Dollinger paused and called, "Jonas, are you awake?"

"Dang right I am." The response came from an open doorway in a hall running toward the back of the house. "I heard two sets of footsteps coming in. Who's that with you?"

Mrs. Dollinger nodded to Smoke. He moved toward the open door and said, "Somebody who hasn't seen you for a long time, Marshal. Too long."

"Smoke—!"

"That's right," Smoke said as he took off his hat and stepped into a neatly kept, homey bedroom with curtains on the windows, a couple of woven rugs on the floor, a framed lithograph of what looked like the English country-side on the wall, a mahogany wardrobe, and a sturdy bed with a quilted bedspread folded back over the legs of the man sitting propped up with pillows against the headboard.

Even under these circumstances, it was evident that the man in the bed had once been a powerfully built hombre. His arms and shoulders and the rest of his bone structure were that of a big man.

But time and illness had wasted away a significant amount of the flesh on those bones and left his silvery hair thinning until there were only a few strands on top of his head. The face that lifted toward Smoke had a haggard look to it despite the surprised smile it wore. At the sight of his old friend, Smoke felt a pang of pity, but he immediately pushed it away.

Jonas Madigan had never been the sort of man who would want anybody to pity him.

"I hoped you'd come," Madigan said, "but I didn't know if my letter would get to you in time."

"It did, and I'm here," Smoke said. He stretched the truth a mite by adding, "I never doubted for a second that you'd be waiting for me, too."

"You never did, eh?"

"No, sir. I knew good and well you were always too blasted stubborn to go anywhere until you were damned well good and ready."

At those words, Smoke heard a soft gasp of surprise behind him from Mrs. Dollinger, but Madigan threw his head back and laughed, a sound hearty enough to belie the impression of weakness his appearance gave.

"By the Lord Harry, you're right about that," he said. He started to push the covers aside. "Let me get up out of this bed so I can shake your hand properly—"

Mrs. Dollinger moved past Smoke and said, "You'll do no such thing. You can shake hands perfectly well from where you are."

She put a hand on his shoulder to reinforce her words. Madigan grunted and sat back.

"No point in arguing with a woman, especially a pretty one. She's accustomed to getting her own way."

"I swear, Jonas, I don't know if you're trying to flatter me or insult me."

"I'll count that as a victory, then. A rare victory, I might add."

"You do go on, don't you?" she said as she patted his shoulder, the affectionate gesture belying the slightly scolding tone in her voice.

Yes, there was definitely *something* more than friendship between these two, Smoke decided.

Madigan lifted his right arm. Smoke stepped forward and clasped the former lawman's hand. Madigan's grip was a shadow of what it had once been, like the man's physical appearance.

"I'm afraid you've caught me when I'm feeling a mite poorly. Seems like that's most days, here lately. But then, I told you in my letter that things have changed." Madigan drew in a deep breath. The action caused him to wince a little, as if it pained him. "I've given up the badge, Smoke."

Smoke nodded and said, "I've met Marshal Cardwell."

"You have, eh? What'd you think of him?"

Smoke hesitated, remembering that Cardwell had served as deputy under Madigan. He didn't figure Madigan would have hired the young man if he didn't believe that Cardwell could do the job.

"Seems like a fine young man. Of course, he doesn't have a fraction of the experience that you do . . ."

Madigan waved a hand. "That'll come, that'll come. Ted's got a good head on his shoulders, and he can handle himself in a fight. Like you say, he just needs some experience and seasoning."

"I'm sure that's right. But I'm sure the folks here in Salt Lick miss having you as their marshal, too. From what I hear, you're mostly responsible for the town being a good place to live."

"Oh, no, that's giving me too much credit. A lot of folks made Salt Lick what it is today, like Miriam here and her husband, Frank. Frank, may the Lord rest his soul, was the mayor here when I first came to Salt Lick and pinned on the badge. He'd already taken some steps to tame the place down. Mighty good man, was Frank Dollinger. We miss him, don't we, Miriam?"

She sat beside him on the edge of the bed for a moment and said, "Yes, we certainly do. But he always praised you as highly as you praise him."

"We made a pretty good team, Frank and me," Madigan admitted.

Smoke had a better sense of things now. Miriam Dollinger was a widow, as he'd suspected. Jonas Madigan, himself a widower, although he had been married for only a short time as a young man before his wife died of a fever, had been a family friend. Smoke was sure that Madigan had been a comfort to Mrs. Dollinger when her husband passed on. A warm friendship had grown from that, as often happened in such circumstances. And then Madigan had gotten sick . . .

Smoke was glad the two of them had been there for each other.

"Well, don't just stand there, Smoke," Madigan said, breaking the brief moment of silence. "Pull up a chair and visit for a spell. You've ridden all this way, and we've got a heap of catching up to do."

"Are you sure you're not too tired for that, Jonas?" Mrs. Dollinger asked. "I imagine that Mr. Jensen plans to be in town for a few days . . ."

"That's right," Smoke said. "After that ride down here

from Colorado, my horse could use some rest. I'll see about a stall for him in the local livery, and then I can hunt a hotel room—"

"No, sir," Madigan interrupted. "You can stable your horse, but no hotel room. There's a spare bedroom right down the hall, so you'll stay here."

"I don't want to put anybody out," Smoke began.

"It's no bother at all," Mrs. Dollinger assured him. "There's always plenty of food."

"That's the truth!" Madigan said. "The ladies of this town keep me mighty well fed. Hardly a day goes by without one or two of 'em showing up with a covered dish of some sort. And the pies! Lord have mercy."

Smoke grinned. "All right, you've talked me into it. I'll go tend to my horse and then be back in a spell."

"You tell Rufus at the livery stable that you're my friend and you're staying here with me. He'll treat you right."

Smoke nodded his thanks and left the room. Mrs. Dollinger followed him out and went to the front porch with him.

"Your arrival certainly lifted his spirits, Mr. Jensen," she said quietly as they paused there. "Jonas has had a hard time of it. He's in a great deal of pain most of the time, although he does his very best not to show it, and he certainly doesn't like to complain."

"Can't the doctor give him something for that?"

"Yes, he can. In fact, he tried to. But Jonas won't take the medicine, not regularly, anyway. He says it makes him feel too fuzzy-headed, like he's not quite actually here. He'll only take it when he just can't stand the pain anymore."

"It's what they've started calling a cancer, isn't it?" Smoke asked.

Mrs. Dollinger nodded. Her jaw trembled, just for a second, but Smoke saw it. She said, "Yes. The doctor doesn't know exactly where it started, but he's convinced that it's spread quite a bit."

"And there's nothing he can do but try to keep Jonas comfortable."

"That's right. Some days are worse than others, but there aren't really any *good* days anymore."

"Maybe another doctor, somewhere else?" Although Smoke didn't live like a rich man, he was actually wealthy enough that he could afford to bring in medical experts from elsewhere, if there was any chance they might help Jonas Madigan.

"Our local doctor assures us there's nothing anyone can do. He offered to send for some other physicians he knows, but Jonas refused and said no one was going to that much trouble for him, especially when it wasn't going to do any good."

Smoke nodded slowly. That sounded like Madigan, all right.

"The way you saw him just now, that's actually the best he's been for a while," Mrs. Dollinger went on. "I honestly doubted that he would be able to hang on until you got here."

"Like I told him, Jonas is a stubborn old cuss."

She laughed softly. "Yes, he is. But stubbornness will only carry a person so far. Are you going to be able to stay in Salt Lick for a while, Mr. Jensen?"

"Yes, ma'am, I can stay as long as I need to."

"It won't be long," she said. "But it will be good for Jonas, having you here." She laid a hand lightly on his forearm. "I appreciate that, Mr. Jensen."

"It's the least I can do, after everything he did for me."

She tilted her head a little to the side. "What *did* he do, if you don't mind me asking? He's never really explained how the two of you came to know each other. I assume it had something to do with his career as a law officer."

"That's right, it did, but it's a pretty long story, and I'd like to get my horse inside at the stable, out of this chilly wind. And you should probably go back inside, too, ma'am."

"All right." She laughed quietly again. "Be mysterious about it. But I still want to hear about it later."

"As long as Jonas doesn't mind, I sure don't." Smoke put his hat on, nodded, and added, "I'll be back in a while."

"We'll be here," she told him.

CHAPTER 7

Smoke didn't bother mounting up. He led the gray stallion back to Salt Lick's main street and turned toward the livery stable he had noticed earlier. As he usually did when arriving at a new place, Smoke had taken a good look at the town when he rode in, before stopping at the SALT LICK TRIBUNE.

A loud, ringing sound came from the blacksmith shop next to the stable, the two businesses being built so that they were adjoining. Smoke recognized the racket as a hammer striking an anvil, so he headed for the open door of the smithy, figuring the same man probably operated both enterprises. He looped the stallion's reins around a hitch rail in front of the blacksmith shop.

Inside, a man wearing a thick canvas apron over his work clothes stood beside an anvil, hammering what looked like a plow blade into shape. He was big all over, broad as well as tall, and had bushy black hair and a prominent beard.

Despite the chilly day, it was warm inside the shop due to the fire in the forge. Smoke thumbed his hat back and said, "Howdy."

The blacksmith glanced at him. "Good day to you, mister." The hammer descended and struck its target with another loud clang. "What can I do for you?"

"Do you own the stable next door, too?"

"I surely do. Rufus Spencer is the name. Got a horse you need stabled?"

"That's right, Mr. Spencer."

The blacksmith lifted his voice and called, "Tommy!" The deep-voiced shout was almost enough to rattle the walls.

A door between the blacksmith shop and the livery stable opened. A slender youngster in overalls, flannel coat, and floppy-brimmed hat looked into the shop.

"Yeah, Pa?" the boy asked in a high, clear voice.

Spencer jerked a blunt thumb toward Smoke. "Gentleman here wants to stable his horse."

Tommy nodded and hurried into the shop, closing the door behind him. "I'll be happy to take care of you, mister," he said.

"Name's Jensen," Smoke introduced himself, leaving off his first name this time.

"Let's get your horse, Mr. Jensen. I'll take mighty good care of him, I promise you that."

When they went out to the hitch rack, Tommy reached for the gray's reins. Smoke said, "Maybe you should let me lead him in. He can be a mite feisty."

"I never met a horse I didn't get along with just fine, and I've been takin' care of them since I was knee-high to you, Mr. Jensen," Tommy assured him. "Anyway, I'll be tendin' to him, so him and me ought to start gettin' used to each other."

Smoke supposed that made sense, but he was ready to step in just in case the stallion started to act up.

However, somewhat to Smoke's surprise, the horse didn't give any trouble at all. In fact, when Tommy untied the reins, patted the stallion's flank, and said, "Come on, big fella, let's find you a nice stall," the horse nudged the youngster's shoulder in a friendly fashion. Tommy grinned as he led the stallion into the barn.

Smoke followed and looked on in approval as Tommy put the stallion in an empty stall, unsaddled him, forked in some fresh hay, and filled the water trough.

"What do you think?" Tommy asked when he had finished and closed the stall's gate. "Worth four bits a night for keeping him here?"

"More than worth it," Smoke said. He took a five-dollar gold piece from his pocket and handed it to the youngster. "That'll cover his bill for a while. I don't know how long I'll be in Salt Lick." He felt a moment of sadness as he thought that depended on how long Jonas Madigan hung on to life. "If I'm around for longer than that, I'll give you some more."

"That'll be fine." Tommy slipped the coin in the pocket of his overalls and then pointed to a good-looking chestnut gelding in one of the stalls on the other side of the barn's center aisle. "That's my horse. I call him Oscar."

"Appears to be a fine animal."

"Oh, he is." Tommy went to the stall and reached over the gate to scratch the horse's nose. "Aren't you, Oscar?"

Oscar bobbed his head as if nodding agreement. Tommy laughed and turned away, and as he did so, Oscar stretched out his neck, clamped his teeth on the brim of the boy's hat, and jerked it off his head.

Tommy exclaimed, "Hey!" and turned around to make a grab for the hat. "Gimme that, you tricky varmint."

Smoke stared. He prided himself on being observant, but he hadn't expected what happened when the mischievous horse plucked the hat from Tommy's head.

Two thick wings of raven hair had tumbled down around Tommy's shoulders. As they did so and prompted Smoke to take a closer look, he realized that Tommy wasn't a boy at all.

Tommy was a girl, or rather a young woman in her late teens, rather than the fourteen or fifteen-year-old boy Smoke had taken her for.

She got the hat away from Oscar and started tucking her hair under it again as she put it on. She must have noticed Smoke's surprised expression, because she asked, "Something the matter, Mr. Jensen?"

"No, I just didn't realize you were a girl," Smoke replied honestly.

"Haven't seen all that many girls in your life, eh?"

Smoke was a little annoyed by the flippant question, but only for a second. Then he saw the humor in the girl's eyes and had to laugh.

"I've seen plenty of girls," he told her, "but I haven't run into many called Tommy."

"It's short for Thomasina," she explained. "My mama named me and thought that was a pretty one."

"It is," Smoke agreed.

She finished tucking her hair under the hat and pushed it down tighter on her head.

"But she died when I was little, so my pa did most of the job of raisin' me," she went on. "He figured that he could make a young lady out of me, on account of that's how my mama would have wanted it . . . but it never really took." She shook her head. "I told him I wanted to help him run the livery stable, since I've always liked takin' care of horses, and he's got enough to do already, what with the blacksmith shop and his fondness for poker games up at the Top-Notch. It took some persuadin', but he came around to realizin' that it was a good idea."

"From what I've seen, that's true."

"And he's always called me Tommy, ever since I was little, so I never saw any reason to ask him to do otherwise."

"I suppose not," Smoke said.

As they walked out of the barn, Tommy asked, "What brings you to Salt Lick in the first place, Mr. Jensen? You don't look like the average sort of saddle tramp we get driftin' through here."

"I'm visiting an old friend. Marshal Jonas Madigan."

"Oh, I know Marshal Madigan. Reckon just about everybody in Salt Lick does. It's a real shame about him gettin' sick. He's not the marshal anymore—"

"Jensen!" a new voice barked from somewhere close by. "I thought I told you to watch your step while you're in my town."

Smoke looked over his shoulder and saw Marshal Ted Cardwell striding toward them. Cardwell had an angry frown on his face, and his back was stiff as a ramrod.

Smoke kept a tight rein on his own temper, turned toward Cardwell, and asked, "What makes you think I'm not watching my step, Marshal?"

Cardwell came to a stop in front of Smoke and Tommy. "For one thing, you're bothering a young girl."

"Mr. Jensen's not botherin' me the least little bit," Tommy said. "He made arrangements to stable his horse here while he's in town. I'm just takin' care of the livery stable's business. That's my job. And I'm not really all that young. Nineteen." She paused and then added significantly, "And you ought to know that about as well as anybody, Ted."

Cardwell drew in a sharp breath that caused his nostrils to flare. As his face reddened, he said, "There's no need to go into that—"

"No, I don't expect you to think there is."

"I just don't want strangers causing trouble for you," the marshal went on stubbornly.

"Well, he's not causing a bit of trouble, so you can put your mind at ease, I reckon."

"Fine," Cardwell snapped. He looked at Smoke again. "I thought you were going to Jonas Madigan's house with Mrs. Dollinger."

"Not that I actually owe you any explanations, Marshal, but I did go see Jonas. And I'm headed back there now. He's asked me to stay at his house while I'm in Salt Lick."

"The city actually owns that house—"

"Yeah, I know."

Cardwell opened and closed his mouth and looked like he wanted to say something else, but no matter how hard he cast his mind back and forth, he couldn't come up with anything. Finally, he just gave the girl a curt nod, said, "Tommy," and turned to walk away rigidly.

They watched him go. Smoke waited until Cardwell was out of earshot to ask, "Your beau?"

Tommy laughed. "He'd like to be, sure enough. I've danced with him some at the town socials, and he asked me on a picnic last summer. He got a little too fresh and I slapped his face for him, and that's the last time he came callin'. But I think he's tryin' to work up his courage to try again." She smiled a bit ruefully. "Ted's not a bad sort of fella, you understand. But I don't think we'd ever hit it off well enough to get married or anything like that." She looked closer at Smoke. "What are you frownin' about?"

"No offense, Tommy, but I'm trying to imagine you at a dance."

"I can dance," she responded, sounding a little indignant. "And I don't wear overalls and work boots to a town social. I may not be most folks' idea of a proper lady, but I *do* own some dresses, you know."

"I reckon I'd better stop digging before this hole gets

any deeper," Smoke said with a smile of his own. "Thanks, Tommy. I'll be by to check on my horse now and then."

"He'll be here and well taken care of," she promised.

"I don't doubt it for a second."

As Smoke walked past the open door of the blacksmith shop, he waved at Rufus Spencer, who gave him a friendly nod in return and called, "Tommy get everything taken care of?"

"That's right," Smoke told him. "I'm obliged to you, Mr. Spencer."

He walked on back to Jonas Madigan's house. When he got there, Miriam Dollinger was sitting in one of the rocking chairs on the front porch.

"Kind of chilly for porch sitting," Smoke commented. The woman wore her coat and had draped a shawl around her shoulders, as well. Smoke figured she must keep the shawl here for moments such as this.

"I know, but I wanted to catch you when you came back," she said as she motioned Smoke into the other wicker rocking chair. "Jonas has dozed off, and he can use all the rest he can get."

"Can he?" Smoke asked as he sat down.

"You mean, since he doesn't have all that much time left, why waste any of it sleeping?"

"Not exactly. A man's got to sleep. But there comes a day when all the time in the world doesn't really mean that much anymore."

Mrs. Dollinger nodded. "That's certainly true. I guess I like to see him sleeping because, well . . . that means that, for right now, anyway, he's not hurting as much as he was."

"I can see that," Smoke allowed. "And when you care about somebody, it's hard to see them in pain."

She looked over at him and asked, "Is it that obvious? That I . . . care . . . about Jonas?"

Smoke shrugged. "Nothing wrong with it, as far as I'm concerned. I think it's good that he has a friend."

They sat there quietly for a few moments, the only sound on the porch the soft creaking of the chairs as they rocked back and forth. From the main street came hoofbeats and the clatter of a wagon passing by. A dog barked somewhere, and a child shouted in play.

Mrs. Dollinger broke that near-silence by saying, "Why don't you tell me how you and Jonas met, Mr. Jensen? I'm sure it's an interesting story."

"I don't know about that," Smoke said. "It happened a long time ago."

"It couldn't have been that long. You're not that old."

"Maybe not in years, but I've traveled a lot of hard miles. Been down many a dark trail."

"I've heard Jonas use that expression. The dark trails. He said he had to follow them, because those were the trails used by the men he was after. Men who had heard the owl hoot." She looked at him as if something had just occurred to her. "Mr. Jensen, I know you're a rancher in Colorado now . . . but were you an outlaw? Is that how you and Jonas met?"

Smoke smiled and said, "Well, the first time I ever laid eyes on him, it *was* over the barrel of a gun. A Henry rifle, in fact, that he was aiming right at me . . ."

Montana, several years earlier

The young man lying on the sloping slab of rock had very broad shoulders and ash blond hair. From where he lay on the rocky hillside, he could see down across the sweep of a valley about five hundred yards wide. A road of hard-packed dirt ran through the center of that valley, twisting around clumps of boulders and thick stands of trees and brush.

A mile to the east, the road emerged from a pass in a range of rugged hills, descended into the valley, and followed it for several miles before climbing into some hills again. The young man on the rock looked back toward the pass and spotted a small cloud of dust. He knew what that dust meant.

The stagecoach was on its way.

A Sharps carbine lay on the rock beside the young man. It was a hot day, with the sun beating down, and when he reached over with a tanned, long-fingered hand and closed his fingers around the Sharps, the metal breech and trigger guard were uncomfortably warm to the touch. He pulled the carbine closer to him. Might be needing it soon, he told himself.

His keen eyes picked up the distant rumble that came from the stagecoach's wheels, as well as the pounding hoofbeats of its six-horse hitch. That team of sturdy, deepchested horses would be capable of considerable speed. Some coaches used four-horse teams, but this one always hitched six, because it carried gold shipments gleaned from the various mining camps and boomtowns in the area and might need to outrun would-be robbers.

The problem was that the team couldn't take advantage of its speed here in this valley. The road twisted and turned too much, seldom running straight for more than fifty yards at a time. If a gang of thieves wanted to hit the coach while it was making one of those lucrative runs, this was the place to do it.

The young man stiffened as he heard a faint clicking sound behind him. Somebody had nudged a rock, causing it to tap against another rock. Most men never would have heard that noise in this vast frontier that almost echoed from emptiness.

This youngster wasn't like most men. He knew he was in danger, and he was about to react with lightning swiftness even as he mentally berated himself for letting anybody sneak up that close to him.

His hand had just started to move toward the .44 revolver on his hip when a man's voice called commandingly, "Hold it right there, son! I'd hate to have to shoot you in the back, but I will if you force me to . . . Buck West!"

CHAPTER 8

Smoke Jensen froze with his hand still a few inches from the butt of the .44. He had adopted the alias Buck West fairly recently. The men he was looking for, the men responsible for the deaths of his father and brother, had the law in their pockets, and they knew he was after them. Hoping to get him off their trail, they had managed to have some reward dodgers distributed with Smoke's name and description on them, along with false accusations of crimes he hadn't committed.

So Smoke had grown a beard to change his appearance somewhat and started going by the name Buck West. The problem was, trouble still seemed to follow him around, and it wasn't long before Buck had a reputation as a gunman and was wanted, also unjustly, by the law as well.

Judging by the stern tone of the man who had told him not to move, that hombre was a lawman. He just *sounded* like he packed a badge.

Without moving, Smoke said, "Take it easy, Marshal. Don't get trigger-happy."

"I never pulled a trigger unless it needed pulling," the man replied. "How'd you know I'm a deputy U.S. marshal?"

"Wild guess," Smoke said dryly.

The man grunted. "Because you know the law's after

you. All right, West. You don't deny that you *are* Buck West, do you?"

"Would it do any good if I did?"

"Not a lick. You match the description on all the posters I've seen. So keep your hands in plain sight and don't reach for that hogleg. Slide away from the Sharps."

Smoke did as he was told. He knew he was fast enough that, more than likely, he could throw himself over onto his back, draw and fire the .44, and drill the marshal before the lawman could get him.

But that would mean killing a man who was just trying to do his job. Probably an honest man, at that. Some of the badge toters who worked for his enemies were every bit as crooked as those men were, but Smoke didn't know that about the man who had the drop on him and couldn't just assume it to be true.

He had never killed a man who didn't need killing, to paraphrase what the marshal had said a moment earlier, and he wasn't going to start now.

"I'm moving," he said. He scooted to the side until the Sharps was far enough away that he would have to make a jump for it to reach it.

"Now stand up," the lawman ordered.

"I'll have to put a hand down to do that."

"Make it the left hand. Keep the right up in the air where I can see it."

The marshal had no way of knowing this since Smoke had been lying on his belly but had a second Colt stuck in his waistband on the left side. He could reach it easily, and he was almost as swift and accurate with his left hand as he was with his right.

But he didn't make the try. He put his left hand on the rock to balance himself and climbed to his feet. Then he raised the left hand, too, without waiting to be told to.

"Turn around. Nice and easy."

Smoke did so. He saw a sturdy figure standing at the edge of some brush on the hillside above him. The man held a Henry rifle in a rock-steady grip. Sunlight reflected from the badge pinned to his vest.

As the lawman came closer, Smoke saw that he was middle-aged, with quite a bit of gray in the brown hair under a tan hat. His face was rugged, with a strong jaw and chin. Bushy brows overhung his eyes. He was an inch or two taller than Smoke.

"Got a hideout gun, do you?" he said in an accusatory tone.

"It's just a spare," Smoke said. "It's not hidden. But I could have reached for it a minute ago, if I really was the outlaw you think I am, Marshal."

"You claimin' you're an innocent man, despite all those reward dodgers on you?" A bark of laughter came from the marshal. "Reckon I've heard *that* one plenty of times before. Try another one on for size, West."

Smoke shook his head. "It would be a waste of time if I did, wouldn't it?"

"Damn sure would."

"So I don't reckon you want to know what's going to happen to that stagecoach headed this way."

The marshal caught his breath. "When I spotted you skulkin' around and watching the road through Eagle Valley down there, I figured you were after that coach! You know it's carrying a load of nuggets and dust."

"I know about the coach," Smoke said, nodding. "But I wasn't fixing to rob it."

"Then why else would you be hiding up here above the trail, in a good place to bushwhack it when it comes along?"

"Because I wanted to see if those other fellas who have been trailing it were going to try a holdup."

"Other fel—"

The marshal had been coming closer as they talked. As he frowned and started to ask Smoke what he was talking about, he got too close. Smoke made his move.

His left arm flashed out and knocked the Henry's barrel upward. He struck even faster with his right, because he wanted to keep the lawman from firing a shot if he could. If the Henry went off now, it might ruin everything.

Smoke's right fist crashed into the marshal's jaw. The man's head snapped back and his hat flew off. Smoke grabbed the Henry's barrel and tore the rifle away from him. Quickly, he slammed the Henry's butt into the marshal's chest, not hard enough to do any permanent damage but with enough force to knock the already off-balance man off his feet. The marshal landed hard on the rock and lay there momentarily stunned.

Smoke stepped back and drew the .44. "Now you're the one who needs to not do anything foolish, Marshal."

The lawman caught his breath enough to sputter some curses. He pushed himself up on an elbow but didn't move after that, because he was staring down the barrel of Smoke's revolver.

"If you're gonna kill me, go ahead and do it, you damned owlhoot," he rasped.

"I'm not going to kill anybody," Smoke said. He lowered the Colt and pouched the iron. "Well, I'm not going to kill you, Marshal. What's your name, anyway?"

"Madigan," the man said with a scowl on his face. "Deputy United States Marshal Jonas Madigan."

"I want you to listen to me for two minutes, Marshal Madigan. If you do, then when I'm finished I'll give this Henry back to you, and if you're still bound and determined to arrest me, I reckon I won't be able to stop you. Maybe not even that long," Smoke added, "because I reckon that stagecoach will be here in less than a minute."

Madigan didn't waste time pondering. He jerked his head in a nod and said, "Talk. Make it fast."

"Earlier this morning, I was back in the hills to the east. I saw that stagecoach stopped at a way station, and I also spotted half a dozen men watching the station from a hiding place on top of a nearby ridge. When the coach left, they followed it. I know the coach carries gold on this run sometimes, and I knew this valley was here with the road that twists around so much. Seemed like a good place to overtake the stage and rob it. They wouldn't want to jump it in the hills. Too big a chance that if the team stampeded, it might go off the trail into a ravine or something where they couldn't reach it."

"You got all of that just from what little you saw?" Madigan asked.

"I've been around enough outlaws to know how they think," Smoke said, then added significantly, "That doesn't mean I'm one of them."

Madigan looked interested despite what probably had been his resolve not to believe Smoke's story. He asked, "What were you gonna do?"

"I was watching to make sure my hunch was right." Smoke shrugged. "If it was, I thought I'd try to stop the holdup. I figured if I picked off one of the varmints from up here, they might come after me instead."

"You can make a shot like that from here?"

"I can make the shot," Smoke said.

After a couple of seconds, Madigan nodded. "For some reason, I believe you."

"About the shot or the robbery?"

"Maybe both."

A sudden rattle of gunfire from out in the valley made

both men look in that direction. Smoke said, "There's proof of some of it, anyway."

Madigan scrambled to his feet with a vitality that belied his years. "Blast it, gimme my rifle!"

Smoke tossed the Henry to him and said, "I'll give you a hand, Marshal."

"I didn't ask for your help."

"Six to one odds are pretty steep."

"Six to two ain't that much better."

"Might be enough," Smoke said as both of them broke into a run toward the trees. Smoke figured Madigan had left his horse tied up close to where his own mount waited.

Since there were two of them now, they wouldn't have to try to draw off the outlaws. They could take the road agents on directly, instead. They were outnumbered, sure, but they would have the element of surprise on their side.

Smoke lunged up the slope and into the trees. His black stallion, Drifter, threw his head up when Smoke appeared. The rangy stallion must have sensed that action was imminent. Smoke yanked the reins loose from the sapling where they were tied and practically vaulted into the saddle.

Horse and rider burst out of the woods. Twenty yards away, Madigan, now in the saddle on a big roan, emerged from the trees, as well. As he and Smoke circled the rock outcropping where Smoke had been lying earlier, Madigan called over the hoofbeats, "If this is a trick, West, I'll make sure you die before I go under."

"No trick, Marshal. I don't have any use for stagecoach robbers."

That was true. Earlier, when Smoke had realized he might have stumbled onto a developing holdup, he had tried to talk himself out of interfering. He told himself it was none of his business, and he dang sure wasn't wearing a lawman's star, so he had no excuse for mixing in.

Trouble was, Emmett Jensen had raised him to be honest, back there on the hardscrabble farm in the Missouri Ozarks. Some of the things Smoke had done since leaving home might be regarded as questionable by some folks, but what was it Cole Younger—also a Missouri boy—had said?

"We were victims of circumstances. We was drove to it."

Yes, sir. Most of what Smoke had done since that day his pa and his brother Luke had ridden away to fight the Yankees, he had been driven to by circumstances . . . or fate, if a man wanted to call it that.

Down below, the stagecoach had come into view, careening along the road with dust from the team and the wheels boiling up behind it. Galloping through that dust came six men on horseback. Flame spurted from the muzzles of their guns as they fired after the racing vehicle.

The jehu on the driver's box leaned forward on the seat to make himself a smaller target as he cracked his whip around the ears of the leaders. He bellowed curses at the horses to urge them on to greater speed.

Beside the driver, a guard knelt on the seat, facing backward so he could fire back at the pursuers with a Henry rifle. The man worked the rifle's lever and sprayed lead at the would-be robbers, but his shots didn't seem to be doing any good. None of the outlaws faltered.

At each bend, the driver had to haul back on the reins. The stagecoach could take those curves only so fast without toppling over. A wreck like that would be the end of the line for the driver and guard.

Smoke wondered if there were any passengers inside the coach.

Just as that thought went through his mind, the question was answered. An arm thrust out through one of the windows. Crimson flame bloomed from the gun the man held, along with a spurt of powder smoke. He fired several more times, but his shots didn't appear to do any good, either. Every time the coach slowed for a turn, the pursuers on horseback closed in a little more.

"They haven't seen us yet!" Madigan called to Smoke.

"Good! Then they won't know what hit 'em!"

Both men had to avoid rocks and brush as they continued their headlong plunge down the hill. The black stallion's nimble-footedness allowed Smoke to get slightly ahead.

They angled their course to intersect that of the stage-coach and the outlaws giving chase. Smoke drew his .44 from its holster, wrapped the reins around the saddle horn, and used his left hand to pull the spare gun from his waist-band. With irons in both hands, he guided Drifter with his knees. The horse lunged onto the road just as the stagecoach flashed past, clattering and bouncing. Madigan reached the road just a few seconds after Smoke.

That put them between the stagecoach and the outlaws. A couple of the horses broke stride for an instant as their riders realized they were facing unexpected opposition.

The next second, all the would-be robbers knew it as Smoke's guns flashed and exploded in a rolling roar of gun-thunder.

Chapter 9

Madigan swung out to the left so he'd have a clear line of fire past Smoke as he opened up on the outlaws, too. He had only one gun, so he triggered at a slower, more deliberate pace so as not to waste bullets.

It wasn't likely the outlaws would give either of them a chance to reload if they ran dry.

The tide of lead from Smoke's guns washed through the gang. One man threw his arms in the air and pitched from the saddle, falling and rolling over in a welter of dust, only to come to a stop in the limp sprawl that signified death.

Another outlaw jerked in the saddle, clearly hit, and grabbed for the horn to keep from toppling off. He managed to stay mounted and even raised his gun to throw more lead at Smoke and Madigan.

Smoke saw one of the outlaws double over and knew that a slug from Madigan's gun had found its target. Then, an instant later, the gap between the two rapidly moving groups had closed, and Smoke and Madigan tore through the gang. The mixture of dust and powder smoke that filled the air stung Smoke's eyes and nose as he fired left and right at dimly seen shapes. Bullets buzzed around his head like angry hornets. Men cursed and cried out in pain.

A fiery finger drew a line of pain along Smoke's left

forearm. He knew a slug had burned his arm, ripping the sleeve of his butternut shirt but not breaking the skin. It stung, but not enough to keep him from putting the pain out of his mind easily. As a man loomed on his right, yelling obscenities through the bandanna that was tied over the lower half of his face to conceal his features, Smoke swung the right-hand Colt in that direction and triggered again.

The bandanna jerked as the bullet tore through it, entered the yelling mouth, clipped the spinal cord, and burst out the back of the outlaw's neck. The man flopped off the horse like a puppet with its strings cut.

To Smoke's left, a horse screamed in pain.

Smoke wheeled in that direction, saw Marshal Madigan's roan rear up on its hind legs in agony from the shot that had mortally wounded it. Then the roan toppled to the side. Madigan tried to leap clear, but the roan came down on his left leg, pinning him to the ground.

On Madigan's other side, two of the would-be stagecoach robbers were still mounted. Madigan had dropped his gun when his horse went down. Smoke spotted the revolver lying on the ground about ten feet from the lawman, but with that horse's carcass lying on Madigan's leg, the gun might as well have been a hundred miles away.

The outlaws spurred toward the fallen marshal and raised their guns.

Smoke jerked his Colts up and triggered them, but the hammers fell on empty chambers. He'd run dry, and there was no time to reload.

"Marshal, keep your head down!" he shouted at Madigan.

The lawman couldn't know exactly what Smoke had in mind. To tell the truth, Smoke wasn't all that sure himself. But he had to do something or Madigan was a dead man. Smoke kicked the black stallion into a run.

Drifter didn't have much room to build up speed, but as

they reached Madigan's sprawled horse, Smoke lifted the black stallion into a jump anyway. Madigan ducked his head and flattened himself as much as possible as Drifter sailed over him.

Drifter actually cleared the obstacle easily and landed running smoothly. Smoke pulled him to the left, into a collision course with the outlaw on that side, while he left the saddle in a diving tackle aimed at the owlhoot on the right.

As Smoke flew through the air, he heard the other outlaw yell in surprise and alarm. Trying to avoid crashing into Drifter had caused him to veer away from Madigan, for the moment anyway.

The next split-second, Smoke slammed into the second outlaw, driving him out of the saddle. Both men landed hard on the ground. The impact was enough to jolt them apart and also knock the air out of Smoke's lungs. He gasped for breath as he rolled over.

As he came up on his left hand and right knee, he saw the man he had tackled scrambling up, too. The man had lost his gun, but he jerked a knife from a sheath at his waist as he lunged at Smoke.

Smoke met the attack by flinging up his left hand and grabbing the man's right wrist as the blade flashed down at him. Smoke's powerful arm and shoulder muscles stopped the potential death-stroke in midair.

At the same time, he drove with his feet and legs and rammed his right shoulder into the man's chest, knocking him back. As they both came upright, Smoke continued holding off the knife while he shot his right hand to the outlaw's throat and clamped his fingers around it. The man caught hold of Smoke's wrist and tried to pry the hand away from his throat.

They swayed there like that, pitting strength against strength, for long moments. Blood roared in Smoke's ears and hammered in his head, but over that racket he heard guns blasting somewhere else. He halfway expected to feel the life-ending smash of lead into his body, but nothing like that happened.

Instead, the outlaw managed to thrust a foot between Smoke's ankles and barreled forward into him. It was an unexpected move and caused Smoke to go over backward.

As he fell, Smoke jerked his right knee up as far as he could and then planted that foot in the man's midsection. He straightened the leg and heaved with the hand that still gripped the outlaw's throat. The man went up and over and, as Smoke let go of him, flipped over completely in the air before crashing down on his back.

Smoke whirled around, saw that the man still held the knife, and dived after him. Both hands locked around the outlaw's wrist, twisting it and forcing it down. The man cried out in shock and pain as the blade went into his chest. He jerked and kicked, and his eyes were so wide they seemed about to pop out of their sockets. Smoke shoved harder. The life went out of those bulging eyes as the knife's point reached the outlaw's heart and pierced it.

Since the guns had fallen silent, Smoke let another moment pass just to make sure the man was dead. Then he let go and pushed himself to his feet, turning to possibly meet a bullet if the other outlaw had survived.

Instead, he saw five more bodies scattered around the road where the battle had taken place.

"Blast it, West, come and give me a hand! Feels like my damn leg might be broke."

That shouted order came from Marshal Jonas Madigan, who still lay trapped under the carcass of his roan. Madigan was not only still alive, but he had the Henry rifle in his hands. He must have been able to reach it in the saddle boot,

Smoke realized, and had finished off the rest of the gang while Smoke was busy with the last one he had killed.

Quickly, Smoke looked around and found his own guns where he had dropped them. Habit told him to check them and reload them before he did anything else, but Madigan might be badly hurt, he reminded himself. He slid one Colt into leather and tucked away the other one.

"You say your leg's broken, Marshal?" he asked as he hurried over to Madigan.

"Said it might be. I don't really know. Can't feel much of anything except this horse layin' on top of me." Madigan's voice softened as he added, "Damn it, Blue, why'd you have to go and get in the way of a bullet?"

"I'm sorry," Smoke said. "It always hurts to lose a good horse. But we need to get him off of you."

"Yeah. Go ahead and do whatever you have to do. I'll keep an eye on those thieving buzzards. I'm pretty sure they're all dead, but men have made mistakes like that before and paid dearly for it."

Smoke whistled for Drifter. The black stallion trotted up. Smoke had a good strong lariat coiled and lashed to the saddle. He took it loose, tied one end around the horn on Drifter's saddle, then fastened the other end to the horn on the roan's saddle. He led Drifter away until the rope went taut, then urged the black stallion on a few more steps.

After telling Drifter to stay where he was, Smoke hurried back to Madigan's side and bent to catch hold of the marshal under the arms. The rope was taking enough of the roan's weight off the trapped leg that Smoke was able to drag Madigan free. He was glad to see that there wasn't any blood on the lawman's trouser leg.

That didn't mean the leg wasn't broken, just that there weren't any jagged bones protruding through the flesh. Smoke helped Madigan sit up.

"What do you think?"

Madigan tried to move the leg and winced. He felt around on it and made a face again. But he said, "Get me up on my feet. That's the only sure test."

Smoke locked his arms around Madigan's chest from behind and lifted him. Carefully, Madigan let his weight come down on his legs. Smoke stepped back but was ready to grab the marshal if he started to collapse.

"It ain't broke," Madigan announced after a moment. "Just bruised and twisted a mite." He took a couple of tentative steps, planting the Henry's butt on the ground to help support himself. "Hurts, but I can walk on it."

"You're a lucky man," Smoke said. "It could've been a lot worse."

"Yeah, I reckon I'm lucky to be alive." Madigan looked at Smoke. "Thanks to that damn fool stunt you pulled, jumping your black over me like that and tackling those last two owlhoots."

"Actually, I just tackled one of them," Smoke pointed out. "Appears you got your hands on that Henry and shot the other one."

"Yeah, and the ones that were wounded but still had some fight in them, too. But that pair charging me would've filled me with lead before I could have done anything, if it wasn't for you, West."

Smoke shrugged. "Does that mean you're not going to arrest me after all, Marshal?"

"Just because I owe you my life? What the hell kind of lawman would I be if I let that affect the way I do my duty?" He swung the Henry up. "I know those guns of yours are empty, so I'll let you keep 'em for now. Gather up those owlhoots' horses and throw the bodies over the saddles. One of 'em will have to carry double, because I'll be riding one."

Smoke looked at Madigan for a moment, then said, "You know, Marshal, somehow I'm not the least bit surprised."

They climbed out of the valley, leading the horses with dead outlaws draped over the saddles and lashed in place. As they rode, Madigan asked, "What made you start ridin' the dark trails, West?"

"You ask that question of all the men you arrest, Marshal?"

Madigan snorted. "Hardly any, as a matter of fact. Most of the men I bring in are just plumb no good, and they've been that way most of their lives. They're too greedy, or too stupid, or just too plain vicious to do anything except become outlaws. A lot of 'em are all three of those things." Madigan glanced over at Smoke. "Thing of it is, you don't seem to fit any of those categories. I don't think I've ever run across a wanted man who would do what you did today."

"Helping you out, you mean?"

"It's not just because I came along. You were gonna try to stop that stagecoach robbery all on your own, before you knew I was anywhere around. At least, that's what you told me, and danged if I don't believe you."

"I don't have any use for thieves," Smoke said.

"But you're wanted for robbery, as well as murder."

Smoke shook his head. "That part's a lie. I've never stolen anything. As for murder, I've killed, but like I said earlier, not anybody who didn't have it coming. It's just that I have enemies, men who want me dead and don't mind using the law to try to accomplish that."

"What did these so-called enemies do to you?"

"To me?" Smoke said. "Nothing. But back during the war, they double-crossed my brother . . . and the Confederacy . . . and killed him. Then, after the war, my pa and I came out here to look for them."

"To settle the score." Madigan's words weren't a question.

"That's right. But they killed my father, too, and then later . . ." Smoke had to stop and draw a deep breath to settle the emotions inside him before going on, "Later, they were responsible for the deaths of my wife and our baby son. The only men I've killed, other than Indians who attacked us, were gun-wolves working for that bunch."

Madigan let out a low whistle. He studied Smoke intently for a moment, then said, "I've heard about a fella who ran into some trouble just like that, but his name wasn't Buck West. There are wanted posters out on *him*, too."

"All lies," Smoke said curtly.

"Maybe so, but the law's still the law. But it sounds like somebody ought to do some looking into your case, West . . . and that other fella's, too . . . and try to find out what justice really is."

"Maybe that'll happen, Marshal . . . one of these days."

A short time after they entered the hills, they came to a way station. The stagecoach wasn't there, having already changed teams and moved on. But as Smoke and Madigan drew rein in front of the squat, log building, they heard an unusual sound coming through the open door.

The wailing cry of a baby.

"What in tarnation?" Madigan muttered.

A short, wiry man with a gray brush of a mustache emerged from the building. He lifted a hand in greeting and said, "Howdy, Marshal. Thought I heard somebody out here." He leaned to the side to gaze past the two riders at the other horses with their grim burdens. "Looks like you been busy. Would that happen to be the varmints who tried to hold up the stage?"

"It would," Madigan answered. "Did the coach make it here all right?"

"It did. And just in time, too." The man jerked a thumb

over his shoulder toward the building, where the crying continued. "Man and his wife were on board, and the lady was just about to, uh, be delivered of a young'un. Seems all the joltin' and jouncin' around in the coach must've got the festivities started a mite early."

Madigan frowned. "You had a *baby* born here?"

"I sure did. My wife delivered it. Whole thing went off slicker'n water off a duck's back, if you don't count the young fella who's the father almost faintin' a time or two. But it's all taken care of now. Mother and child appear to be healthy. They're gonna stay here until the next westbound comes through, on account of my wife says the lady hadn't ought to be travelin' so soon."

"Well, Lord have mercy," Madigan said. "A baby." He frowned. "But that don't change what we've got to do. You got a couple of shovels, Schofield?"

"You know I do," the station man said. "You gonna plant those owlhoots?"

"Unless you want to keep 'em like daisies."

"Whoo-ee! No, sir. Shovels are in the barn. You and your deputy help yourselves, Marshal."

Madigan glanced at Smoke, then nodded and said, "Obliged."

While they were digging graves a couple of hundred yards from the station, Smoke said, "I notice you didn't correct that hombre when he assumed I was your deputy, Marshal."

"It's none of Schofield's business who you are," Madigan snapped. The shovel in his hands bit into the earth. He tossed the dirt aside, then leaned on the shovel and regarded Smoke solemnly.

"You didn't just save my life," he went on. "You helped save the lives of that driver and guard, and a man and his wife and their baby. There's a good chance that bunch would've killed 'em all."

"Could've happened that way," Smoke allowed.

Madigan drew a deep breath, frowned in thought, and said, "Here's what we're gonna do. We're gonna finish puttin' these no-good skunks in the ground, and then I figure on going in the station and paying my respects to the lady and her new little one. While I'm doing that, you can tend to the horses."

"You think so?" Smoke said.

"I know so. You should pay special attention to that black of yours, and maybe one of the horses those owlhoots were ridin'. Pick out the best of the bunch."

"And what should I do with those two horses?"

"Whatever you think is best," Madigan said. "And here's one more thing. Anybody who wants to get word to me can write to the chief marshal's office in Denver. I like to get letters, too."

"All right," Smoke said slowly. If Madigan needed to talk around what he was actually saying, that was fine.

"I was wrong," Madigan went on. "I got one *more* thing to tell you, West. I know what today's date is. I keep up with such things. If I ever come across any wanted posters on Buck West . . . or that other fella . . . that were issued after today, I won't take it kindly. You understand what I'm sayin'?"

"Yes, sir, Marshal, I do. I can't promise anything, though, except that I'll try."

"See that you do." Madigan lifted his shovel again. "Let's get to work. These desperadoes won't bury themselves."

CHAPTER 10

Salt Lick

"So he just let you go," Mrs. Dollinger said. "Allowed you to take your horse and a spare mount and ride away while he was inside the stagecoach station fussing and cooing over a newborn baby."

"That's right," Smoke said with a smile. "I think it pained him a whole heap to do it, too. But that baby tipped the scales in my favor. If that little girl hadn't been born when she was, Jonas might have taken me in, and then there's no telling what might have happened. I had some mighty powerful enemies back in those days."

"Did you write to him? Wait, of course you did, I know that. The two of you became good friends over the years."

"Yeah, I let him know what happened to me and how the whole thing played out. And we kept in touch, so I was able to follow his career as a lawman, too. The letters sort of dwindled over the years, though. I knew he'd taken a job as a town marshal in Texas, but that was the last I'd heard from him until I got his recent letter."

"That was quite an exciting tale. Did you embellish it,

the way those men do who write yellowback novels about you?"

Smoke grunted. "You've seen some of those, have you?"

"Jonas has a collection of them. He's quite proud of knowing the hero of all those stirring tales."

"Well, most of those fellas do more than embellish what actually happened. They just make things up out of thin air, and nine times out of ten, it's so outlandish that nobody with any sense could believe it." Smoke shrugged. "Folks seem to enjoy them, though. Nothing wrong with something that helps to pass the time."

"And you didn't actually answer my question."

"No, ma'am, I did not," Smoke said.

A footstep caught the attention of both of them. The front door opened, and Jonas Madigan stepped out onto the porch with a blanket wrapped around him.

"Thought I heard somebody talking out here."

Mrs. Dollinger got quickly to her feet, followed by Smoke. "Jonas, you shouldn't be up and about, especially not in this chilly air."

"I've slept away most of the day," Madigan growled. "A man can't sleep all the time. And in the long run, I don't reckon a little cold air will have any effect on what ails me, good or bad."

"Perhaps not, but still, you should go lie down—"

"No, I've done that enough for a while," he said firmly. "But I'll tell you what I *will* do. I'll sit in that comfortable armchair in the parlor, and you can tuck this blanket in around my legs if you want to, Miriam. Then Smoke and me will have ourselves a talk, get caught up on everything. Maybe even have a cigar or two. How's that sound, Smoke?"

"I'll pass on the cigar, Jonas, but I could do with a cup of coffee."

"It's settled, then," Madigan said. "Come on in. I want to

hear all about how things are going up there on that ranch of yours, Smoke."

Several miles south of Salt Lick, Sid Atkins and Bart Rome hunkered next to a tiny fire, trying to stay warm without attracting any attention. The flask of whiskey they passed back and forth helped with that.

In addition, every slug of the Who-hit-John they downed made the plan they had come up with seem even better and more likely to work.

Rome was still worried, though. He said, "You know the boss won't ever forgive us for double-crossing him. That means there's a good chance he'll never stop trying to hunt us down and get his revenge."

Atkins waved the flask dismissively. "He'll have other things to worry about. Anyway, there'll be other banks, with bigger hauls than this one. Sure, he'll be mad, but he'll get over it." Atkins tipped the flask to his mouth and took a swallow. "Besides, neither of us rode with him for all that many years. We owe more loyalty to ourselves than we do to him."

"Maybe . . . but I can't help but worry he won't see it that way."

"Then we just need to stay far enough ahead of him that he won't ever have a chance to catch up to us." Atkins handed the flask to Rome. "I'm thinkin' after we get over in New Mexico Territory, we can cut south, maybe head down across the border into Old Meh-hee-co. Away from all these cold winds. Plenty of tequila to warm your innards and hot-blooded little señoritas to warm your bed . . ."

His voice trailed off in a wistful sigh.

"All that's fine," Rome said after he'd taken a drink, "but first we've got to take care of business here."

"We will, don't worry about that," Atkins assured him. "As soon as it gets good and dark."

They had some jerky and stale biscuits and made a sparse supper on that as the afternoon light faded. When night fell, they put out the fire, which made the air feel even colder. But there were still a few renegade Comanches roaming the high plains, and the sight of a fire might be too tempting if any of those warriors happened to be where they could see it.

"The stars are out," Rome said. "It's late enough, Sid. Let's go get this done."

"You're right," Atkins agreed. "Salt Lick looked like the sort of place where they roll the boardwalks up as soon as the sun goes down. I don't reckon anybody will be around to give us any trouble."

"As long as we don't make too much racket getting into the bank. Are you sure you've got enough dynamite to blow the vault door open?"

"Sure, I'm sure! If you know what you're doin', all it takes is one stick of the stuff, and I know what I'm doin'. I used to work in a mine, and we set off charges all the time."

"Back in the days when you were an honest man, eh?"

"Well," Atkins said with a chuckle, "I may have had an honest job, but I ain't sure I was ever what you'd consider an honest man."

Earlier in the day, after that arrogant pup of a lawman in Salt Lick had put the run on them and they had ridden out of town to wait for dark, the two men had unsaddled their horses. Now they got the rigs back on their mounts.

"I wish there was some way to pull this job without the people in town even knowing we were there," Rome commented as they rode north, into the wind.

"Well, there ain't," Atkins said, "unless you want to hang around these parts long enough to find out who the bank president is, so we can grab him and force him to open the vault. And we don't have that much time to waste."

"No, we don't," Rome agreed with obvious reluctance.

"So that means all we can do is blow the vault, grab as much loot as we can, and light a shuck outta there. Even though we'll have to move fast, we ought to have a pretty good payday."

"You know, it's not too late to turn around and go back to join the others, like we were supposed to."

"Thinkin' like that is why we ain't ever in charge of anything, Bart. A fella who just does what he's told never gets to decide anything for himself. He's just half a man, really . . . the order-followin' half."

"All right, all right," Rome said, sounding like he was getting irritated. "Let's get on to town and rob that damn bank."

Windy Whittaker drove up late in the afternoon with a wagon that had chunks of firewood stacked in the back. Smoke helped him unload the wood and carry it around to the rear of the house, where there was a bin in which it was stored. The chunks were small enough they could be used in the wood-burning stove in the kitchen.

"Did you cut and split this wood, Windy?"

"Naw. Where would I do that?" The bearded old-timer waved a hand at the surrounding countryside. "There ain't what you'd call an abundance o' trees in these parts. Fella name of Fred Cunningham has it freighted in from elsewhere in the state, and then he sells it." Windy sniffed and rubbed his nose with the back of his hand. "When folks first started settlin' in these parts, they burned mostly buffalo dung, on account of that's what there was more of than anything else. It ain't the best-smellin' stuff in the world, though, so these days, folks prefer firewood when they can get it. When they can't, they make do."

"Have you been around Salt Lick since it was founded?" Smoke asked.

"Me? Shoot, no. I've always been fiddle-footed. Reckon I've roamed over most o' the frontier from the Rio Grande to the Milk River. I just blew into these parts a couple o' years ago." He laughed. "Blew into. On account o' folks call me Windy."

"Yeah, I got that," Smoke said dryly. "For some reason, it just seemed like you might have been around here longer."

"That's 'cause I'm the sort o' fella who, once you get to know me, you feel like we been pards for years an' years."

Smoke nodded and said, "Yeah, I can see what you mean."

They had just put the last of the wood in the bin when the back door opened and Miriam Dollinger looked out.

"Windy, Jonas wants you to stay for supper."

Windy jerked his hat off. His whiskery face creased in a grin as he said, "Why, ma'am, I'd be plumb honored to do so. If I wouldn't be puttin' nobody out, that is."

"Not at all," she told him. "There's plenty of food, and Jonas enjoys your company."

"I always enjoy visitin' with him, too." Windy glanced at Smoke. "But the marshal's already got comp'ny . . ."

"A man can't have too many friends," Smoke said. "You're welcome as far as I'm concerned."

Windy bobbed his head. "In that case, then, Miz Dollinger, I'll sure be happy to accept the kind invite."

"The two of you come on in," Mrs. Dollinger said. "I've just put on a fresh pot of coffee."

Supper was an enjoyable affair with the four of them sitting around the kitchen table. Madigan wore a thick robe and groused about how he should have gotten dressed, but he had to admit the robe was comfortable. Miriam kept the coffee cups filled. They had beans and cornbread and thick slices of ham, simple fare but very good and filling. They finished off the cornbread with glasses of cold buttermilk that made for good dunking.

When the meal was over, Madigan leaned back in his chair and sighed contentedly. "I have to say, between that fine food and even better company, this is the best I've felt in quite a spell. I'm mighty obliged to all of you for lifting the spirits of a decrepit old man."

Miriam was sitting to his right. She rested her hand on his and smiled as she said, "You're not all that decrepit, Jonas."

"I wouldn't say that. But I don't mind *you* saying it, Miriam."

Windy Whittaker had kept the conversation going during supper with a series of colorful stories about his travels and adventures. To hear Windy tell it, he was acquainted with every famous frontiersman from Kit Carson to Wild Bill Hickok to Buffalo Bill Cody.

"Ever run into an old mountain man called Preacher?" Smoke asked the old-timer when he, Madigan, and Windy had moved into the parlor while Miriam said she would clean up.

"Preacher?" Windy slapped his thigh. "Why, sure, me an' that ol' reprobate go 'way back. I know I don't look near old enough to have been out here durin' the mountain man days, but I got in on the tail end o' that time. Went to one of the very last rendezvous they had on the Green River, and Preacher was there. Shinin' times, son, shinin' times."

As far as Smoke could recall, he had never heard Preacher mention anything about someone called Windy Whittaker, but he supposed it was possible Windy was telling the truth. Smoke had heard plenty of stories about and from the old mountain man, but he didn't know everything Preacher had done, or everyone he had met.

"What about Jamie Ian MacCallister?"

"Rode the river with that ol' boy many a time!"

Smoke hadn't met Jamie MacCallister, although Preacher had shared numerous adventures with Jamie. Smoke was fairly well acquainted with Jamie's son Falcon. Again, he didn't recall any connection between the MacCallisters and Windy Whittaker. But it didn't really matter, Smoke mused, whether Windy was stretching the truth or not. He was an entertaining old codger, and Madigan seemed to enjoy having him around, so that was good enough for Smoke.

Windy spun a few more yarns, and then Madigan began to yawn. "Sorry, boys," the former lawman said. "I shouldn't be sleepy, as much as I napped during the day, but I'm startin' to get a mite weary."

"You should turn in, then," Smoke suggested.

"I think that's an excellent idea," Miriam said as she came into the parlor. She had put on an apron while she was cleaning up, but it was off now, signifying that she was through with the chores. "I'll go straighten up your bed."

"Blast it, that's not necessary," Madigan said. "It's not like I waller around so much that I turn it into a rat's nest."

"You'll be more comfortable and sleep better if I freshen it up." Miriam smiled and turned to leave the room.

Madigan waited until she was gone to say quietly, "That woman sure does like to fuss over me."

"Yeah, you'd think she was married to you or something," Smoke said with a smile.

Windy said, "Any fella who was lucky enough to get hitched to Miz Miriam could sure enough count hisself fortunate. She's darned near about the nicest, prettiest woman I ever saw in all my borned days."

"She is that, all right," Madigan agreed. "Give me a hand, Smoke."

Smoke helped his old friend out of the chair where he sat

and then went with him down the hall to the bedroom. With assistance from Smoke and Miriam, Madigan got into bed. Miriam pulled a chair up close and said, "I've brought a new book for us to read, Jonas, by Mr. Twain. It's called *The Prince and the Pauper*. It's supposed to be quite a thrilling historical adventure."

Madigan chuckled. "I'll bet it's not as thrilling as *Smoke Jensen Battles the Bandits of Buzzard's Canyon*."

"You'll be better off sticking with Mark Twain," Smoke told him with a grin.

Miriam turned down the lamp slightly, then picked up the book she had placed on the bedside table earlier. As Smoke left the room and eased the door closed behind him, he heard her reading in a soft but compelling voice.

The smell of tobacco smoke drew him out to the porch, where Windy sat in one of the rocking chairs, puffing on an old corncob pipe. Smoke took the other chair. The air was chilly, but the wind had died down, so it was fairly pleasant, a crisp late autumn evening.

"She readin' to him?" Windy asked quietly.

"Yep. Something by Mark Twain."

Windy nodded. With the pipe stem still clenched between his teeth, he said, "Them two ought to get married while they still can. I ain't never been much of a believer in what you call your matrimonial bliss, but they was made to pull in double harness, if you ask me. Damn shame they never found each other as more than friends until it was this late."

"Better late than never, they say."

"You a married man, Smoke?"

"I am. To a beautiful girl named Sally. I don't know what I'd do without her. Hope I never have to find out. How about you, Windy?"

"Me?" The old-timer waved a hand. "Shoot, what woman with a lick o' sense would ever get hitched to a crusty ol' badger like me? I wintered with Injun tribes a few times and had squaw wives for a spell, and there was this redheaded gal who run a sportin' house up in Cheyenne and me and her got along real well, well enough that we decided to set up housekeepin' together for a while, so she gave up the sportin' house and I, uh, gave up the line o' work I was in just then. If we'd stayed together, we might've got hitched someday, but after a spell we didn't get along as well as we used to, so we decided . . . well, *she* decided . . . that it'd be better if I was to sort of mosey along, and by that time, to tell you the truth, I was kinda ready to take off for the tall an' uncut my own self, so I give her a big ol' goodbye smooch and she told me to rattle my hocks 'fore she trimmed these whiskers o' mine with a Bowie knife." Windy sighed. "Yes, sir, she was a good ol' gal, Roberta was, even if she was a mite on the pestiferous side now and then."

Smoke had listened to the torrent of words, wondering when Windy was going to run out of steam, and since it appeared that the old-timer was finished, at least for now, Smoke indulged his curiosity by asking about something that had caught his attention while Windy was talking.

"What line of work was that?"

"What line o' work was what?"

"The one you gave up when you moved in with Miss Roberta."

Windy cleared his throat and said, "Oh, well, that was so long ago, I don't hardly remember—"

The sudden, totally unexpected sound of an explosion somewhere in Salt Lick dropped the curtain on the old man's clearly reluctant answer. Both men bolted to their feet, and Smoke's hand dropped to the gun on his hip.

CHAPTER 11

A short time earlier, Sid Atkins and Bart Rome had ridden into Salt Lick, circling to the east so they could come in on one of the cross streets. That was Rome's idea. He figured they would be less likely to be noticed that way, rather than entering the settlement on the north-south trail that became the main street.

They didn't get in any hurry. A couple of horses moving through the night at easy walks wouldn't draw much attention. A dog barked somewhere. The two men heard a few notes from a piano, but the music ended as abruptly as it began. Somebody must have opened the door at Apple Jack's saloon, or one of the other saloons, and then closed it again quickly.

"Most of the town's gone to bed," Atkins said.

"Yeah, just the way we want it," Rome agreed.

"They'll get woke up soon enough."

Before reaching the center of town, the two men turned their horses and rode into an alley cloaked in thick shadows. They knew from their visit to Salt Lick during the day that this alley ran behind the bank building. Since the bank was the most impressive structure in town, it was easy to spot, even at night.

They reined in behind the bank. A couple of posts supported a small awning over the back door, so they made sure their horses were tied securely to one of those posts. They would need the mounts in a hurry, and it would be disastrous if they came out of the bank and the horses had gotten loose and wandered off.

"Got the stuff?" Rome whispered.

Atkins patted the front of his coat. "Right here."

"Let's see if we can get in there, then."

Banks tended to put most of their trust in their vaults, rather than the buildings in which those vaults were housed. Sure, the doors were locked, but breaking in usually wasn't that difficult. Rome, who was better at such things than Atkins, drew a slim-bladed knife from a sheath at his waist and went to the door. He slipped the knife into the gap between the door and the jamb and began probing.

After a moment, he cursed under his breath.

"What's wrong?" Atkins asked.

"The damn thing's barred, not just locked."

Atkins made a face in the darkness. "So you can't unlock it?"

"Doesn't matter if I do or not. We still can't get in with that bar in place."

"How about tryin' the front door?"

"Too good a chance of being seen. A few people are still moving around."

Atkins stepped back and looked up at the rear wall.

"Give me a boost up," he said. "I can stand on that awning and reach one of the second-floor windows. I'll get in there and come downstairs to open the back door."

"Those windows are liable to be locked, too."

Atkins shrugged. "So I'll wrap my bandanna around my

gun butt and break out the glass. I can do that without making a lot of racket."

Rome thought it over for a moment, then said, "I suppose it's worth a try. Our only other choice is to ride back out empty-handed and go back to the others, like we were supposed to. We'll still have our shares coming to us."

"If we do that, we'll have money, all right . . . but we'll never be rich."

Rome slid the knife back into leather and bent over to lace his fingers together in a makeshift stirrup. "All right, come on. I'll boost you up there."

An awkward minute later, Atkins was standing on the awning, hoping that it wouldn't collapse under him or prove so weak that he fell through it. He was able to reach one of the second-floor windows, but when he tried to shove the pane up, it refused to move. After trying to lift the window for a minute or so, he drew his gun, swathed the Colt's butt in his bandanna, and tapped firmly on the glass.

If the window was nailed shut, he might have to knock all the glass out in order to climb through. But if it had a latch, all he needed was a big enough hole to reach in . . .

That was how it turned out. The glass shattered under the blow and fell into the room. The noise might have been loud enough to hear on the street, but Atkins didn't think that was likely. He reached in, found the latch, and shoved it back. The window went up smoothly then, and a moment later he was inside.

The place was dark as the inside of a black cat. Atkins felt his way out of the room, which seemed to be an office of some sort, judging by the desk he banged his hip on. He risked snapping a lucifer to life long enough to locate the stairs. Since he was in an inner corridor with no windows, as he saw as the match flared up, it was safe to have a light.

Two minutes later he was downstairs, lifting the bar out of its brackets on either side of the back door. The key was in the lock. Atkins twisted it and let his partner in.

"Any signs of trouble outside?"

"No," Rome said. "As far as I can tell, nobody heard that window break."

Atkins grinned and said, "See, I told you. Luck's on our side tonight."

"Let's hope it stays that way. Where's the vault?"

"I don't know, but the place ain't that big. We can find it."

Since the bank had two big front windows, they couldn't risk striking another match. But the glass also allowed in a faint glow from other buildings along the street, so the two men were able to fumble their way through the lobby, behind the railing that separated the president's desk from the rest of the room, and finally to the massive steel door of the vault, which was tucked away in the back of the lobby.

Rome rapped his knuckles against the door a couple of times and said, "Are you *sure* you can blow this thing open, Sid? It sounds mighty solid. Might be better to wait until the others are here and we can force the banker to open it, if it's not already open then."

"There you go, thinkin' small again." Atkins reached inside his coat. "All I got to do is wedge one of these sticks of dynamite right here beside the lock. It'll blow the sucker right open. I've seen what this stuff can do, plenty of times."

Rome sighed and said, "Well, all right. We've come this far, so I guess it'd be foolish not to go whole hog."

Working mostly by feel, Atkins took a blasting cap and a length of fuse from his coat pocket and fixed them to the end of the explosive cylinder.

"Go out and get behind that counter where the tellers' cages are," he told Rome. "That's far enough away and sturdy enough that it ought to protect us from the blast."

"Will you have enough time to get away from it before it goes off?"

Atkins chuckled and said, "I'd damned well better, or else you'll be scrapin' me off the walls, Bart. Naw, don't worry, I'm just joshin' you. It'll be fine."

Rome hurried to shelter while Atkins placed the dynamite to his satisfaction. He had to drag over one of the ladder-back chairs in front of the president's desk and angle it on its front legs so the back was wedged against the dynamite to hold it in place. The explosion would blow that chair to splinters, but that would hardly be the bank's only loss.

Satisfied with the dynamite's placement, Atkins stepped back a little and dug out another lucifer. He snapped the match to life with his thumbnail and held the flame to the end of the dangling fuse. With a sputter of sparks, it caught right away and began burning up toward the dynamite.

Atkins shook out the match and turned to hurry out of the railed-off area where the vault was located. He broke into a run as he headed across the lobby toward the tellers' cages. From behind the counter, Rome said in an urgent whisper, "Come on, Sid."

"I'm comin', I'm—"

Atkins tripped on something and fell forward, sprawling on his face.

Terror shot through him, but a small part of his brain told him that he still had plenty of time. All he had to do was get up and take those last few steps to the counter. He scrambled to his feet, slipping once more as he did so, and he had to put a hand on the floor to steady himself.

He had just come upright for the second time when the dynamite went off with a huge roar that shook the floor and rattled the windows in the bank building.

* * *

Marshal Ted Cardwell was in his office with its adjoining cell block, nursing a cup of coffee and nibbling on a roast beef sandwich he had picked up at the Red Top Café, a few doors along the street.

He usually ate his supper here in the office like this, before heading out to make his final rounds of the town. Night rounds had been his job when he was a deputy, and since he didn't have a deputy of his own after taking over for Marshal Madigan, he had continued with the chore.

He could have taken his meals at Ma Haskell's boarding house, where he had a room, but he didn't really like any of the other boarders . . . and they didn't like him since he'd become marshal. He knew they resented him, since it was his job to enforce the law and he might have to arrest them someday. That possibility set a man apart and made other people nervous around him. Cardwell sometimes wished that wasn't the case, but there was nothing he could do about it.

As he took another sip of coffee, he thought that things would be different if he had a house of his own. A house with a woman in it, maybe . . . a woman like Tommy Spencer.

Not for the first time, Cardwell fervently wished that he hadn't let his emotions get the best of him that day when they'd gone on the picnic. He had been too forward with her; he wasn't going to deny that. She had slapped his face for him, and he'd had it coming.

But he had apologized up one way and down the other, and he knew good and well that Tommy was smart enough to realize he was sincere. So why hadn't she accepted his apology? Why had she refused all his invitations to have supper with him or to go for a ride in the countryside?

Maybe, he told himself, *she just doesn't like you that much.* And if that was the case, he would just have to learn to live with it . . .

To distract himself from those thoughts, he opened one of the desk drawers and took out a stack of wanted posters. Nearly every time the stagecoach came in, the mail pouch brought more reward dodgers. Cardwell added them to the collection that Marshal Madigan had started, and every so often—like tonight—he got them out and went through them, studying the names, descriptions, and occasional photographs or drawings that adorned them. As a lawman, it was his job to be familiar with as many wanted men as possible.

There was no telling when some of them might show up in Salt Lick.

Cardwell flipped through the stack of posters as he finished off the sandwich and drank the rest of the coffee. He tried to time things so he would reach the end of his supper and the last wanted poster at the same time, but he didn't quite make it. A few posters remained in the stack as he set his empty cup on the desk next to the sheet of butcher paper where the sandwich had been.

He was about to just flip those posters over and add them to the rest of the stack, then put all of them away, but since he was this close to the end, he decided to look at the few pieces of paper left from the original bunch. He turned one over, glanced idly at the next one, and then sat back in his chair and drew in a sharp, surprised breath.

A drawing of a familiar face was looking up at him from the reward dodger.

Cardwell stared back at it for a long moment.

Then he began to curse, soft but heartfelt, under his breath.

BART ROME was the name printed on the poster. *Wanted for Murder, Attempted Murder, Bank Robbery, Train Robbery, and Grand Larceny*. The charges covered

Texas, Indian Territory, Kansas, and Missouri. Rome was known to be associated with the Snake Bishop gang.

"He didn't even give me a fake name, the brazen son of a gun," Cardwell said. "I should have recognized it. I wonder if . . ."

He started going through the remaining posters.

Sure enough, only two dodgers later, he saw a familiar name: SID ATKINS. Atkins' poster had no photo or drawing on it, but the description matched. And Atkins hadn't bothered with a false name, either. Cardwell groaned at this indication of how little regard they had for him as a lawman.

But why should he expect any different from a couple of owlhoots, he asked himself? Why would Rome and Atkins think any more highly of him than everybody else in Salt Lick? The townspeople all doubted his ability to enforce the law, despite the fact that he had worked for Marshal Jonas Madigan for more than a year and a half. He was too young, he had overheard some of them say. Just a wet-behind-the-ears pup.

So when he'd tried to show them all that he could be just as tough and hard-nosed as Madigan, they had called him full of himself and arrogant. What in blazes did people *want* from him, anyway? Couldn't they see he was doing the best he could?

Maybe they were right to doubt him, he thought as he stared at the two wanted posters he placed side by side on the desk. He stood up, leaned forward, rested his knuckles on the desk, and glared at the reward dodgers.

He had had two wanted outlaws right in his grasp today, two members of the notorious Snake Bishop gang . . . and instead of arresting them, he had let them go! Worse than that, he had run them out of town.

The reward for each man was $500. If he had just locked them up, he would be a thousand dollars to the good, Cardwell thought bitterly. Some lawmen didn't take bounties out of personal preference, but there was no law against it. More important, Atkins and Rome would be behind bars where they couldn't commit any more crimes and couldn't hurt anybody else.

If he had just done that, Tommy Spencer might feel differently about him. She might actually respect him, and from respect could grow something else . . .

Cardwell sighed. "Too late now," he said aloud. Those two owlhoots were long gone.

The sound of the explosion that rolled through Salt Lick at that moment was so loud and powerful that Cardwell took an involuntary step back from the desk, almost as if the force of the blast had pushed him. His eyes got huge. He had no idea what had happened, but anything that sounded like that couldn't be good.

The bank! Somebody might be robbing the bank. As soon as that thought flashed through his mind, others tumbled crazily after it.

Rome and Atkins were known to be members of the Snake Bishop gang. Cardwell had heard of Bishop and his band of marauders. They had raided towns across several states and territories, looting and burning and killing. Why would Rome and Atkins have come to Salt Lick, unless they were scouting the place for their leader, Snake Bishop?

Maybe the Bishop gang was raiding the town right now!

Ted Cardwell hesitated, knowing what a reputation Bishop and his men had for being ruthless, bloodthirsty killers. And he was only one man, who had never faced anything like that . . .

But the hesitation lasted only for a split-second. He had a job to do, and he was going to do it.

Without pausing to put on his coat, Cardwell grabbed a Winchester from the rack behind the desk. The rifle was fully loaded, but he jerked open a drawer and grabbed a box of cartridges anyway. If the Snake Bishop gang was attacking Salt Lick, he'd probably need the extra ammunition.

Then he ran out of the marshal's office into the night, leaving the door open behind him. A wind drifted into the room, played for a moment with the wanted posters scattered on the desk, and then fluttered several of them to the floor.

CHAPTER 12

The blast had filled the bank's lobby with smoke. Coughing, Bart Rome rushed out from behind the counter and waved his hand in front of his face, trying to clear enough of the thick, choking stuff for him to locate Atkins. Rome's ears rang so much from the explosion that a terrible clamor filled his head.

He spotted Atkins sprawled face-down on the floor where the force from the blast had thrown him. As Rome dropped to a knee beside his friend, the ringing in his ears subsided enough for him to hear the groan that came from Atkins. That told him Atkins was still alive, anyway.

"Sid!" Rome said as he grasped Atkins' shoulders. "Sid, can you hear me?"

Atkins started to fight as Rome rolled him onto his back. It was too dark and smoky in the bank to tell how badly Atkins was hurt, but he seemed fairly spry as he struck out at Rome in confusion. Rome grabbed his arms.

"Sid, stop it! Damn it, Sid, it's me, Bart! Come on. We got to get that money out of the vault."

Atkins stopped fighting. "B-Bart?"

"Yeah. Come on."

The smoke made both men cough as Rome helped Atkins to his feet. They stumbled toward the vault. Rome got a match from his pocket and lit it. The glare gave the smoke a hellish tint, but the stuff was starting to clear and they could see the vault door through the gaps in it.

Both men groaned in despair at the sight that met their eyes.

"I thought you said it would blow the door wide open!"

"It should have," Atkins insisted. "I don't know what went wrong."

But something obviously had, because the vault door, while showing signs of scorching and pitting around the lock and handle, was intact and still separated the two out-laws from the loot they sought.

Atkins had lost his hat, and the back of his neck was bloody from the flying splinters that had gouged it, the result of the chair being blown to bits. Other than that, he appeared to be shaken up but unhurt. As he stared at the vault door, he muttered, "I can try again—"

"No! Damn it, Sid, there's no time. We've got to get out of here—*now*!"

"Yeah, you're right. That blast must've woke up the whole town."

They turned away from the vault. It was a shame that their efforts had come to nothing, but they couldn't afford to hang around Salt Lick. Even if the marshal was an arro-gant little pissant, he still represented a threat. The citizens would all turn out to see what the commotion was, too.

Stumbling runs carried the two outlaws to the back door and out of the bank. The horses were still there, even though the explosion had spooked them, and they tossed their heads nervously. Atkins and Rome jerked the reins loose and leaped into the saddles.

"Head south?" Atkins said. "Back to the gang?"

"We can't risk it," Rome said. "When Snake finds out

what we did, he'll kill us for trying to double-cross him, even though we failed."

Atkins bit off a curse. "Reckon we'd better head for New Mexico anyway, then," he said. "I'm sorry, Bart—"

"Save it. It was worth a try. Like you said, probably our only chance to ever get rich."

They hauled their horses around and galloped out of the alley, turning to the left so they could follow the cross street through the center of the settlement and on to the west.

They hadn't quite reached the corner when a man appeared on the boardwalk to their left, brandishing a Winchester and shouting, "Stop! Hold it right there, you two!"

Smoke was coming out through the cracks around the bank's double doors when Marshal Ted Cardwell ran past the building's entrance. One of the front windows had a big, jagged crack running across it but hadn't shattered.

That was enough to confirm Cardwell's hunch that the blast had come from inside the bank. Somebody was trying to rob it, all right. But he didn't see anything else going on, so maybe Salt Lick wasn't under general attack from the Snake Bishop gang after all. Maybe the bank was the only target.

Cardwell hesitated long enough to wonder if he ought to kick the doors open. The robbers could still be in there.

But then he heard rapid hoof beats from around the corner. They were trying to get away. He ran to the end of the boardwalk and saw two men on horseback to his right, racing along the cross street as fast as they could.

They had to be the bank robbers. Nobody else would be riding hellbent-for-leather like that. They were trying to escape, and he had to stop them.

He yelled for them to stop and then flung the Winchester

to his shoulder. The riders didn't rein in. They didn't even slow down.

Instead, they opened fire, muzzle flame from their guns blooming like crimson flowers in the darkness.

Cardwell fired once and heard the Winchester's wicked crack as the butt kicked back against his shoulder. He worked the rifle's lever and jerked the trigger again, but the Winchester's barrel was rising already because slugs pounded into Cardwell's body and knocked him backward. He felt a couple drive deep into his chest, and another ripped through his guts like somebody had just shoved a huge, jagged pole into his body. Pain the likes of which he had never known rampaged through him as he dropped the rifle and crashed down on his back.

He had enough of a lawman's instinct left to fumble with the Colt on his hip and claw it out of its holster, but he was too weak to lift it. It twisted out of his fingers and fell on the planks of the boardwalk beside him as he died.

Smoke drew his gun as he clattered down the steps from the front porch of Jonas Madigan's house. Windy Whittaker was close behind him, exclaiming, "What in the Sam Hill? Are the damn Yankees invadin' us again?"

"That wasn't artillery," Smoke said. He reached the gate in the picket fence and threw it open. "Sounded more like a stick of dynamite going off to me."

"Dynamite! What in blazes—"

"You've got a bank in this town, don't you?"

Smoke gazed toward the center of Salt Lick. He didn't see anything on fire.

"I'd better go and find out—"

Windy gripped his arm. "Look there! Couple o' riders comin' fast!"

Smoke caught a glimpse of the men on horseback, silhouetted against a few faintly glowing windows behind them. Then, a heartbeat later, tongues of flame lashed out from their guns as they opened fire on someone. Smoke heard a rifle crack and saw a muzzle flash from the boardwalk at the corner.

In the reflected glow of that flash, his keen eyes recognized the face of Marshal Ted Cardwell. The lawman was trying to stop the fleeing riders, and they were equally determined to escape past him.

Cardwell was outgunned. Smoke's grip tightened on the Colt in his hand as he saw the young marshal go down under the onslaught of lead from the two horsemen. Smoke knew Cardwell must have been hit hard, but he didn't have time to worry about that now.

The two riders flashed past the intersection and pounded on toward Smoke and Windy.

"Get back inside," he snapped at the old-timer, but Windy ignored the order.

"The hell with that!" he said. "I got an old horse pistol in the wagon!"

The wagon Windy had used to deliver the firewood was still parked in front of the house, with a couple of mules standing stolidly in their traces. Windy ran to the vehicle and thrust an arm over the sideboards into the back.

Smoke moved behind the wagon, as well, to use it for cover. He didn't know who those riders were, but he had watched them gun down Marshal Cardwell, so he was certain they belonged to the owlhoot breed and he didn't want them to get away. He lifted the Colt and called in a loud, clear voice, "Stop and throw down your guns!"

Instead, more red eyes winked in the night as the two men tried to blast their way past. Smoke had called on them to surrender and they'd ignored that chance, so as bullets thudded into the wagon, he lined his sights and triggered twice.

One of the riders screamed and flung his arms out to the sides. He went backward out of the saddle and landed in the street with a sodden thump.

At Smoke's side, the old cap-and-ball pistol Windy had gotten from the back of the wagon went off with a boom like a cannon. The second outlaw jerked under the impact of the heavy lead ball, but he kept coming, and the gun in his hand continued to spout flame.

Smoke fired while Windy reloaded and fired, too, and this time the attacker lifted up out of leather and turned a backward somersault to land face-down behind the galloping horse. Both mounts charged on past the wagon where Smoke and Windy had taken cover.

Their former riders lay motionless in the street.

"Jonas, wait! You can't go out there!"

Smoke looked over his shoulder to see Miriam Dollinger struggling to keep Madigan from charging out onto the porch in his night clothes.

"Blast it, woman, let go of me," the former lawman roared. "I've got to see what all that shootin' is about."

"Windy, go give Mrs. Dollinger a hand," Smoke said. "Jonas doesn't need to be rushing around out here in the cold."

"What about those varmints?" Windy asked as he jerked his whiskery chin toward the men lying in the street.

"I'll check on them and make sure they're dead."

"I . . . I seen 'em shoot somebody there in town. I think it was Marshal Cardwell."

"Looked like it to me, too," Smoke said, "and I'll see

about him once I've made sure those men are no longer threats."

Windy swallowed, nodded, and hurried up the walk toward the house. Smoke kept his Colt leveled in front of him as he stepped out from behind the wagon and approached the fallen men.

The closest one lay face down. Smoke kicked away the gun the man had dropped, then hooked a boot toe under his shoulder and rolled him onto this back. The way the man's arms flopped loosely as he went over told Smoke that he was indeed dead, just as expected.

Smoke moved on to the other man and confirmed that he was dead, too. As he was finishing that grim task, he saw Windy coming toward him. The old-timer held a lit lantern in his upraised left hand. His right still clutched the long-barreled old cap-and-ball pistol.

"Are both of the varmints done for?" Windy asked as Smoke joined him near the other body.

"That's right. I guess you and Mrs. Dollinger were able to get Jonas back to bed?"

"Yeah, he didn't much want to go, but—Holy jumpin' horned toads!" Windy burst out as the circle of light from the lantern he carried washed over the dead man's face.

"What's the matter? You know him?"

"No, I . . . I just . . . He's an ugly varmint, ain't he?"

Smoke looked down at the angular face, frozen now in a grimace of pain and death. Although all the features were different, this man reminded Smoke of scores of other hardened outlaws he had encountered. The unmistakable stamp of the owlhoot trail was on his visage.

"Let's take a look at the other'un," Windy suggested.

He took the lantern over to where the second outlaw lay and gazed down at him for a moment.

"How about this one?" Smoke asked.

"Never seen him before, but you can tell he's a bad one just by lookin' at him."

By now, several people were hurrying along the street toward them. As they came into the light, Smoke recognized a couple of them: Edward Warren, from the SALT LICK TRIBUNE, and Rufus Spencer, the burly, bearded liveryman and blacksmith. Spencer carried a shotgun, and some of the other men were armed with rifles or handguns, as well.

"Mr. Jensen," Warren said, "what's happened here? Who are these men?"

"I don't know," Smoke replied, "but we saw them shoot down Marshal Cardwell."

A big man with curly dark hair and a high-pitched voice said, "We know. We found poor Ted back up yonder on the boardwalk."

"Is he . . . ?"

"I'm afraid he's dead," Warren said in reply to Smoke's unfinished question. "He had a number of bullet wounds." The newspaperman shook his head. "He never had a chance."

Smoke's jaw tightened. He hadn't particularly liked Ted Cardwell and thought he was handling the job of marshal the wrong way, but with experience, Cardwell might have learned how to be a decent lawman. He'd certainly had a good example to follow in Jonas Madigan. Smoke was sorry that Cardwell would never get that chance.

"Do any of you know what it was about?" he asked. "What was that explosion?"

"We're, uh, not sure," Warren said. "Some of us thought it came from the bank. We were about to check when we saw you and Windy down here."

Smoke nodded. "Let's go take a look." He headed in that direction, and the other men came along. He wasn't trying to take charge, necessarily, but people recognized his naturally commanding personality.

And with Cardwell dead and Jonas Madigan in no shape to step back into the role, *somebody* had to take the lead.

When they reached the bank, they found a man wearing a nightshirt over a hastily pulled on pair of trousers bobbing up and down agitatedly on the balls of his feet.

"Have you been inside, Mr. Hawkins?" Edward Warren asked him.

The man shook his head. "No, I was worried that some of the robbers might still be in there."

"You're the president of this bank?" Smoke asked.

"That's right, sir. Abner Hawkins. And who might you be?"

"He's Smoke Jensen," Warren said. "The famous gunman and adventurer."

Hawkins stared at Smoke for a second, then said, "I'll unlock the doors, and some of you men can go inside if you want. I . . . I can smell smoke, but I'm not sure the place is on fire . . ."

"That's dynamite you smell," Smoke said. "I've had occasion to use the stuff before." He nodded toward the doors. "Go ahead and unlock them, if you don't mind, Mr. Hawkins."

The banker hesitated, and Rufus Spencer said, "I know Mr. Jensen's new in town, but he's got more experience with trouble than all the rest of us put together, so he's sort of running things right now. Go ahead and unlock 'em, Abner."

"Very well." Hawkins thrust a big key into the lock and twisted it. He stepped back out of the way while Smoke, Windy, Spencer, and a couple of other armed men went inside.

It was obvious this was where the explosion had taken place. A few wisps of smoke still drifted in the air. The banker's desk was lying on its side, pushed over by the force of the blast. Papers and smaller pieces of debris were scattered around the lobby. As the light from Windy's lantern reached the vault door, they all saw the blackened area around the lock.

"The varmints tried to blow the door," Windy exclaimed.

Outside, Hawkins heard that and rushed in. "Did they get into the vault?" he asked excitedly. "Did they take the money?"

"You can rest easy, Mr. Hawkins," Smoke told him. "Your vault door held up to the blast."

"Thank heavens," Hawkins muttered. "It should have. It cost enough." He looked around. "There aren't any more of the outlaws in here?"

"Looks like there was just the two of 'em," Windy said. "And they won't rob no more banks, thanks to Smoke and me."

"They won't gun down any more marshals, either," Warren added. "Poor Ted."

The men drifted back outside, except for Hawkins and one of the others who worked as a teller in the bank, Windy explained to Smoke. The two of them started cleaning up the mess inside the lobby.

A few yards away, just before the boardwalk ended at the corner, someone had spread a blanket over Ted Cardwell's body, but it was still lying there, a grim reminder of the violence that had erupted on this chilly night.

"Does anybody know who those killers were?" a man asked.

"I do," the man with the high-pitched voice replied. "They came into my saloon earlier today and had a drink. Friendly enough fellas. You could tell they were saddle tramps, but they seemed like decent sorts."

"You think anybody's decent who's buying your whiskey, Apple Jack," Spencer said.

"Now, that ain't exactly true!"

As if he hadn't heard the saloonkeeper's objection,

Spencer went on, "Since you mention it, I remember them, too. They came in just before that poker game I was playing in broke up."

"And Marshal Cardwell mentioned something about running a couple of drifters out of town," Smoke said. "That had to have been the same pair. I guess they didn't like what happened, and came back to settle the score by robbing the bank."

"Could be," Windy said. "But what's got me worried is this. How do we know they was by theirselves?"

That was an odd question to ask, Smoke thought, and as the group of men began to break up, he put a hand on the old-timer's shoulder and said, "Why don't you come down to the marshal's office with me, Windy? I think we need to have a talk."

CHAPTER 13

Somebody had already gone to fetch Salt Lick's undertaker. The man's wagon rolled up at the corner, and he and an assistant hopped down from the seat to tend to Marshal Cardwell's body. They would deal with the bodies of the two dead outlaws, as well.

"Don't you reckon we ought to stay here in case they need any help?" Windy asked.

Smoke tightened his grip on the old-timer's shoulder. "I'm sure they can handle things," he said. "That's their job, after all. And if they do need help, there are probably plenty of men around who'd be willing to volunteer."

"Yeah, yeah, I reckon so," Windy muttered. With his eyes downcast, he allowed Smoke to steer him along the boardwalk toward the marshal's office. The office door was open. Lamplight spilled through it from inside.

As they went in, Smoke saw papers scattered on the desk and across the floor. So did Windy, who hurried forward and started gathering them up.

"Looks like the wind made a mess in here," he said. He balled the papers together and reached for one of the desk drawers, as if he were about to shove them in there.

"Hold on a minute," Smoke told him. "What's that you have there?"

"This?" Windy waved the jumbled sheaf of papers. "Oh, nothin' important. Looks like some wanted posters. That's somethin' you'll find in just about any lawman's office."

"Yes, it is," Smoke agreed. "Put them down there on top of the desk."

For a second, Windy looked like he might argue, but then he swallowed, his Adam's apple bobbing up and down under the brush of white whiskers. He set the reward posters on the desk. Smoke leaned over and spread them out, smoothing them down where Windy had crumpled them.

"I admit I haven't known you that long, Windy," he said, "but it seems to me that you're acting a little strange. You have been ever since you got a good look at the faces of those men we were forced to kill. You *do* know them, don't you?"

"No, I . . . I . . ." Windy glanced down at the papers and suddenly jabbed a gnarled finger toward them. "I thought I recognized one of 'em from those reward dodgers, that's all. I'll bet a hat they're somewhere in that bunch."

"Are you in the habit of studying the marshal's collection of wanted posters?"

"Not lately. Ted Cardwell didn't want me around. But I told you, I used to work as a jailer sometimes, back when Jonas was wearin' the star, and I'd go through the posters to pass the time when I was on duty at night. Sometimes, when you read about all them bad men and all the terrible things they done, it's almost like readin' a story."

Smoke nodded slowly as he thought about Windy's answer. That was actually a reasonable explanation the old-timer had offered him, he decided. He had no reason to doubt that it was the truth. Windy had seemed more surprised than recognizing a wanted owlhoot really warranted, but as Smoke had said, he didn't know the old-timer well enough to say for sure what was or wasn't out of character for him.

Smoke spread the wanted posters out more. One with a drawing on it caught his eye. He separated it from the others and pulled it closer.

"Look familiar to you?" he asked Windy after he had studied the drawing for a moment.

"That's him! The fella we shot. I was right. He's got paper on him." Windy's eyes widened. "And a five hunnerd dollar ree-ward!" He leaned over the desk and pawed through the posters. "What about the other one? Is he— Dadgum, look there! That matches the description of the other varmint, don't it?"

"Sid Atkins," Smoke read from the poster. "And the other man was Bart Rome. I wonder if they mentioned their names to that saloonkeeper who saw them."

"Reckon we can ask ol' Apple Jack and find out," Windy suggested. "But whether they did or not, there ain't no doubt these are the fellas."

"I agree."

"And they're worth five hunnerd apiece. We can split that—"

Smoke waved a hand. "Don't worry about that. You can have the reward."

Windy practically licked his lips in anticipation. "Are you sure?"

"Yeah. I'm more worried about something else."

"What's that?"

Smoke tapped one of the wanted posters, then the other.

"These dodgers say that Rome and Atkins are both members of the Snake Bishop gang. I've heard of Bishop and his bunch. And from what I've heard, giving Bishop the nickname of 'Snake' is an insult . . . to all the snakes in the world."

"He's a lowdown sidewinder, all right. From, uh, what I've heard about him, I mean. And you think that since these two are supposed to be ridin' with him . . ."

"It sure makes me wonder where Bishop and the rest of the gang are," Smoke said.

Fifty miles south of Salt Lick, flames shot high in the night from half a dozen burning buildings. This settlement didn't have an official name. There was no post office here; it wasn't on any stagecoach line, and no railroad ran anywhere nearby. It was just a little wide place in the trail, with a trading post, a blacksmith shop, a saloon, and several houses where the people who ran those businesses lived.

They were the ones who had decided to call this tiny settlement Thatcher's Crossing, after the fella who had started the trading post. The crossing part came from the fact that an even smaller east-west trail intersected the sparsely traveled north-south trail here.

After tonight, nobody would call it anything, unless, before the elements swallowed up the ruins entirely, somebody might point at them and say, "That's where Thatcher's Crossing used to be. Before Snake Bishop and his gang rode in."

Bishop himself strode back and forth, the whip he carried in his left hand coiling and hissing around his booted feet like a live thing. Folks assumed he had gotten the "Snake" name because of how mean and ruthless and deadly he was, but that wasn't the case at all.

Early on, down there in New Orleans, he had gotten a reputation as being a dangerous man to cross because of the way he handled a blacksnake whip. He didn't care if somebody came after him with a gun; he was fast enough with that whip to cut a man to ribbons before the fool could draw and fire. And anybody who tried to use a knife against him was an even bigger fool. They'd never get close enough before Bishop had them on their knees, screaming because that whip had sliced their faces open, leaving them bloody and blind and ruined.

That whip had tasted plenty of blood over the years, a mighty damned lot.

And nobody wielded it better than Blacksnake Bishop.

Eventually, people had shortened the name to just Snake Bishop, and even in the cesspit of crime and corruption that was New Orleans, things got too hot with the law for Bishop to hang around. He had lit a shuck for Texas, or, as some of the old-timers from plantation days called it, the Texies.

But he took that whip with him, and it had helped him assemble the gang he led now, nearly four dozen of the toughest hombres west of the Mississippi. As the gang grew, they had ranged up through Indian Territory to Kansas and over into Missouri. They had held up numerous trains and stagecoaches, but what Bishop liked best was raiding towns, targeting banks in particular but looting whatever money and valuables they found in all the businesses, killing anybody who tried to stop them and then leaving the places burning behind them.

Unlike some men he'd known, Bishop didn't get any particular pleasure out of burning things. It was just a good tactic; that was all. Folks with their lives destroyed around them, turned into smoldering heaps of ash, were too demoralized to even think about going after the men responsible for that atrocity. Mostly they just sat in huddled heaps and cried, until necessity forced them to get around to burying the dead.

By then, Bishop and his followers were long gone.

This place, with only a handful of businesses, had barely

been worth the trouble. Once they counted the loot, more than likely they'd find that the take amounted to no more than five hundred dollars. Not even ten dollars a man, split evenly . . . which they didn't, because Bishop always got a fifth of the loot off the top.

But hell, it was on the way to where they were going. Might as well hit it for the practice, if nothing else, Bishop had decided.

And so they had, sweeping out of the night, an unexpected storm of death and destruction. Now the buildings were on fire, half a dozen bodies were sprawled on the ground, motionless in the hellish glare of the flames, and another fifteen prisoners pressed together in a terrified cluster, surrounded by Bishop's cold-eyed killers.

Bishop walked up in front of them and regarded them with no emotion on his face. He was a tall man, handsome in a brutal way, well-dressed in stovepipe boots, whipcord trousers, a frock coat, a white shirt, and a flat-crowned black hat.

He'd been raised in an expensive parlor house, the son of a whore and some unknown but no doubt well-to-do customer. His daddy had to be rich, because his mama was so beautiful, and as a boy Calvin Bishop had dreamed about the day that rich man would show up to claim him and take him and his mama off to a better life.

That had never happened, of course, and when Bishop was eight years old his mama had died of a fever, and he was left to survive on his own, whatever it took and whatever he was willing to do.

It hadn't taken him long to realize that he was willing to do *anything*, as long as it got him what he wanted.

He swung his left hand back and forth, just a little, and the whip writhed at his feet. He lifted his voice and said over the crackle of the flames, "Do you people know who I am?"

No one answered.

Bishop didn't delay. His left hand came up and the whip flashed out, and a middle-aged man with a drooping mustache shrieked in pain and dropped to his knees, pawing at the eye that the whip had just turned to jelly.

"I said, do you people know who I am?"

"You . . . you're Snake Bishop," another man forced out.

"That's right. So you know I won't hesitate to kill any of you who fail to cooperate with me."

"What do you want from us?" a woman cried. "You've already taken everything!"

Bishop smiled and shook his head slowly. "Not everything, ma'am. True, my men went through the businesses and your houses and collected everything of value before they set them on fire, but I still see . . ." Bishop pointed with the whip as he counted quickly. "One two three four . . . young women who can be of comfort to my men on a chilly night such as this."

That brought terrified cries from the women and angry shouts from the men, but with a whip-wielding madman in front of them and gun-hung outlaws all around, nobody dared move.

Bishop nodded curtly. Some of his men grabbed the girls he had indicated, tearing them away from their husbands or parents, and dragged them off.

One of the male prisoners found enough courage somewhere inside to step forward and rage, "Someday justice will catch up to you, Bishop! Someday you'll get what's coming to you!"

"But this," Bishop said, smiling and shaking his head slowly, "is not that day."

He cracked the whip. His men knew that signal. Guns came out and began to roar. The captives tried to flee into the night but had no chance before the flying lead scythed them all down. A few twitches and it was over, all but the echoes rolling away across the Panhandle plains.

Sometimes Bishop allowed the survivors of one of his raids to live; sometimes he didn't. Unfortunately for the people of Thatcher's Crossing, this had been one of those times when he didn't.

The gang rode away a short time later, leaving death and ruins behind, taking with them the four sobbing girls, who probably wouldn't live through the night either. Stopping here had barely been worth the time and trouble, Bishop thought again as he rode at their head . . . but it had livened up a long, boring ride.

The real payoff still lay ahead of them . . . in a town called Salt Lick.

Jonas Madigan had refused to go to bed until Smoke got back, but at least he was sitting in the parlor in a comfortable armchair with a blanket over his legs. He looked up, his dark eyes snapping with anger, and demanded, "What happened?"

Miriam Dollinger, sitting close beside him, reached over and took his hand. "Please don't get too worked up, Jonas," she cautioned.

He pulled his hand away. Miriam looked down quickly, Smoke noted, probably so Madigan wouldn't see that he had hurt her feelings.

Smoke, who had just walked in, took his hat off and sighed. "I hate to tell you this, Jonas, but Ted Cardwell is dead."

Miriam gasped. Madigan's face grew even more haggard, but he said, "Go on."

"A couple of outlaws tried to rob the bank. That explosion was them using dynamite in an attempt to blow open the vault door. They failed."

"Well, there's that, anyway, I reckon," Madigan muttered. "What else?"

"Marshal Cardwell did his job," Smoke said. "He tried to stop them from escaping. But they shot and killed him."

"So the varmints got away?"

Smoke shook his head. "No. They tried to ride right down the street outside, past me and Windy."

Madigan stared at Smoke for a second, then a grim chuckle escaped his lips. "Damn fools," he said.

"They're both dead."

"I don't reckon you had to tell me that. Is Windy all right?"

"He's fine," Smoke said.

"Good. I like that cantankerous old cuss. Where is he?"

"He walked down here with me to get his wagon," Smoke explained, "and then he was going back to the marshal's office. We figured somebody needed to be there, and Windy used to be the jailer, at least, even if he wasn't an official deputy."

Madigan nodded and said, "He's a good man. I reckon he can hold down the fort for now."

Smoke drew a chair up and sat down. Madigan had a right to know the rest of it.

"There's more, Jonas. Windy recognized one of the outlaws from a wanted poster he'd seen, and we figured out who the other one was by going through the posters in the marshal's office. They were both members of the Snake Bishop gang."

Madigan's eyes widened. He started to stand up, jolted out of the chair by what Smoke had just said. Miriam caught hold of his arm and kept him from standing.

"Please, Jonas—"

He ignored her and repeated, "Bishop! Good Lord, Smoke, over the past few years, he's been the worst outlaw in this whole part of the country!"

"I know," Smoke said, nodding. "We've heard plenty about him and his gang, even up in Colorado."

"The varmints who hit the bank . . . you think Bishop sent them here to scout out Salt Lick and see if it's worth raiding? I've heard rumors that that's how he operates."

"It's possible," Smoke allowed. "But remember, those two already tried to rob the bank. It could be that they've split off from Bishop and he's nowhere around here."

"Or it could be that he sent 'em and they decided to double-cross him and pull a job of their own," Madigan said stubbornly. "That would've been a mighty foolish thing to do, considerin' how loco he's supposed to be, but the thought of gettin' their hands on some loot might've made them a little crazy, too."

"I don't reckon we can rule that out," Smoke said.

Madigan sat back, breathing heavily but more composed now. "In that case, there's only one thing we can do. If there's even the slightest chance that Snake Bishop is headed here, the town's got to be ready for him. And that means we have to have a lawman."

"Jonas, you're in no shape to take over that job again," Miriam said. "I know you still think of Salt Lick as your town—"

"It *is* my town, blast it!" Madigan thumped a fist on the arm of the chair. "It always will be, as long as I'm on this side of the dirt." He shook his head. "But I wasn't talkin' about me. I'm not completely loco, Miriam. Hell, the town would be better off with Windy Whittaker as the marshal than with me!"

"I thought about Windy—" Smoke began.

"And you knew, even though you just rode in today, that he's not up to the job, either." Madigan glared at Smoke. "One of us might as well say it. If Snake Bishop is on his way here, then Salt Lick's only got one chance, Smoke . . . and that's you. You got to pin the badge on. You got to be the new marshal of Salt Lick."

CHAPTER 14

The situation hadn't magically improved by morning. The threat of Snake Bishop and his gang still loomed, although nothing had happened since the attempted bank robbery the previous night.

Miriam Dollinger arrived early at Jonas Madigan's house to prepare breakfast for Smoke and the former marshal. Smoke had told her before she left the night before that he could rustle up some grub for himself and Madigan, but she'd insisted.

"I've gotten in the habit of looking after Jonas," she'd said. "I don't see any reason to stop now. Besides, I make excellent flapjacks and bacon."

"I don't doubt that for a second, ma'am," Smoke had told her with a smile. "And I already know how good your coffee is, so I'm not going to argue with you."

"You're a married man, so I suspect you know that arguing wouldn't do you any good."

"Yes, ma'am."

Madigan insisted on getting up and having breakfast with them at the kitchen table, rather than allowing Miriam to bring him a tray. As they ate, he said, "Have you given any more thought to what we discussed last night, Smoke?"

"You mean about me taking over as marshal? Shouldn't

the mayor and the town council have something to say about that?"

Madigan waved that away. "Roy Trout and the other members of the council will do whatever I suggest when it comes to the law around here. They gave the job to Ted, didn't they? And he would've done fine if . . . if he'd had the chance . . ."

The emotional catch in Madigan's voice made him look down and clear his throat. After a moment, he raised his eyes to gaze once more across the table at Smoke.

"You can't honestly believe that there's anybody in Salt Lick better suited to handle this kind of trouble than you, Smoke."

"Well, if we're being honest . . . I've probably had to deal with more shooting scrapes than anybody else around here, except for you."

Madigan snorted and said, "You've tackled more badmen than I ever will. Just say you'll pin on the badge."

Smoke nodded. "I'll do it. With some reluctance, I might add. And the town should move quickly on the matter of finding a *real* lawman to take over."

"The stagecoach will be coming through tomorrow," Madigan said. "I'll get the mayor to write a letter and send it to the governor, asking him to send a Ranger up here until we can find somebody to take the job permanent-like. But it'll take a week or more for anybody to get here from Austin, and we probably don't have that long."

If anybody wanted to get precise about it, Smoke *had* been a real lawman several times during his life, wearing the badge of a deputy United States marshal for a short while as well as filling in for a few local star packers, as he was about to do here in Salt Lick.

But none of those instances had lasted very long, and he had never considered upholding the law to be his real job. It just coincided with his natural desire to see justice done and the innocent protected.

"If it would make you feel better," Madigan continued, "you can go see Mayor Trout and get him to appoint you officially, but that isn't really necessary. You can just pin the badge on and tell folks that you're takin' over for Ted, and nobody's gonna argue with you. *Especially* once they find out there's a chance Snake Bishop and his bloody-handed bunch are on their way here."

Miriam frowned and said, "Should you even tell people about that now, at this point? You don't *know* that Bishop is coming, and if you tell people he is, it's liable to cause a panic."

Madigan poked his fork in the air a couple of times, toward Miriam, and said, "The lady is smart as well as beautiful. Maybe it *would* be better to keep that possibility under our hats for now, as much as we can. Some folks have got to know, of course, so we can get ready to defend the town if Bishop does plan on raidin' it."

"I agree," Smoke said with a nod. "But remember, Windy knows about it already."

Madigan let out a groan. "Oh, for Pete's sake! I'd forgotten about Windy. If he knows, there's a chance half the town knows by now. At least half."

"Maybe not. He was going to stay in the marshal's office until I stopped by there this morning. Maybe no one came in and he hasn't had a chance to talk to anybody." Smoke's plate was empty. He picked up his cup and drank the rest of the coffee in it. "I'd better go ahead and get down there, though, just in case somebody might come along."

"Good idea. If he's got any questions about you takin' over, or problems with how things are gonna be, you tell him to come and see me."

"All right, Jonas." Smoke stood up and dropped his

napkin beside the empty plate. "I don't think he'll have any problems with it, though."

"No, I don't expect he will. Windy Whittaker has never seemed all that ambitious. He won't want a bunch of responsibility."

Neither did Smoke, but somebody had to take over. The threat of Snake Bishop loomed as threatening as a storm racing down on a helpless community.

If there was a storm bound for Salt Lick—an actual storm—there was no sign of it this morning as Smoke walked toward the center of town. In fact, the sky was a clear, dazzling blue, and the breeze had turned around to the south and was warmer than it had been the day before.

Quite a few people were moving up and down the boardwalks. Wagons were parked in front of some of the stores. Men on horseback rode along the street. It looked like a typical day in Salt Lick, despite all the excitement the night before.

However, the bank had a CLOSED sign on its door, Smoke noted as he reached the corner. Abner Hawkins and his employees probably were still cleaning up inside.

"Howdy, Mr. Jensen," a deep voice rumbled at Smoke. He looked to his right and saw Ralph Warren coming along the street toward him, pulling a small, red-painted wagon with stacks of folded newspapers in it.

"Are you delivering papers this morning, Ralph?" Smoke asked the youngster.

"Yes, sir. Pa and me got up early and put out an extra. It's all about the bank robbery and the shootin' and poor Marshal Cardwell gettin' killed. I'm takin' copies around town and droppin' 'em at the stores that sell 'em."

"Well, I'll buy a copy directly from you, if that's all right."

"Shoot, you ought to get one free! It wouldn't be near as good a story without you in it. If it hadn't been for you, those damn bank robbers would'a got away."

The boy glanced around quickly, as if worried that someone who would report it to his mother might have overheard his profanity. No one seemed to have noticed, though.

"I'll pay for a copy," Smoke said as he took a dime from his pocket and handed it over.

"Paper's only a nickel."

"Close enough," Smoke told him. He took the paper Ralph handed him and glanced at the headlines:

MARSHAL SLAIN BY OUTLAWS.
BANK ROBBERY ATTEMPT FAILS.

ESCAPE FOILED BY FAMOUS ADVENTURER SMOKE JENSEN.

"Everybody's talkin' about all the excitement last night," Ralph said. "This is the biggest thing to hit Salt Lick in . . . well . . . forever!"

If Snake Bishop and his gang attacked the town, that would be an even bigger story, Smoke thought, but for now the possibility of that happening had to remain a closely held secret among only a few people.

"Thanks, Ralph," he said. "I'll read this more closely later. Right now, I have things to do."

"How about if I follow you around so I can tell my pa what you're doin' and he can write about it? I'm gonna be a reporter myself one of these days."

"I'll bet you will be." Smoke nodded toward the wagon. "But right now your pa's counting on you to deliver those papers, I expect."

"Well, yeah, I reckon. But if you have any exciting news, you be sure to look me up and tell me. I'll be in the newspaper office or around town somewhere."

As the boy started to pull the wagon away, something occurred to Smoke. He asked, "Ralph, why aren't you in school?"

"No school right now. The teacher ran off with a cowboy and they got married. We're supposed to get another teacher sometime, but they haven't found one yet. My ma said she'd take over the school temporarily, but folks won't allow that. They say you can't be a teacher and have a husband."

That was the policy in a lot of places, Smoke knew. Sally had been a teacher when they first met, but she had given it up when they got married. As far as Smoke was concerned, the rule didn't make a lot of sense—he knew good and well Sally would be just as good a teacher now as she had been before they were hitched—but he didn't decide such things.

Ralph went on his way, and Smoke walked across the street to the marshal's office. He heard snoring as soon as he opened the door.

Windy had the marshal's chair tipped back and his legs crossed at the ankles with the boot heels resting on top of the desk. His head hung back and his mouth gaped open as awesome snores issued from it. The white whiskers jutting from his chin quivered in time with the racket.

Under other circumstances, Smoke might have gone on his way quietly and let the old-timer sleep. But they needed to talk about things, so he stepped inside and said, "Rise and shine, Windy. Time to rattle your hocks."

Windy's head jerked up hard enough to make his hat fall off backward, but the rawhide chin strap caught it. His feet came up off the desk, and for a moment he was balanced precariously on the chair's rear legs. Smoke didn't want him to hurt himself, so he stepped forward quickly and came around the desk to catch hold of the chair. The front legs came down with a thump.

Windy got his feet on the floor and stood up. He pawed through his disarrayed white hair and then jammed the battered old hat back down on it.

"Dadblast it, Smoke, you like to scared me outta ten year's growth! And an old fella like me ain't got any extra years to spare!"

"Sorry, Windy," Smoke said. "I'll try to be more gentle about it next time."

Windy raked fingers through his beard and said, "See that you do. Why, 'tain't safe to spook a dangerous ol' lobo like me. I might'a whipped out this hogleg o' mine and commenced to blazin' away with it."

He slapped the old cap-and-ball pistol, which now rested in an equally ancient holster attached to a gun belt strapped around the old-timer's scrawny hips.

"Well, I wouldn't want that," Smoke said.

Windy snorted. "Durned right you wouldn't."

"So I'll be more careful in the future. Right now, though . . . was there any more trouble last night?"

Windy shook his head and said, "Nope. I made the rounds two or three times, and everything was quiet as could be. Town seems back to normal this mornin'." He made a face. "Just wish it'd stay that way."

"Maybe it will."

"Not if Snake Bishop is headin' this way," Windy said. His weathered face was gloomy now. "Only question is what's gonna hit Salt Lick first, them bloodthirsty outlaws or that hellacious blue norther that's bearin' down on us."

"What blue norther? The weather's better out there today. It's actually almost pleasant."

"That don't mean nothin'. That's just a trick Ol' Man Winter likes to play on Texas. It'll be nice and sunny and warm, and folks walk around goin', oh, lah-de-dee, ain't this just the prettiest weather, and then the norther comes crashin' through and the wind howls like a thousand starvin' wolves and the temperature drops like the bottom come out of it. I've seen it happen a heap o' times, and my bones tell me it's on the way again."

"Well . . . that might be a good thing," Smoke suggested. "If the weather's really that bad, Snake Bishop might hunt some place to hole up instead of coming here to raid the town."

"Yeah, but even if he did, that'd just slow him down, not stop him. Once he's got his mind set on somethin', he always goes through with it. Uh, so I've heard tell, anyway."

Smoke nodded slowly. "I suppose that's possible. But even a delay like that would give us more time to get ready. And speaking of that . . . Jonas thinks that I should take over the marshal's job for the time being."

"Well, shoot, of course you're gonna be the marshal. Ain't nobody else in Salt Lick who's fit for the job, lemme tell you." Windy opened the top drawer in the desk and took something out of it. "Teel Wilkins, he's the undertaker, brung this by a little while ago, along with Ted Cardwell's other things."

He held out the marshal's badge.

Smoke took the badge, studied it for a moment. "Some folks may think you should be wearing this, not me."

"Now, *that's* a real knee-slapper! Everybody in Salt Lick knows I ain't cut out to be in charge. But they'll respect you and do what you say, 'specially when they hear that Snake Bishop's on the way."

"That's another thing," Smoke said as he pinned on the badge. Madigan and Windy were both right: he was the best man for the job, so there was no point in discussing it. "Jonas and I agree that we don't want to say anything about

Bishop right away. That could start a panic. Have you told anyone about Rome and Atkins being part of his gang?"

"Nope. Ain't really seen nobody to talk to except Teel, and I didn't say nothin' to him. But Smoke . . . folks *got* to know. We got to get ready to fight, and they need to know who they'll be fightin'."

"We'll have to tell them, all right, but I want to get a better idea what we'll be working with, first. I've met some of the people in town already, but I want to meet more of them, especially the ones who might have some experience in fighting. I imagine there are some veterans of the war who live here, and maybe some former soldiers, even if they haven't been in combat."

Windy brightened up a little. "Yeah, I can help you with that. I know most of the fellas in town."

"You probably need to get some breakfast first, though. You haven't eaten, have you?"

"No, and I am a mite ga'nted. But we can do some of both at the same time. Come on down to the Red Top with me. Fella who runs it, Mickey Shaw, used to be a sergeant in the cavalry. He just retired a couple years ago. He was with Mackenzie down there at Palo Duro Canyon, so he's seen some fightin'."

"That's exactly the sort of man I want to meet," Smoke said. "Come on."

CHAPTER 15

Mickey Shaw was a short, stocky man with grizzled, close-cropped hair and a jaw like a chunk of rock. His grip was powerful as he reached across the counter in the Red Top Café and clasped Smoke's hand.

"'Tis pleased I am to be meeting you, Mr. Jensen," he said. "I've heard a lot about you. Never really thought we'd run into each other, though."

Shaw wore a canvas apron, and the sleeves of his work shirt were rolled up to reveal brawny forearms. He went on, "Excuse me a minute," and turned his head to bellow through the window in the wall behind him, "Where the devil are those eggs?"

An equally loud reply came from the kitchen on the other side of the window. "I'm gettin' 'em done, you big-mouthed Mick! Just keep your shirt on!"

Shaw grinned at Smoke and jerked a thumb over his shoulder. "Me wife. Her bark is worse than her bite, as they say."

"I heard that! And I wouldn't bet on it!"

Shaw ignored the comment from the kitchen. "What can I do for you, Mr. Jensen? You want some breakfast? It'll be on the house, after what you did for the town last night, stoppin' those robbers from escapin' after they gunned down Marshal Cardwell."

"I've eaten already," Smoke told him, "but I could use a cup of coffee. It's Windy here we came to feed." Smoke nodded toward the old-timer.

"Oh." Shaw frowned at Windy. "You have any money?"

Before Windy could answer, Smoke said, "You can put it on the tab for the marshal's office. I'm holding down the job temporarily, and Windy's my deputy."

"I am?" Windy said in obvious surprise.

"You are. I'm going to need an experienced man backing me up."

"Oh. Well, I, uh, appreciate that, Smoke. I'll try not to let you down." Windy licked his lips. "I could use a couple eggs and some biscuits and bacon."

Shaw shrugged and nodded. "Comin' up. You hear that, Charlotte?"

"I heard," the reply came from the kitchen. "I'll get it done as soon as I can. There's only one of me, you know."

"I know," Shaw told her, then added under his breath, "The world couldn't handle more than one of you."

He poured coffee for Smoke and Windy, who took seats at the counter. Smoke glanced around. Several of the café's booths were occupied, but no one else sat at the counter. He leaned forward and said quietly, "There's something else I need to talk to you about, Mr. Shaw."

"Call me Mickey. And you look mighty serious all of a sudden, Mr. Jensen. Or should I call you Marshal Jensen?"

"Make it easy on all of us and just call me Smoke." He took a sip of the coffee, which was good but not as good as Miriam Dollinger's, and went on, "Windy tells me you were a sergeant in the cavalry."

"That's right. Was in eighteen years but finally had enough of it and came here to open this café."

"Salt Lick may be facing some trouble, the kind where military experience could come in mighty handy."

"Well, that doesn't sound good," Shaw said. "Maybe you'd best just speak plain, Smoke."

"All right. Those two who tried to rob the bank, more than likely they're part of the gang that rides with Snake Bishop."

Shaw's jaw tightened and jutted out even more. "Bishop," he repeated. "He's supposed to be a mighty bad sort."

Windy said, "He is. Don't you ever doubt it, Sarge."

"We don't know that Bishop is headed for Salt Lick," Smoke said, "but there's a good chance he is. If he raids the town, we'll need to be ready for him, and that means rounding up some good fighting men . . . and someone to take charge of them."

"And you want me to do that?"

"From what I've heard, you're the best man for the job."

Windy said, "I told Smoke about you bein' down yonder at Palo Duro Canyon with Colonel Mackenzie."

Shaw nodded slowly. "I was there, all right. It was quite a fight against the Comanche. From what *I've* heard, though, Bishop may be even worse than they were. And we don't have several troops of cavalry to work with."

"How many good fighting men do you think you can find here in Salt Lick?"

Shaw pondered Smoke's question for several seconds, then said, "Maybe two dozen who are worth much, and are still young enough to fight. Throw in some green kids who *might* have what it takes, and some like Windy, who have the experience but are past their prime, and there might be twenty-five or thirty more."

"Past my prime?" Windy said indignantly. "Why, I'll have you know I can still lick my weight in wildcats—"

"So we're talking about a force of approximately fifty men," Smoke said, breaking into the old-timer's protest.

Shaw nodded. "Yeah. One good thing is that there ought to be plenty of rifles and ammunition among the stock of the mercantiles here in town. We shouldn't run short of firepower."

"That is good," Smoke agreed. "Why don't you and Windy put your heads together and come up with a list of men we can recruit? For now, though, don't say anything to them. We're trying to keep the possibility of a raid quiet for the time being."

"You don't want folks so scared they start running around like chickens with their heads cut off."

"That's right."

A swinging door into the kitchen opened, and a woman came out with a tray loaded with plates. After hearing the way she and her husband shouted at each other, Smoke halfway expected Charlotte Shaw to be a middle-aged harridan, but he was surprised to see that she was at least ten years younger than the former sergeant and very attractive with long, dark hair done into a thick braid.

"Here you go, Windy," she said as she took one of the platters from the tray and placed it in front of Windy.

"Miz Charlotte, that looks plumb delicious," he told her. "Smells like it, too."

"Thank you." She glanced at Shaw. "It's nice to know that *somebody* around here appreciates my efforts."

Shaw just snorted. Then, as his wife picked up the tray and went to deliver meals to some of the other customers, he turned back to Smoke and said, "I'll tell you somebody else you need to talk to. Apple Jack."

Smoke remembered hearing one of the men from the night before referred to by that name. "Saloonkeeper, isn't he?"

"That's right. Owns the Top-Notch. But he has the sort of background you're looking for, too."

Windy glanced up from the eggs he was cutting with a fork and said with a puzzled frown, "He does?"

"That's right. But I don't want to talk out of turn, Smoke, so he can tell you about it if he wants to."

"I appreciate that, Mickey."

"Call me Sarge. Everybody else does."

"All right, Sarge." Smoke turned to Windy. "Finish your breakfast, work on that list of men with Sarge here, and then go on back to the office. I'll be there in a while, after I've talked to Apple Jack."

"All right," Windy said. "And I was thinkin', Smoke, that somebody ought to ride out and do a little scoutin', just to make sure they ain't already tryin' to slip up on us."

"I agree. I'll do that later this morning."

Smoke said so long and left the Red Top. He didn't know if the Top-Notch Saloon would be open this early in the day, but he could find it, anyway.

When he located the saloon, he saw that the doors were open and the batwings had been unfastened so that they hung across the entrance. Taking advantage of the nice weather while it was here, he supposed.

He wondered if Windy might be right about a powerful blue norther having the town in its sights, despite there being no indication of it at the moment. If Preacher had told him something like that, he wouldn't have doubted the prediction for a second. He had complete faith in the old mountain man's instincts. He supposed that Windy might be correct, too. Old men's bones were usually pretty good at predicting the weather.

Smoke pushed through the batwings. The Top-Notch was like scores of other saloons he had been in. Even at this hour, a poker game was going on at one of the tables. A couple of men stood at the bar. They had coffee cups in front of them instead of beer mugs or shot glasses, but a sleepy-looking bartender stood on the other side of the hardwood and an uncorked bottle was within reach, so Smoke figured the coffee had been doctored a mite.

A man sat at a rear table by himself, also with a coffee cup. He wore a brown tweed suit and a string tie. Smoke recognized him from the night before.

Obviously, the recognition was mutual, because the man got to his feet and lumbered forward with his hand out-stretched.

"Good morning, Mr. Jensen," he greeted Smoke in his squeaky voice. "Welcome to the Top-Notch."

Smoke shook hands with him. "You're Apple Jack?"

The man laughed. "Jack Appleton is actually my name," he said, "but if that wasn't enough, the way my head looks a little like an apple has had people calling me that since I was a boy." The affable expression went away, replaced by a more solemn look. "What can I do for you?"

"You can see by the badge that I'm filling in for the late Marshal Cardwell."

Apple Jack nodded. "Yeah, and I'm glad to see it, too. Salt Lick needs a lawman, and I don't reckon anybody around here is more suited for the job than you. Shame we can't keep you permanent-like, but I know you have a ranch up in Colorado."

"Can we talk for a few minutes?"

"Sure." Apple Jack waved a hand toward the table. "Have a seat. I'll get you some coffee."

"No, that'll all right. I've had plenty already this morning."

"Well, then, sit down and tell me what's on your mind . . . Marshal."

When they were both seated, Smoke said quietly, "Salt Lick may be in for more trouble. Those two men who tried to rob the bank last night normally ride with Snake Bishop's gang."

Apple Jack started breathing harder. "Snake Bishop," he repeated. "From what I've heard, he's a really bad hombre. And two of his men were in my place yesterday?"

"That's what it looks like."

"I never would've been so friendly to them if I'd known that. Good grief, I even bought 'em a drink!"

"You didn't have any way of knowing," Smoke said. "The important thing now is that it's possible Bishop and the rest of his bunch are on their way here. He's been known to send men ahead to scout a settlement before he raids it."

Apple Jack frowned. "If those two fellas were scouts, why'd they try to rob the bank?"

"We don't know. Could be they decided to try to clean it out themselves before the others got here. Or they could have split off from the gang and been on their own. We just don't have any way of knowing, since they're both dead."

"But Bishop *could* be headed here."

"He could be," Smoke agreed.

"Lord have mercy on all of our souls, then. That man is a monster." Apple Jack looked even more puzzled. "But what's that got to do with me?"

"We're not spreading the word about Bishop just yet, not until I can talk to some of the men in town and put together a force of volunteers who'll be ready to meet the trouble head-on, if it comes. Sarge Shaw over at the Red Top Café suggested that I talk to you."

"He did?" Apple Jack shook his head. "I don't know why he'd do that. I'm just a simple saloonkeeper. I . . . I don't know anything about fighting battles."

Smoke didn't think the man's words had the ring of truth. He considered himself a pretty good judge of character, and although he might not have noticed it if Shaw hadn't suggested he come here, Smoke thought now that he caught a glimpse of something else in Apple Jack's eyes.

"Sarge said you'd have to be the one to tell me, Mr. Appleton," Smoke said quietly. "If you wanted to. If you don't, I reckon I'll go on my way and not bother you anymore."

Apple Jack fidgeted with his coffee cup for a moment, then sighed and said, "All right. I reckon this business with Snake Bishop is important enough I ought to trust you, Mr. Jensen."

"Make it Smoke."

"All right. And you can call me Apple Jack like everybody else. Folks didn't always call me that, though. For a while, during the war, they called me something else." The saloonkeeper looked down and then back up to meet Smoke's eyes. "They called me Colonel Appleton."

"You were in the army?"

"Well . . . the Confederate army. Does that make a difference to you, Smoke?"

Smoke shook his head. "Not a bit. I was just a boy when it was over, but I remember hearing that President Lincoln said we were all countrymen again. Robert E. Lee said the same thing. Men like that, I tend to take them at their word. Where did you serve?"

"All over Missouri, Arkansas, Kansas, Indian Territory . . . I commanded an artillery brigade in what they called the Trans-Mississippi District. The biggest battle I was in was the one at Pea Ridge, where we got beat. It was never the same after that." Apple Jack sighed. "Sarge Shaw was in that battle, too . . . on the other side. I never knew about that . . . never knew him . . . until he came here to Salt Lick. Then one day he said something while he was in here that made me think he'd been there, so we got to talking about it. You know, the way old soldiers do. There aren't any hard feelings between us. We've always gotten along and still do. But I've got a business to run, and folks from all over live in Salt Lick these days, including Yankees. Some of them still hold grudges, even all these years later, so I don't go out of my way to let 'em know I fought for the Rebs."

"All I care about is that you're accustomed to command," Smoke said.

"I told you, I was an artillery man. I never was in the thick of any battle."

"But you're heard the cannon roar and given orders. That puts you ahead of some of the men in town."

"I suppose so," Apple Jack admitted with obvious reluctance. "I figured I'd put all that behind me forever, though."

"Maybe you have," Smoke said. "There's a chance Bishop and his gang aren't headed in this direction. But if they are, I'd like to know that I can count on you, Apple Jack."

The saloonkeeper shook his head and practically moaned, "All I wanted to do was just run this place. I saw enough of war to last me the rest of my life."

"I'm sure you did. But sometimes fate doesn't give us much choice in what we're called on to do. And I suspect you have a lot of friends here in Salt Lick. They're more than just customers to you, aren't they?"

Apple Jack drew in a deep breath, let it out in a sigh, and nodded.

"That's right. I guess . . . if it comes down to it . . . a man's got to fight when his home and his friends are in danger, doesn't he?"

"If he wants to call himself a man," Smoke agreed.

"Then count me in, Smoke. What do you want me to do?"

"For the moment, nothing except think about how you'd defend this town from an attack. Windy Whittaker and the sarge are putting together a list of men who they think will be willing and able to fight. You must have been there for plenty of councils of war with the other officers, so you know strategy and tactics. Figure out a plan and get together with Windy and Sarge later to go over it and see what they think."

"I can do that," Apple Jack said with what seemed to be a bit more enthusiasm. "What are you going to do?"

"I need to take a ride," Smoke said, "and make sure trouble's not nearly on top of us already."

CHAPTER 16

"This horse of yours and I are getting along just fine, Mr. Jensen," Tommy Spencer said a short time later as she stroked the rangy gray stallion's shoulder. "And you acted like he was a one-man horse."

"Well, you're not exactly a man," Smoke pointed out to the girl.

She grinned. "No, I'm not." She grew more solemn as she went on, "I'm glad you killed those skunks who gunned down Ted. Maybe he and I weren't ever going to get together the way he wanted, but he didn't deserve what they did to him."

"No, but he died doing his duty, for whatever consolation that is."

Tommy drew in a deep breath, then said, "What can I do for you, Mr. Jensen? You want this big fella saddled?"

"That's right."

"You're not leaving town, are you?"

"No, just going for a ride," Smoke said.

She nodded and said, "It's a mighty good day for it."

She got to work. Smoke could have saddled the horse himself, of course, but he had a hunch she might have been offended if he suggested it. This was her job, and she was going to do it.

A short time later, he rode out of Salt Lick. No one he'd talked to had noticed Atkins and Rome the previous day until they were already in town, so he didn't know from which direction they had come. Under those circumstances, one starting point was as good as another, so he headed north and rode a couple of miles before swinging to the west and starting a large circle around the settlement.

Out here on these high plains, a man could see a long way. The breeze out of the south wasn't very strong. Smoke knew that if a large group of riders was approaching Salt Lick, he ought to be able to see the dust cloud their horses would raise. There wasn't enough wind to completely disperse any dust.

Instead, the horizon was clear every direction he looked. No one was approaching the settlement.

That was no guarantee the town was safe, of course. Snake Bishop and his gang could still be on their way. But it didn't seem likely they were sneaking up on Salt Lick right at this moment.

The bank had two stories and was the tallest building in town, Smoke recalled. He needed to post a couple of men on the roof to keep watch on the surrounding countryside. As flat as the terrain was, those sentries would be able to see a long way. No one would be able to get close without being spotted.

He would take care of that as soon as he got back to town and consulted with Windy Whittaker and Sarge Shaw, he decided.

Once he had made a complete circuit of the town, he headed back in. It was midday, so after turning over the stallion to Tommy at the livery stable, he walked along the street to the Red Top Café, which was considerably busier at this hour. Smoke found an empty stool at the counter and nodded to Sarge when the proprietor came over.

"Any sign of trouble?" Shaw asked.

Smoke shook his head. "Not yet."

"Do you think there's a chance we might actually dodge it?"

"That's hard to say. It's certainly possible." Smoke smiled slightly. "That's not what my gut tells me is going to happen, though."

Shaw grunted and said, "Mine, either. Well, Windy's got that list of men we came up with. Like you asked, we haven't talked to any of them yet."

"I'll see him at the office in a little while, after I've eaten."

"For all her faults, my Charlotte puts together a pretty good pot of stew. Want a bowl?"

"Sounds good to me," Smoke said.

The stew *was* good, piping hot and full of savory chunks of beef and plenty of vegetables. Smoke enjoyed a full bowl, washed down with another cup of coffee and helped along by a couple of fluffy rolls. When he was done, he paid for the meal even though Shaw said that as the marshal, he didn't have to. Smoke waved to Charlotte through the opening into the kitchen as he stood up and left the café.

Windy stood in the open door of the marshal's office, hatless, with his thumbs hooked in the old gun belt as he looked up and down the street.

"Ain't nothin' but peace and quiet as far as the eye can see," he reported as Smoke walked up. With a sigh, he added, "Sure wish we could count on things stayin' that way, but I don't reckon we can."

They went inside and Smoke closed the door behind them. Windy went over to the desk and tapped the sheet of paper lying there.

"This here's your army," he told Smoke. "Them that'll go along with it, that is."

Smoke picked up the paper and read the names printed on it in a neat script. "Did you write this?" he asked Windy.

The old-timer nodded. "Yeah, I can read and write and even do some cipherin', too. Learned most of it out on the trail. I never went to school but just a little bit, 'way back when I was a younker."

Most of the names didn't mean anything to Smoke, but he spotted several he recognized: Edward Warren, Rufus Spencer, and Apple Jack. Smoke pointed to that last one and said, "I talked to Colonel Appleton, and he agreed to help us. You and Sarge get together with him when you can and go over the defensive plans he said he'd work up."

"Colonel Appleton, is it? I never would'a figured him for an officer. Not an easy-goin' type of fella like him. But Sarge said we needed to put him on the list, so we did."

"Folks will surprise you," Smoke said. "In the meantime, can you pick a couple of good men from this bunch and see if they'll climb on top of the bank to keep watch on the countryside around town?"

"That's a mighty good idea," Windy agreed. "I know just the fellas to do it, too. Shug Russell and Enoch Jones. Both of 'em used to do some buffalo huntin'. They got good eyes and don't get spooked easy. Well, Shug's only got one eye, but it's a good'un."

Smoke nodded and said, "Sounds like just the sort of men we need."

"I'll take care of it," Windy said.

Smoke indulged his curiosity and said, "Before you go . . . what's the story on Sarge and his wife? The way they were fussing at each other, when I saw her she wasn't really what I expected."

Windy chuckled. "They go at it hammer and tongs sometimes, sure enough, but I reckon that's just the way they are.

If you talk to either of 'em when the other one ain't around, you can tell they plumb love each other. They just don't like to show it around other folks for some reason. She was with the sarge when he moved here a couple years back, not long after I did. But I got the feelin' they hadn't been hitched very long at the time. If I had to guess, I'd say he met her in a sportin' house somewhere and took her outta there and married her. Matches like that work out pretty well sometimes, if you got the right people involved."

"That they do," Smoke said, having been around a few unions like that himself.

Windy went off to recruit the two men he had mentioned as lookouts while Smoke walked back to Jonas Madigan's house to bring the former lawman up to date on what was going on. That meant leaving the marshal's office unattended for the moment, but Smoke wasn't expecting any trouble just yet.

If any broke out, he would be close by and could get back to the center of the settlement in a hurry.

Not surprisingly, Miriam Dollinger was at Madigan's house and had prepared lunch for him. She offered to warm up some food for Smoke, but he assured her that he had already eaten. Madigan was back in bed. Smoke sat with him for a while and told him the preparations that had been made so far.

"It sounds like you're doing a good job of getting ready," Madigan said. "I thought about puttin' men on the bank roof to watch for Bishop and wished I'd mentioned it to you. I should've known you'd come up with the idea yourself. I agree with Windy; Russell and Jones are good men for the job." Madigan paused. "Speakin' of jobs . . . what's mine?"

"How do you mean?" Smoke asked.

"Well, with a horde of bandits about to descend on the town at any minute, you don't expect me to just sit here in this bed, do you?" Madigan snorted dismissively. "That ain't hardly gonna happen!"

Miriam had come to stand in the doorway and listen to the conversation. She joined in by saying, "That's exactly what you're going to do, Jonas. You're in no shape to do anything else. You shouldn't even be walking to the kitchen for your meals."

"Dadblast it, I ain't dead yet! I can still walk, and I can damn sure still pull a trigger if I need to."

"I'm not sure if I will or not. And I know you don't want to admit it, Jonas, but your fighting days are over."

Madigan sat back, glaring, but Smoke saw hurt in his eyes as well as anger. After the adventurous, eventful life Madigan had led, this forced inactivity had to rankle. Smoke figured it left a bad taste in the older man's mouth. He knew that was the way he would feel about it, if he had been in Madigan's place.

"You've already helped, Jonas," he said. "If you hadn't written that letter to me, I wouldn't be here now."

"And those bank robbers would've gotten away, and we wouldn't have any idea that Bishop and his gang may be in these parts. I know, I know. That's true, Smoke, but it ain't enough. It just ain't. And *you* know *that*."

"Let me think on it, Jonas," Smoke said, ignoring the warning glance Miriam slanted toward him. "I'll keep you informed, you can count on that."

When Smoke left a few minutes later, Miriam followed him onto the porch.

"You shouldn't get his hopes up like that," she said quietly. "The days of him being able to go out with a gun in his hand and fight badmen are over and done with."

"Maybe," Smoke said. "But if you get right down to it . . . is it really going to make that much difference?"

Miriam caught her breath. "That . ... that's a rather callous way of looking at it, isn't it?"

"Jonas would say it's a realistic way. He knows he doesn't have much time left, no matter what he does. He wants to spend it in a way that means something to him, the same way he's spent his life up to now."

Miriam's hands knotted together. "I know you're right, Smoke, but he . . . he's come to mean so much to me, I just hate to think about . . . about . . ."

"I know." His voice was gentle now. "We want to keep those we care about with us as long as we can. But we have to think about what's best for *them*, too."

"So if the town's attacked, he should go out with guns in both hands and blaze away at those outlaws?"

Smoke smiled and said, "That might take them by surprise. And Jonas might acquit himself better than you think. You've got to remember, he's had a *lot* of experience taking on owlhoots."

Miriam sighed. "Well, perhaps it won't come to that."

"Maybe not," Smoke said. But he couldn't quite make himself believe it.

CHAPTER 17

A meeting was held that evening at Rufus Spencer's livery barn. Forty-seven men were there, not counting Smoke and Windy. They were the ones Windy had talked with during the day, advising them that more trouble might be on its way to Salt Lick and asking if they would be willing to join the fight against it, although he hadn't gone into details about what—or *who*—that trouble might be.

To a man, every one of them had said yes.

When Smoke looked around, he saw men of all shapes and ages, ranging from fresh-faced youngsters barely in their twenties to leathery old-timers who had been around the frontier for a long time.

Two such veterans, Shug Russell and Enoch Jones, were still atop the bank, standing guard over the town. Smoke had told them about Snake Bishop, so they would know what they were getting into and what they needed to look out for.

Russell, a tall, lanky man with a tuft of gray beard, blind in his left eye from a knife wound suffered in a fight with another buffalo hunter at Adobe Walls several years earlier, had responded by saying, "I'll take my Sharps up there with me, and if that Bishop scoundrel comes within a mile of Salt Lick, I'll give him a Big Fifty welcome!"

Jones, rotund and a little softened up from town living but still keen-eyed, had expressed a similar sentiment. Even though Smoke had just met the two men, he immediately liked and had confidence in them.

A low hum of conversation filled the barn this evening. These men were aware that something was wrong but knew just enough to be worried.

Smoke stepped up on a bale of hay and raised his hands. "Men, if I could have your attention . . . Thanks for coming this evening. I want to thank you, too, for trusting me to fill in for the marshal. Most of you don't know me, but my name is Smoke Jensen, and I'm an old friend of Jonas Madigan."

Edward Warren said, "I believe most, if not all, of us know who you are, Mr. Jensen, even the ones who haven't met you personally. And we're very glad that a man with your reputation is in Salt Lick right now to give us a hand in our time of trouble."

A general mutter of agreement went through the crowd, and one man called, "Damn right!"

"I appreciate that, fellas," Smoke said with a smile. "Windy Whittaker, who's agreed to serve as my deputy for the time being, has spoken to all of you today and let you know that the town may soon be facing even worse trouble than that attempted bank robbery last night. Those two outlaws who were killed were members of the Snake Bishop gang."

Stunned silence greeted that blunt announcement and gripped the group of men for a long moment. Then a flood of exclamations, curses, and questions broke out.

Smoke let it continue for several seconds before he raised his hands for quiet again. When he didn't get it right away, Sarge Shaw said, "Settle down!" and his commanding tone got immediate results.

"We don't know for sure that Bishop and his men are headed this way," Smoke went on. "But they could be, and we need to be ready for them if they show up."

"They've raided a bunch of towns," Rufus Spencer rumbled, "and they've killed a bunch of folks in every one of them. Some of those settlements were burned to the ground!"

Smoke nodded and said, "That's right. He took those places by surprise, and folks weren't able to put up much of a fight. But we're not going to let that happen here, are we?"

For a second there was no response, then an angry, defiant roar welled up.

In the silence that followed that, however, a man said, "Wouldn't it be better if we . . . well, if we just packed up our families and got out of town, while there's still time?"

"And abandon everything you've built and worked for?" Shaw asked. "I don't know about any of you boys, but I'm sure not prepared to do that!"

"You don't have kids, Sarge," another man said. "I do."

Smoke said, "I understand that. Of course, all of you want what's best for your families. But it's just not practical for everybody to leave, especially when we're not sure Bishop is even headed this way."

Windy spoke up. "Besides, you don't want to be headin' anywhere else right now, not with that bad weather fixin' to set in."

"What bad weather?" a man asked. "It's about as nice as it ever is at this time of year."

"Yeah, but that ain't gonna last. Sometimes these blue northers are even worse when the weather's nice right before they get here."

Several looks of derision were cast toward Windy, but he ignored them, obviously supremely confident in his ability to know what the weather was going to do.

One of the men said, "What do you think would be best, Mr. Jensen? Or Marshal Jensen, I reckon I should say."

"We have a plan to defend the town that's been put together by Colonel Appleton—"

"Who?"

Shaw barked, "Don't interrupt the marshal that way."

Smoke went on, "Colonel, would you step up here?"

He hopped off the hay bale and, with some effort, Apple Jack took his place. At the sight of the heavyset saloon-keeper climbing onto the bale, laughter came from several of the men.

"Colonel?" one of them repeated. "That's just Apple Jack."

"Colonel Appleton to you, mister," Shaw said, "and to all the rest of you, too. You may not know it, but the colonel here was the commander of an artillery brigade during the late war, and a fine officer, to boot!"

It was hard not to be impressed by that endorsement from the former sergeant. Shaw hadn't mentioned which side Apple Jack fought on, but no one asked.

Apple Jack began, "You fellas all know me—"

"Not as well as we thought we did!"

"Quiet down." Despite the natural squeak in Apple Jack's voice, the words had a tone of authority to them, as well. He reached inside his coat and drew out several folded papers. "Sergeant Shaw and I have drawn up a plan of the town and marked the best positions for defending it in case of an attack. We need volunteers to man those positions. If you have your own weapons and ammunition, that's fine, but if you don't, we'll requisition some from the general stores. We want men who can shoot, but more than that, we need men who can keep a cool head and not panic in the face of trouble. We don't know exactly how many enemies we'll be facing, if it comes to that, but this group here . . ." He waved a hand to encompass all of them. "I know good and well we can take on those outlaws and beat 'em!"

Those words, calm but forceful and then building in intensity, got through to the doubters. A cheer went up from the men when Apple Jack clenched one pudgy hand into a fist and thrust it into the air in front of him. Only a few still appeared skeptical.

Shaw looked over at Smoke, gave him a curt nod, and said quietly, "They'll come around."

"I think so, too."

Apple Jack went on, "Now, I'm gonna climb down from here, and if you fellas will gather around, we can figure out who's going to be assigned to which position . . ."

While they were doing that, with Shaw assisting, Smoke and Windy stepped back to give them room. The old-timer scratched at his whiskers and said, "I know we're doin' the right thing, but I ain't sure these fellas will ever be a match for Bishop's gang. They're the meanest bunch this side of a rattlesnake den!"

"I don't know what else we can do," Smoke said. "Jonas is sending a letter to the governor when the stagecoach comes through tomorrow, but it'll take a while for any help to get all the way up here from Austin."

"Yeah, that's one thing about Texas . . . ever'where is way the hell an' gone away from ever'where else!" Windy shook his head dolefully. "Wiped out by outlaws or froze by a blue norther. If it ain't one thing, it's another!"

Salt Lick was the end of the run for the stage line that ran north from Amarillo. When the stagecoach reached the settlement, it turned around and retraced its route southward.

Luther Blassingame was the regular jehu on this route

and had been for several years. J.J. Hanesworth normally rode shotgun. Both men were on the driver's seat the next morning as the coach rolled northward toward Salt Lick.

They had been making this run for several years and had never encountered much trouble. Renegade Comanches had chased them a couple of times, but on both occasions, Hanesworth's deadly accurate fire with a Winchester had knocked some of the warriors off their ponies, and the rest had given up the pursuit.

Outlaws had also tried twice to hold up the stage. It wasn't a very tempting target, except for the rare occasions when it carried a money shipment bound for the bank in Salt Lick. Blassingame and Hanesworth had blasted their way through one of the attempted holdups, Hanesworth blazing away with the Winchester and then cutting loose with a double-barreled coach gun, Blassingame handling the team with one hand while firing his Colt with the other.

The second time, the masked varmints had killed both leaders in the team, so Blassingame didn't have any choice but to stop. The outlaws had taken the mail pouch and what valuables they could find on the passengers. It wasn't much of a haul, but still, it rankled the driver and guard that the bandits had gotten away with it. At least they hadn't killed anybody other than the horses, so there was that to be thankful for.

But Blassingame's resentment meant that he was in no mood to stop for road agents after that. He had sworn many times that they'd have to shoot him off the seat to get him to stop.

He wasn't thinking about that today as the coach rocked along the trail. The weather was still pleasant, although the breeze from the south had died down to nothing and the air was still. The dust kicked up by the team's hooves and the coach's wheels went almost straight up in the air and hung there in a slowly moving column.

Blassingame looked off to the northwest, blew a breath through his drooping walrus mustaches, and said, "You see that up yonder, J.J.?"

"See what?" Hanesworth asked. His mustache was a match for Blassingame's, but that was the only physical similarity between them. Blassingame was short and built like a barrel. Hanesworth was taller and one of those fellas who could turn sideways behind a fence post and practically disappear.

"I'm talkin' about those clouds to the northwest."

"I don't see any clouds. Sky's clear all the way down to the horizon."

"No, it ain't," Blassingame insisted. "Look down really close to the ground. See that thin blue line?"

Hanesworth squinted for a moment, then shook his head and said, "No, I don't. What do you reckon you're seein'?"

"That's a blue norther. I'd bet a new hat on it."

"Well, I wouldn't. And I've been around the Panhandle and seen as many blue northers as you have, Luther. I think that's one of those, what do you call 'em, mirages."

"A mirage is what you see when you're out in the desert and it's really hot."

"Yeah, but it's somethin' that ain't really there, even though you see it, right?"

Blassingame shook his head and said, "I ain't gonna argue with you. Anyway, if we just keep goin' toward Salt Lick, we'll find out, won't we? Because it'll get here, sooner or later."

"If it really is anything."

Blassingame glared for a second, then shook his head and concentrated on his driving. The trail ran flat and mostly straight through miles and miles of prairie dotted with clumps of hardy grass and occasional thickets of scrub brush. Stunted, gnarled trees were even rarer. Here and there, shallow, rocky ridges thrust up and the trail swung wide around them. In another ten miles or so, they would pass the little salt flat to the west of the trail that gave the settlement of Salt Lick its name. Blassingame had seen much bigger salt flats out in West Texas, but this one was large enough to attract the cattle from various spreads in the area. A good number of critters could be found around the flat most of the time.

"Ain't nothin' between the Panhandle and the North Pole except a slat fence," Blassingame mused.

Hanesworth grunted. "What?"

"Just somethin' I heard a fella say once. Ain't nothin' between the Panhandle and the North Pole except a slat fence. The North Pole is where all the cold air is."

"I know what the North Pole is."

Blassingame went on as if he hadn't heard. "So when one of those blue northers blows through, there ain't nothin' to stop all that cold air from pourin' in, because there's nothin' between here and there."

"Nothin' except part of Indian Territory and Kansas and Nebraska and—"

"It's just a sayin', for Pete's sake! You don't have to take it so damn literal—"

A fist-sized chunk of J.J. Hanesworth's skull flew off, spraying blood, brain matter, and shards of bone into the side of Blassingame's face. Hanesworth jerked back, dropped his rifle, and then toppled forward, landing on the edge of the floorboards and rolling off to the side.

Just like that, not much more than the blink of an eye, he was dead and gone, and a stunned Luther Blassingame was left alone on the rocking, swaying stagecoach seat, staring straight ahead as some of his old friend's brain slid down his cheek and dripped off his jaw.

Then Blassingame's own shocked brain started working again. He grabbed the whip from its holder, leaned forward, popped the lash over the team's heads, and slashed at their rumps with it as he yelled at them. The six horses lunged forward, picking up speed. The coach began to jolt even more on the broad leather thoroughbraces that ran underneath it.

Blassingame hadn't heard the shot that killed Hanesworth. That didn't surprise him. The hoofbeats from the team and the clank and rattle of the coach itself created quite a racket. The two men had had to almost shout to hear each other, and they had been sitting side by side. A single gunshot from a distance easily could have gone unnoticed.

For that matter, they could be shooting at *him* right now, Blassingame realized, and he wouldn't know it until one of the bullets smashed into him. He hunched lower on the seat, trying to make himself as small a target as possible.

He faintly heard a shout from inside the coach but couldn't tell which of the three passengers it came from. The coach was carrying three men today, a couple of drummers headed to Salt Lick to get orders from regular customers there and a lawyer from Amarillo who had a meeting with one of his clients, a rancher who owned a spread up along the border with Indian Territory.

Blassingame didn't figure any of the three would be worth much when it came to putting up a fight against outlaws.

So their only real chance, especially with Hanesworth gone, was for him to outrun the bandits.

He risked raising up enough to cast a glance back over his shoulder. What he saw made terror well up inside him.

At least two dozen riders were pursuing the stagecoach.

It was like he had a damn army on his tail, Blassingame thought wildly. There might be even more riders back there; the dust made it difficult to tell.

But the leaders in the bunch were less than fifty yards behind the coach . . . and gaining steadily. Even though Blassingame had caught only a glimpse of him, the driver had seen the man who seemed to be the leader.

The man was galloping just ahead of the others and *popping a whip* like a crazy man. Who would do such a thing?

And then Blassingame remembered rumors he had heard and realized who was after him, and he let out a groan of despair.

That was Snake Bishop back there, closing in on him!

CHAPTER 18

Smoke felt the difference in the air as soon as he stepped out of Jonas Madigan's house that morning. It was only a little cooler than it had been the day before, but it held a still heaviness that promised change.

Maybe Windy Whittaker had been right.

The meeting had broken up the night before with two men, Harold Lomax and Cliff Lawson, heading for the bank to relieve Shug Russell and Enoch Jones. Lomax and Lawson would stand guard during the night. Another pair of men would be relieving them soon, if that hadn't happened already. Sarge Shaw had drawn up a roster of guard shifts. Smoke trusted him and was more than happy to let him do that.

Also before the men left the livery barn, Smoke had asked them to keep what he had told them to themselves. He knew it would be difficult for some of the men not to say anything about the Bishop gang to their wives. If word got out, he wasn't going to be overly surprised. He wanted to postpone a panic as long as possible, but the volunteers had to be aware of what they were facing. It wouldn't be fair to them, otherwise.

For now, most of the men seemed to know what they

were supposed to do in case of an attack. Smoke had suggested that they figure out what to do about their families if they had to go and fight. Apple Jack had suggested that they gather at the bank, since it was the sturdiest building in town. The front window that had been cracked in the explosion had already been boarded up, and it would be easy enough to nail some boards over the other window to make it more secure.

The bank was also the most tempting target for the outlaws, which was why a dozen volunteers had been given the assignment of heading there right away in case of trouble and holding it at all costs.

Several men were tasked with moving wagons into the street at both ends to block it and prevent outlaws from mounting a devastating charge through the center of town. Those wagons were positioned in strategic alleys with teams already hitched to them, ready to be led into place.

The rest of the men, more than thirty in all, would scatter to various defensive positions around town. Everyone knew to keep their guns and ammunition handy.

As far as Smoke could see, they had done everything they could to get ready for a raid . . . a raid that might not happen, he reminded himself as he walked toward the marshal's office. But they couldn't count on that.

When he walked into the marshal's office, he was surprised to see that Windy's normally tangled thatch of white hair had been combed, and it looked like the bushy white whiskers had been trimmed a little, too. Not only that, but the old-timer was wearing a clean flannel shirt, too.

"What are you getting all spiffed up for?" Smoke asked with a grin.

"Dagnabbit, can't a fella decide to clean up a mite?" Windy demanded.

Smoke noticed something else. "I see you're wearing a badge, too."

Windy looked down at the star pinned to his fringed buckskin vest. "Yeah, I found this in the desk," he said. "Ted Cardwell used to wear it when he was the deputy. You've been tellin' folks that you deputized me, but I didn't figure it'd hurt to wear the badge, so's people who ain't heard the news yet would know I got at least some authority around here."

Smoke nodded and said, "I think that's a very good idea."

He understood now why Windy had tried to make himself look more respectable. Before, the old-timer had been just an eccentric local character. Now, he held an official position, and it made sense that he'd want to look the part.

"No trouble overnight, I suppose?" Smoke went on.

Windy shook his head. "Nary a bit."

"The bank's open again this morning, I noticed."

"Yeah. Just to look around town, you wouldn't know anything had ever happened." Windy paused, then added, "Well, unless you spotted them fellas standin' guard on the roof o' the bank."

Smoke took an envelope from his pocket and placed it on the desk. "This is the letter Jonas has written to the governor asking for help from the Rangers. I told him I'd make sure it goes out in the mail pouch on the stage. What time does the coach usually get here?"

"Around the middle of the day, unless ol' Luther Blassingame gets in a hurry for some reason. I hope he gets here, switches teams, picks up the mail and drops off any passengers, and heads back south before the storm rolls in."

"You still believe there's a blue norther on the way?" Smoke asked.

Windy snorted. "It ain't a matter of believin'. It's comin', sure as shootin'. Didn't you feel the change in the air this mornin'?"

"I have to admit, it does seem a little different out there."

"That's because one ring-tailed roarer of a blue norther is rollin' right toward us like a runaway freight train. It'll be here before the day's over, Smoke. You can mark my words on that."

"I suppose we'll find out, one way or another. Right now, have you had breakfast yet? If not, I'll stay here for a spell while you go have some of Mrs. Shaw's flapjacks."

Windy stood and hitched up his baggy denim trousers. "That sounds like a mighty fine idea. This is liable to be a busy day. *Quien sabe* when I'll get a chance to grab some grub again!"

Even though he knew it probably wouldn't do any good, Luther Blassingame leaned over and turned his head to shout through the coach window, "If any of you fellas got guns, now's the time to use 'em!"

To his surprise, one of the drummers stuck an arm and his head out the window, thrust a long-barreled Remington .44 revolver toward the outlaws, and fired. The gun went off with a heavy boom. Blassingame wondered for a second where the gent had been carrying the Remington. In his sample case, more than likely.

Then Blassingame turned his attention to trying to get more speed out of the team. The horses were already running valiantly, straining against their harness, but Blassingame knew the effort was doomed. Even on a straightaway like this, those draft horses couldn't outrun the outlaws' speedy mounts.

But miracles had been known to happen in this world, even though they were rare. If he could just manage to stay in front of the pursuers for a while, maybe somebody else would come along to help him and the passengers. Maybe they would run into a cavalry patrol, or a whole company of Texas Rangers . . .

Might as well hope those horses would sprout wings and fly to the moon, he thought bleakly. That was just about as likely.

Despite knowing that, Blassingame continued to pop the whip and shout encouragement to the team. Behind him, the drummer's Remington blasted several more times. Then the man cried out in pain, and when Blassingame glanced back, he saw the drummer withdrawing an empty hand into the coach. A couple of fingers were gone, sheared off by the bullet that had knocked the gun out of the hand, and blood spouted from the stubs where the fingers had been.

A shot like that was pure luck, and whether it was good luck or bad depended entirely on which side of it a fella found himself.

Up ahead, a gully that meandered across the plains swung over fairly close to the trail, maybe fifty yards away. Blassingame wondered if he and the passengers could abandon the coach and take cover in that gully. Maybe the outlaws would be content to loot what they could from the vehicle and leave him and the passengers alone.

Blassingame didn't think that was likely—from everything he had heard, Snake Bishop was a loco, kill-crazy human buzzard who would kill a man for the sport of it, and his followers weren't much better—but what other chance did they have? The outlaws were close now, still sending a hail of slugs after the coach, and Blassingame knew it was only a matter of time until they shot him off the box.

Without wasting any more time thinking about it, he hauled on the reins and sent the coach plunging off the trail toward the gully.

The terrain might *look* pretty flat, but once off the trail, it was a lot rougher for the stagecoach. It bounced so hard that Blassingame lifted up off the seat a few times. It seemed like the whole thing might fly apart at any moment. Blassingame had to slow down to keep from losing control entirely.

"When we stop, run for the gully!" he shouted to the passengers. "I'll cover you!"

That was crazy, but those gents were his responsibility, and even though he had originally planned to dive into that gully and try to hide as fast as he could, he realized he couldn't do that. If he slowed down the outlaws, it might give the passengers a better chance to get away.

Not that any of them actually had much of a chance. He knew that . . . but Luther Blassingame wasn't the sort of man to give up a fight as long as he had breath in his body.

There was the gully! Ten feet deep and thirty or forty wide, it was choked with brush. If a fella got down into that growth, he might be able to give those outlaws the slip. Blassingame hauled on the reins again, pulling the team sharply to the left, so that the coach swung around and stopped sideways to the gully. That would give the fleeing passengers a little shelter, maybe.

Bullets thudded into the vehicle and sent splinters flying. Blassingame dropped the reins and bent over to grab the Winchester poor J.J. had dropped when the varmints killed him. He worked the rifle's lever and twisted on the seat to face the charging horde as he yelled, "Get out, get out! Run!"

He expected to feel the coach shift under him as the passengers jumped out and fled, but it didn't move. After firing a couple of shots as swiftly as he could work the Winchester's lever, he realized that as many times as the coach had been hit, all three men might be dead by now. The vehicle's thin walls wouldn't stop many bullets.

Placing a hand on the seat, Blassingame vaulted down on the far side of the coach with a spryness that belied his years. A fella was capable of a lot when he was being shot at. He landed hard and awkwardly but didn't fall. Grabbing the door handle, he jerked it open.

The sight of three bloody, bullet-riddled corpses met his horrified gaze. The passengers were all dead.

So he was free to get the hell out of here if he could, he realized. He turned and ran for the gully. The hoofbeats of the outlaws' horses sounded mighty loud . . .

More shots crashed. Blassingame felt the hammerblows of the slugs as they struck him. He was close to the gully's edge. Somehow he stayed on his feet, and momentum carried him forward. Then a third bullet hit him, twisted him around, and suddenly he was rolling down the steep, sandstone slope. Brush clawed at him as he came to a stop.

Pain the likes of which he had never experienced raced through Blassingame, but he knew that if he just lay here, Bishop's men would come to make sure he was dead.

The part of his brain that wasn't too stunned to think seized on a desperate idea. Forcing uncooperative muscles to work, he fumbled with the long duster he wore and wrestled it off. It was ripped by the brush, torn by bullets, and stained with blood. He thrust it into the brush and looked around for his hat. He found it and put it at the top of the duster. Tugging off his bright red bandana, he left it there, too.

Then, using his toes and elbows, he pushed and dragged his screaming body deeper into the brush until he couldn't move anymore. Lying on his belly, his head dropped forward and he tasted dirt in his mouth. It was in his eyes and nose, too. He made himself lie still.

A man yelled, "There he is! See!"

Instantly, guns began to go off again. It sounded like a war, there on the edge of that gully.

But none of the bullets found Luther Blassingame. He knew they had spotted his coat and hat in the thick brush and believed they were filling his body full of lead. He was ten or fifteen feet away, though.

He didn't budge as they whooped and laughed and fired their guns into what they believed was his riddled corpse.

Then, as the shots faded, a man called, "He's dead, Snake! He's got to have a pound of lead in him, at least."

"Then leave him there and come on." That had to be Snake Bishop himself. "We still have an appointment in Salt Lick."

That was the last thing Luther Blassingame heard as a tide of darkness washed over him and swept him away.

CHAPTER 19

Smoke saw a lot of nervous looks on the faces of the townspeople as he walked around Salt Lick that morning. Rumors had to be spreading that more trouble loomed over the town, even if folks didn't know all the details yet.

The tension wasn't totally due to the possible threat from the Bishop gang, either. One of the storekeepers commented to Smoke, "Folks are about to empty my shelves because they've started talkin' about bad weather coming. Everybody wants to be prepared. When the temperature gets down close to zero and the wind is howlin' and the snow's comin' down so thick you can't hardly see, nobody wants to go out. They just build up the fires in their stoves and fireplaces and huddle at home, and I don't blame 'em."

"So you think there's a storm coming, too?" Smoke asked.

"It sure looks like it, back off to the northwest."

That was true. A line of dark blue clouds lay off in that direction. They hadn't been there first thing that morning, but they were now, and they appeared to be moving steadily closer to the settlement.

Smoke mentioned that to Windy when he checked in at the office. The old-timer nodded, obviously satisfied with himself.

"I won't say I told you so . . ." he began.

Smoke grinned. "That's all right, Windy. You can say it. I'm perfectly willing to admit that your weather predicting powers are accurate . . . this time, anyway." Smoke took his watch out of his pocket and opened it to check the time. "But that stagecoach ought to be coming in pretty soon, shouldn't it? I thought I'd walk down to the station and wait for it, so I can be sure to get that letter to the governor in the mail pouch."

"I'll come with you," Windy offered. "It'll feel good to stretch my legs. Especially because we're liable to be cooped up for a while once that norther gets here."

"That's what I'm hearing around town. Everybody's getting ready for it."

As they walked along the street toward the stage line office, a gust of wind pushed through, stirring up the dust into small whirlwinds around them. Smoke turned his head to look in the direction it came from.

"Air's got a little bite to it."

"Gonna be a big bite before it's over," Windy said.

Folks on the street began hurrying more as they went about their business, Smoke noticed. They had felt that fresh chill in the air, too.

As they reached the stage station, the door into the office opened and a balding man in spectacles, vest, white shirt, and bow tie stepped out. He held an open watch in his hand.

"Howdy, Eugene," Windy called. "Stage ain't late, is it?"

"Not just yet," the man replied. He snapped the watch closed and slid it back in his pocket. "But it should be getting here any time now."

Windy introduced Smoke to Eugene Hardisty, the manager of the stage station. Hardisty wasn't one of the men they had recruited to defend the town if Snake Bishop's gang attacked. Smoke could tell by looking at him that the man's eyesight wasn't very good. His eyes were watery and he blinked frequently behind the rimless spectacles.

"How long does it take for the stage to pick up a new team and head back south?" Smoke asked.

"Not long," Hardisty replied. "My hostlers are good at their jobs. Of course, Luther and J.J.—that's Luther Blassingame and J.J. Hanesworth, the driver and guard—usually get something to eat while they're here, since they arrive around midday. However, today I'm going to advise them to pick up some food from the café and take it with them, instead of lingering over a regular meal. They need to get started back to Amarillo so they can stay ahead of the storm."

Windy said, "You reckon a stagecoach team can outrun a blue norther?"

"Well, perhaps not completely," Hardisty allowed. "But if they don't waste any time, I believe they can beat the worst of it."

Smoke hoped that turned out to be the case. But as the minutes ticked past, he could tell that Hardisty was beginning to worry. He felt unease stirring, too.

After a while, Hardisty took out his watch, checked the time, and snapped it closed again.

"That's it," he said. "The stagecoach is late now."

Windy scratched his beard and shuffled his feet nervously. "Lots of things can happen to slow down a stagecoach," he commented. "Don't have to mean it was anything really bad."

"Perhaps not, but I've never known Luther to be late without a good reason. Today of all days is not a good time for this to happen."

Smoke and Windy exchanged a glance. Smoke figured the old-timer was thinking the same thing he was.

Not only did they have to worry about all the normal delays that could befall a stagecoach, but there was also the possible threat from Snake Bishop and his gang to worry about. According to the reward posters, Bishop had held up and robbed a number of stagecoaches. The gang had murdered drivers, guards, and passengers, too.

"Was anything particularly valuable supposed to be on today's stage?" Smoke asked the station manager.

Hardisty hesitated before answering but then said, "I shouldn't be talking about it, but since you're the law in Salt Lick now, Mr. Jensen . . . Yes, there's supposed to be a shipment of cash for the bank. Payday for the ranches in the area will be here before the next run, so the money has to be brought in today."

"Would anybody who might be inclined to hold up the stage know that?"

Hardisty shook his head. "I don't see how. I was aware of it, as was my counterpart in Amarillo, and a few people at the bank there, I suppose, as well as Abner Hawkins here. But we're talking about honest, trustworthy individuals, most of whom I've known for a long time."

"What about the driver and guard?"

"Are you implying that Luther or J.J. might have tipped off some outlaws?" Hardisty asked as he glared at Smoke. "I'd trust my life to either of those men." One shoulder rose and fell slightly. "Of course, I realize that you aren't personally acquainted with them, Marshal, so naturally you might be suspicious. But I can vouch for them, I assure you."

"Good enough for me," Smoke said with a nod.

"Besides, neither of them would have known until the last minute that the cash was going out today, although they might have surmised as much from previous instances of such shipments."

"Reckon we ought'a ride south and see if we can find out why the coach is late?" Windy asked Smoke.

"I'm not sure it's late enough yet to warrant that, Marshal," Hardisty said. "But of course, that's up to you."

"We'll give it another few minutes," Smoke said. "But if it doesn't show up pretty soon, I think we should saddle and ride, Windy."

The old-timer nodded.

Smoke had another idea. "I'll walk down to the bank and go up on the roof. That way I ought to be able to see a good long way to the south. Maybe I can spot the coach, or at least the dust from it."

"If you don't, maybe we should head on out."

"I agree. I'll be back in a few minutes."

The day before, Shug Russell and Enoch Jones had placed a ladder in the alley behind the bank and used it to reach the roof. The ladder was still there, being employed by the guards who had taken over since. Smoke climbed it easily and swung his leg over the low wall around the bank's flat roof. Two men he hadn't met stood there, each with a pair of field glasses. They had taken over for Lomax and Lawson earlier in the day.

The sentries knew who Smoke was, of course. They shook hands and introduced themselves as Griff Adams and Ben Sinclair.

Smoke said, "Have either of you noticed any dust off to the south?"

"You mean from that outlaw gang?" Adams asked.

"Actually, the stagecoach is late," Smoke said. "I was hoping maybe you'd spotted it."

Sinclair shook his head and said, "Not a thing, Marshal." He held out his pair of field glasses. "But you're welcome to have a look."

Smoke took the glasses and lifted them to his eyes as he faced to the south. He turned his head slowly from left to right, studying the flat terrain that stretched as far as the eye could see. Nothing out there, he told himself.

Then he stiffened as he spotted something. At first, he

wasn't sure if anything was actually there, but after a moment he was confident that his eyes weren't playing tricks on him. There really was a column of dust rising and moving toward Salt Lick.

The two sentries had seen Smoke's reaction. Ben Sinclair asked, "Do you see something, Marshal?"

"Is it that no-good Bishop gang?" Griff Adams added with a mixture of worry and anticipation in his voice.

"I don't think it's the outlaws," Smoke replied. "There's not enough dust for a bunch as big as that one is supposed to be. More than likely it's the stagecoach." He handed the field glasses back to Sinclair. "Something must have happened to slow it down, but maybe it wasn't too bad."

Smoke said so long to the two men and climbed back down the ladder. He walked quickly to the stage station, where Windy and Eugene Hardisty waited for him with anxious expressions on their faces.

"See anything?" Windy asked before Hardisty could ask the same question.

"I did," Smoke said. "There's a little dust cloud headed this way. Looks about the right size to be coming from a stagecoach."

Hardisty let out a heartfelt sigh of relief. "Oh, thank heavens. I'll tell the hostlers to get the fresh team ready." Another gust of wind blew along the street. "Luther's going to have to hurry on his way back to Amarillo if he wants to stay ahead of that norther."

He hurried off into the barn next to the office while Smoke and Windy waited in front of the building. While they were standing there, Windy asked, "You didn't see nothin' suspicious while you was up there on the bank roof, did you, Smoke?"

"Not a thing. The two men posted there seemed pretty

alert. I'm sure they'll let us know if they spot any signs of trouble."

In a few minutes, the column of dust was close enough to be seen with the naked eye. It rose and then flattened out and streamed off to the south, an indicator of the rising wind from the north. After another couple of minutes, Smoke's keen eyes were able to make out the dark shape at the base of the dust cloud and knew that was the stagecoach.

Windy saw the same thing and said, "Here it comes."

The coach rolled into Salt Lick and came up the main street. Smoke tensed as he realized only one man was on the box, instead of the two that were expected.

"What in thunderation!" That startled exclamation came from Windy, who had noticed the same thing. "That's just Luther Blassingame on the box. Where's Hanesworth?"

The jehu swayed wildly back and forth with every bounce of the stagecoach. Smoke said, "He looks like he's hurt. I don't know if he can stop that team."

Indeed, the coach hadn't slowed down. A few people in the street had to scurry to get out of its way. A man shouted angrily at the driver, but Blassingame didn't seem to hear.

Smoke strode out into the street, took off his hat, and waved it over his head. The horses saw him and spooked a little. That accomplished Smoke's goal of getting them to slow down. He dodged out of the way but was able to grab the harness on one of the leaders and haul the horse to a stop. The other members of the team halted as well.

"Luther!" Windy called as he ran forward. "Luther, what in blazes happened?"

Blassingame didn't respond. Smoke saw the dark bloodstains on the man's faded blue shirt. Blassingame swayed again, and this time he didn't even try to catch himself. He fell over on his side and then rolled off the seat to fall heavily to the ground next to the coach's left front wheel. Neither Smoke nor Windy could get there in time to break his fall.

They arrived at his side a second later, though, and Windy dropped to his knees beside the jehu.

"Damn it, Luther, you're shot all to pieces!"

Windy was right about that. Smoke saw that Luther Blassingame had at least three bullet wounds in his torso and had lost quite a bit of blood from each of them. He must have suffered quite a bit of damage internally, too. With those injuries, Smoke wasn't sure how the man was even still alive.

"Luther!"

That shout came from Eugene Hardisty, who had emerged from the barn and seen his driver's bloody shape sprawled on the ground next to the coach. Hardisty rushed forward and dropped to a knee on Blassingame's other side.

Windy got an arm around Blassingame's shoulders, lifted him slightly, and propped him up on a leg. Looking around at the crowd that was starting to gather, Windy said, "Somebody fetch a bottle from Apple Jack's! Luther needs some bracin' up!"

A few shots of whiskey weren't going to do Blassingame any good in the long run, Smoke knew, but in a way Windy was right. The liquor might revive the wounded man and give him enough strength to allow him to tell them what had happened.

More townspeople crowded around. The stagecoach's arrival would have drawn a considerable amount of attention, anyway. Such things always did, because they broke up the monotony of life in a frontier settlement. With word already spreading that the driver had been shot, more and more people hurried up to see what was going on.

Smoke thought that Blassingame might have died before falling off the coach, but a groan came from the driver, proving that he was still alive. Windy propped him up a little higher and said, "Luther, can you hear me? Luther!"

Blassingame's eyelids fluttered a few times, then opened. His lips moved, but no sound came out, at least none that Smoke could hear. He gave the muttering crowd a stern look and said, "Everybody quiet down."

His commanding tone got results. A hush fell over the street. When Blassingame opened his mouth again, Smoke leaned forward to hear what the man had to say.

"Out . . . outlaws . . . jumped . . . the coach," Blassingame rasped. Every word cost him an obvious effort. Blood trickled from both corners of his mouth. "Twenty men . . . maybe more . . . shot . . . J.J. . . . killed . . . passengers."

One of the bystanders reached over, grasped the handle of the coach's door on this side, and twisted it. A woman screamed at the sight of the three corpses lying in bloody heaps on the vehicle's floor.

Smoke stepped over and closed the door. "Everyone stay back," he ordered. "Somebody fetch the undertaker for these gents."

Then he returned his attention to Luther Blassingame, who was still painfully gasping out words.

"Salt lick . . . south . . . of town," he said, and Smoke figured he was referring to the geographical feature that had given the settlement its name. That must have been where the outlaws attacked the coach. "Was able . . . to hide . . . in that gully . . . near there . . . They thought . . . I was dead . . ."

So that was how Blassingame had escaped from the bandits when the guard and the passengers had been killed. He wasn't going to survive for long, however, as badly wounded as he was.

A man pushed through the crowd and announced, "Here's that bottle you wanted, Windy!" He held out an uncorked bottle of whiskey.

Windy snatched it and held the bottle to Blassingame's mouth. He dribbled a little of the fiery stuff between the jehu's lips. Blassingame choked and coughed, but then he swallowed more of the whiskey and appeared to strengthen slightly.

"Once they was . . . gone . . . I crawled outta . . . the brush . . . got back on the stage . . . headed for town . . ."

That must have required a herculean effort, Smoke knew. During the drive into Salt Lick, Blassingame would have lost even more blood and gotten even weaker, but he had clung to life somehow . . . and clung to the reins, as well, to guide the team the rest of the way here.

Windy gave him another drink, and from that Blassingame was able to find the strength to lift a bloody hand and clutch at the old-timer's arm.

"Had to make it . . . had to warn you . . . Bishop! . . . It was . . . Snake Bishop . . . and his gang! . . . And they're . . . they're headed . . . here . . . headed for . . . Salt Lick!"

Blassingame stiffened in Windy's arms and his eyes went wide. Another breath rasped in his throat as he drew it in. It came back out in the sort of rattling sigh that Smoke had heard too many times in his life. He didn't have to see Blassingame's eyes glaze over to know that the man was dead.

Blassingame's final words hung there in the shocked silence surrounding him.

CHAPTER 20

That stunned reaction lasted for a moment that probably seemed longer than it actually was.

Then a woman cried out and a man yelled, "Snake Bishop! Snake Bishop's comin'!"

Noise welled up from the crowd as men cursed and shouted questions and women whimpered and cried and clutched at their husbands.

Some of the men knew about the potential threat from the Bishop gang, of course, because they were part of the defensive force Smoke had put together. But they were only a small fraction of the group. Most of these folks had had no idea of the danger looming over their heads . . . until now.

Once Snake Bishop's name was out there, however, the news began to spread like wildfire. Already, some members of the crowd were running to tell friends and family about what they had just heard.

As Windy eased Luther Blassingame's head and shoulders back to the ground, he looked up at Smoke and shook his head in dismay.

"We knew we couldn't keep it from 'em forever," he said, "but I reckon it would've been all right if it'd been a mite longer before folks found out."

"I'm actually surprised we kept it as quiet as we did, for as long as we did." Smoke extended a hand, clasped Windy's wrist, and helped the old-timer to his feet. "We'd better go talk to Sarge and Apple Jack and let them know the cat's out of the proverbial bag."

"Reckon they'll likely know before we get there," Windy commented as he looked around. The crowd was scattering in a hurry now. It wouldn't be long before the news reached every corner of Salt Lick.

The Top-Notch Saloon was closer, so they headed there first, leaving Eugene Hardisty to watch over the bodies until the undertaker arrived. As they walked, Windy said, "I'm mixed up about somethin'. If Bishop's bunch jumped the stage earlier today and were headed this direction, why ain't they here yet? They should've beaten Luther to Salt Lick."

"The only explanation is that they didn't come straight here to raid the town," Smoke said.

"But why not? You reckon somethin' happened to delay them?"

Smoke shook his head. "We don't have any way of knowing. It could be that Bishop decided to wait until night-fall to launch his attack. Remember, he believed Blassin-game was dead along with the others. He didn't have any way of knowing that Blassingame was going to warn us, just like he didn't know about Atkins and Rome tipping us off with their failed bank robbery. So he didn't have any reason to hurry."

"Maybe," Windy said as he ran his fingers through his whiskers, "but I never knowed Snake to worry that much about day or night. He was always just as liable to attack in broad daylight."

Smoke frowned slightly as he glanced over at his deputy. Once again, Windy had sounded a little more familiar with

Snake Bishop's way of doing things than he should have been.

Windy must have realized the same thing, because he went on hastily, "Judgin' by what I've read about him on the wanted posters, I mean, and in the newspapers."

"Yeah," Smoke said. A gust of wind tugged at his hat and caused him to lift a hand to the brim and tug it down tighter on his head. "What about the weather? Maybe he changed his mind because of that blue norther headed this way."

"Maybe," Windy said slowly, but he didn't sound convinced.

The sun was still shining in Salt Lick, but the clouds were close enough now that they could be seen over the rooftops, moving fast enough that their progress could be tracked with the naked eye. With the sun shining on them like that, their color had darkened from blue to almost black. It was as ominous-looking a storm front as Smoke had ever seen.

"Hard to believe that yesterday was almost as pleasant as spring, ain't it?" Windy said. "But that's Texas for you."

When they went into the Top-Notch, they found that the saloon was busier than usual for this time of day. Men were lined up at the bar, and Apple Jack and one of his bartenders were busy pouring drinks and drawing mugs of beer. The rush had to be prompted by the news that had broken a short time earlier. Men wanted to get together and talk . . . and fortify themselves with some liquid courage.

Apple Jack spotted Smoke and Windy and waved them toward the far end of the bar. He went along the other side of the hardwood to join them there.

"Well, we knew it wouldn't last," the saloonkeeper said, "but folks are even more worked up than I thought they would be."

Windy said, "Most of these fellas never fought Injuns or

owlhoots and are too young to have been in the war. They've never had to think serious-like about pickin' up a gun and defendin' themselves and their homes and families." He shook his head. "They just never knowed how lucky they really had it. The wolves have always been out there, just waitin' for their time to come around again."

"What's our next move, Smoke?" Apple Jack asked.

"We'll get our force together and put the men on alert. The ones in the outer ring can go to their positions and get settled in. The men responsible for the wagon barricades can go ahead and move those into place. We'll wait to move the families to the bank and establish the inner ring until it's necessary. The important thing is that Bishop and his gang aren't going to take us by surprise. I think we'll put up a lot stiffer fight than they're expecting."

"Maybe they'll pass us by because of the storm," Apple Jack suggested, unknowingly echoing what Smoke had said earlier.

"That might happen," Smoke said, "but we can't count on it."

Apple Jack nodded. "I'm gonna close the saloon. We've got enough on our plate without having half the fellas in town drunk as skunks."

"That's a good idea," Smoke agreed. "Although you'll probably get some arguments about that."

Apple Jack snorted and said, "Anybody gives me too much trouble, I'll break a bungstarter over his head!"

As Smoke and Windy left the saloon and headed for the Red Top Café, Smoke said, "I'm a little surprised Bishop just left the stagecoach there and didn't take the horses, at least."

"I ain't," Windy replied. "Once they'd looted the coach, they didn't have no more use for it. And big ol' draft horses like the ones in that team wouldn't do 'em any good. They'd never make good saddle mounts. Sure, they might be able to sell horses like that, but they wouldn't bring enough to be worth the trouble."

Those same thoughts had crossed Smoke's mind, but he wanted to find out what Windy would say. Again, Windy had phrased his comments in a way to make it sound as if he knew how Snake Bishop's mind worked . . . and Smoke found that very intriguing, as well as a little worrisome.

He didn't have time to follow up on that line of thought, however, because he spotted Sarge Shaw hurrying along the street toward them before they reached the Red Top. The former non-com looked upset about something.

"I heard about what happened with the stagecoach," Shaw said as he came up to them, "so you don't have to tell me. I'm hearing some really disturbing talk, Marshal."

"What's that?"

"Some folks are considering packing up their families and leaving town before Bishop gets here."

Windy said, "We done talked to 'em about that at the meetin' last night!"

"Most of the people in town weren't at that meeting," Smoke pointed out. "And they don't know about our plans, either. They just know that they want to protect their families, and they think the best way to do that is by running."

"Well, it ain't."

"We know that, but—"

Angry shouts from down the street interrupted what Smoke was saying. The three men turned and looked in that direction. A couple of wagons had been moved into the street to form part of the barricade at that end of town. Near them was a knot of men locked in a struggle. Fists flew as the battle swayed back and forth.

"Come on," Smoke said. "We need to break that up."

They ran toward the wagons. Smoke shouted for the

men to stop fighting, but they were too caught up in their emotions and ignored him.

"Stay back, Windy," Smoke told the old-timer, then he and Shaw waded into the fight. They grabbed men by their collars, jerked them away from their opponents, and slung them to the ground.

A couple of those hombres tried to scramble back to their feet, but Windy moved in quickly behind them and rapped them on the head with the butt of his old cap-and-ball pistol. The massive revolver was pretty heavy and the well-placed blows sent the men back to the ground, too stunned to try it again for a few minutes.

One of the battlers made the mistake of swinging a wild, roundhouse punch at Smoke's head. Smoke easily ducked beneath it and stepped closer to hook a hard left into the man's midsection. When the man bent forward from the impact with his eyes bulging, that put his chin in perfect position for the uppercut that Smoke brought whistling up. The blow landed perfectly and lifted the man's feet a couple of inches off the ground before dumping him on his back, out cold.

A few feet away, Sarge Shaw caught two men by the neck and drove their heads together. The skulls collided with a solid *thunk!* and those men dropped senseless to the hard-packed dirt street, too.

The fight ground to a halt then. The men who were still on their feet stood in a ragged half-circle around Smoke and Sarge Shaw. Windy hovered nearby, ready to wallop somebody else with that gun butt if he needed to.

Smoke glared at the men and said, "What in blazes is wrong with you fellas? Don't you think there's enough trouble in Salt Lick right now without you fighting each other?"

One of the men pointed and said, "They're tryin' to block the street so we can't get out!"

"That's what they were told to do. They're blocking the street so outlaws can't get *in*."

"Yeah, but those outlaws aren't here now," the townsman argued, "and some of us want to leave before they get here."

"You mean to abandon your homes?" Smoke demanded. It was the same argument that had been raised during the meeting in the livery stable the night before. "That's probably the worst thing you can do right now."

"Snake Bishop's got a reputation for burnin' down towns," another man said.

"That's right," the first one put in. "But at least our families would be safe. We can rebuild houses and businesses."

Windy said, "If it's your families you're worried about, they'll be safer here than out yonder on the prairie somewhere. What if you was to run into Bishop's bunch while you're out in the open, with no place to hide or take cover? What kinda chance do you think you'd stand then?"

"According to what Luther Blassingame said before he died, Bishop is south of town," a man said. "We'll just go north, away from him. Ain't that right, boys?"

Shouts of agreement went up.

Smoke shook his head and leveled an arm to point toward the onrushing clouds.

"If you go north, that's what you'll run into," he said. "I don't think you want that."

At that moment, as if they had been waiting for a cue, the clouds reached the sun and swallowed it in one gulp. Gloom fell over the town like a curtain, and the temperature seemed to drop perceptibly between one breath and the next.

Windy said, "Maybe you fellas ain't ever been caught in a blue norther. I have. Let me tell you, the only thing that ever scared me more was a blasted cyclone. When that norther hits, the wind's gonna howl like you never heard it before. It'll be so cold it'll steal ever' last smidgen of warmth right outta your body. Your blood'll get so thick it won't hardly flow through your veins. And if there's snow behind it, which I reckon there is behind that one, it'll come down so hard and thick you won't be able to see your hand in front of your face. I've seen fellas freeze to death five feet away from the door to the buildin' they were lookin' for. They never knowed it was there." Windy let out a disgusted snort. "And *that's* what you want to go draggin' your families off into!"

The men looked more subdued now. Some even seemed to be ashamed of their panic. They shuffled their feet as the wind began to blow harder and colder.

"It *does* seem like the weather's fixin' to turn bad," one man said.

"Might be best to stay inside," another added.

"But what about those outlaws?" a third man asked.

Smoke nodded. "They're a threat, too, no doubt about that. That's why we're getting ready as best we can. We're going to block the streets so Bishop's gang can't charge straight through town and shoot the place up. We have men on the bank roof keeping an eye out for trouble. Men will be posted on top of other buildings and in strong defensive positions to fight back if the town is attacked. We plan to make Salt Lick too big a bite for Snake Bishop to swallow."

"That sounds good . . . but we're just ordinary folks, Mr. Jensen, and Bishop's got a big gang of hard-case killers. Are we really any match for them?"

"Well," Smoke said, "we kind of have to be, if we want to fight them off. I don't know about you boys, but when the Good Lord was handing out qualities, he didn't put a whole lot of back-up in me."

"Nor in me," Sarge Shaw added. "I saw plenty of fighting in the war. Some hard defeats, sure, but more victories, and in every one of them, most of the fighting was done by fellows who were scared and didn't figure they had any business being there. They didn't think they had what it took. But they did."

"And a lot of 'em died, too," a man said sourly.

"That's true. But they figured the fight was worth it." Shaw looked around. "I think this town is worth it. I think your families are worth it. And I think each and every one of you is worth it. And that's why I'll fight for you. For all of us."

Nobody cheered. But looks of resolve began to appear on the faces of the gathered men.

"We all have work to do," Smoke said. "Let's get at it. Some of you men help these others finish moving the wagons into place. The rest of you go home and make sure your guns are loaded and ready. If you don't have any guns, stop at one of the general stores. You can pick up rifles and shotguns and ammunition." He smiled. "There's always a chance that trouble won't come. But if it does, we need to be ready for it."

The crowd began to scatter, except for the men moving the wagons and the new volunteers who stayed to help. Even though it was still early afternoon, the dark clouds had covered the whole sky from horizon to horizon, and it looked more like twilight. The temperature had dropped enough that men's breath began to fog in front of their faces.

"I'm going to talk things over with Apple Jack," Shaw said.

Smoke nodded. "You two are our commanders," he said. "If you see something that needs to be done, make sure it is. Windy and I will be at the marshal's office if you need us."

As they walked along the street, Windy shook his head dolefully and said, "This is gonna be a bad blow. You can feel it already, and I can smell the snow that's on the way. But the town could get through the storm all right, if that was all we had to worry about. But with Snake Bishop on top of it . . ."

The old-timer's sigh of dismay was eloquent.

"I don't reckon we need to give up just yet," Smoke said. "But there is something I want to talk to you about, Windy, as soon as we get back to—Wait a minute. Is that who I think it is?"

The question was prompted by the sight of a man standing in front of the marshal's office, evidently waiting for them with his hat pulled down and his hands plunged into the pockets of a thick flannel coat.

Windy chuckled and said, "It sure is. Jonas Madigan, his own self. Are you surprised, Smoke?"

"No," Smoke admitted. "No, I'm not."

CHAPTER 21

As they walked up to Madigan, Smoke said, "I know somebody who's not going to be happy with you, Jonas."

"Did you sneak out?" Windy asked.

Madigan glared and said, "I don't have to sneak out of my own house, you old rapscallion." He paused, then went on, "I just, uh, waited until Miriam had gone back to her house to get a few things. With the weather about to turn bad, she wanted to be able to stay over at my place for a few days without having to go back and forth. And don't you dare say anything to sully that noble woman's reputation—"

Windy held up both hands defensively. "I wasn't about to say nothin', Jonas. Shoot, as far as I'm concerned, the two o' you might as well be married."

"Well, we're not," Madigan snapped. "Although I've come around to thinkin' that we ought to be. And once we get past this storm and deal with Snake Bishop's gang, I'm gonna see if we can do something about that."

"I think that's a good idea," Smoke said. "As long as Mrs. Dollinger goes along with it."

"I reckon she will, unless I miss my guess." Madigan shared his shoulders. "But first we've got to deal with other things, and we might as well get in out of this damned cold wind while we do it, hadn't we?"

"Sounds good to me."

They went into the office. Earlier, Windy had started a fire in the pot-bellied stove to boil some coffee, but it had burned down to embers during the day. Still, a little bit of heat came from it, so it wasn't quite as chilly in the office as it was outside. While Smoke went behind the desk, Windy put some more wood in the stove, added kindling, and snapped a lucifer to life to get a blaze going again.

Smoke reached for the badge pinned to his shirt and said, "Now that you're back, Marshal, I reckon I should give this to you."

"Wait just a blasted minute there," Madigan said. "Just because I came to help doesn't mean I'm takin' over the marshal's job again. That's still yours for now, Smoke."

"But by rights, the job's more yours than mine," Smoke objected. "I was just filling in."

"And you still are." Madigan heaved a sigh. "I can sit in an office, and if I have to, I reckon I can hold up a gun and pull the trigger, but to tell you the truth, son . . . just walkin' the short distance here took a hell of a lot out of me. There's no way I can be runnin' around town directin' the fight against Bishop's gang if they hit us. That's gonna be up to you."

"Colonel Appleton and Sarge Shaw are in charge of our defense."

Madigan snorted. "Apple Jack and Sarge were good men in their day. Still are good men, I expect. But they're not Smoke Jensen. There's only one of those. They broke the mold when they made you, Smoke, and you know it."

Smoke wasn't going to waste time arguing about that. He had never thought of himself as anything special, just a fella who used his God-given skills to try to do the right thing.

"Whether you want the badge back or not, Jonas, I'm mighty glad to have you here," he said. With a smile, he added, "When this is all over, I'll put in a good word for you with Mrs. Dollinger, if you think it'll help."

"I don't know about that," Madigan said, "but I reckon it couldn't hurt."

Windy had the fire going in the stove. He stood there for a moment with his hands extended toward it, warming them, then turned and put his backside to it to warm that.

"Smoke, you were sayin' outside that there's something you wanted to talk to me about . . ."

"That's right."

Smoke took off his hat and placed it on the desk as he sat down in the chair behind it. Jonas Madigan went over to sit on the old divan along the front wall, to the left of the door. That was the corner where the stove was, so he could soak up some of the warmth from it.

Smoke clasped his hands on the desk, looked at Windy, and asked, "How long ago was it that you rode with Snake Bishop and his gang?"

Windy's eyes widened in shock. He swallowed hard. Madigan stared at Smoke and said, "Have you gone loco? Windy's no owlhoot!"

"Not now, maybe," Smoke said. He nodded toward the old-timer. "But he's not denying it, is he?"

"I didn't . . . I never . . ." Windy forced out. "What in tarnation, Smoke?"

"You didn't just recognize Bart Rome from his picture on a wanted poster," Smoke said calmly. "I think you knew him, and Atkins, too, from your time with the gang. You just thought up that story about knowing them from their wanted posters when we came in here and found reward dodgers scattered all over the desk and floor.

"Don't get me wrong, it could have happened that way," Smoke went on, "but that was the first thing that made me wonder. Ever since then, though, you've been saying that

Bishop would do this or Bishop wouldn't do that, and then as soon as the words were out of your mouth, you'd realize you'd said too much and make sure to add that you were just going by what you've read or heard about him. But the way you were so quick to throw in those excuses just made me wonder more about you, Windy."

Windy's normally affable face was set in cold, hard lines now as he looked across the room at Smoke. "You're forgettin' that we've fought side by side, ain't you?" he asked. "Would I have blazed away at Rome and Atkins like that if they were my pards?"

"I never said they were your pards. But remember, when we were shooting at them, we didn't know who they were. All we knew was that they gunned down Ted Cardwell and were trying to get away, and that was enough to tell us they had to be stopped. We didn't see their faces until later."

Madigan said, "Now, just hold on a minute. Windy's been here in Salt Lick for two years or more. I can't believe Bishop would've sent him here that long ago—"

"Bishop didn't send him here," Smoke broke in. "I never thought that. It wouldn't have made any sense. But you don't know what he was doing before he showed up in Salt Lick, do you, Jonas? He's told a lot of stories about the places he's been and the things he's done—"

"And ever' word of 'em was true, too!" Windy said indignantly. "Well, 'most ever' word, anyway."

"And I believe you," Smoke assured him. "But that still doesn't mean you couldn't have spent some time riding with Bishop's gang."

The two of them locked eyes for a long, tense moment, before Windy finally broke off his stare and turned his head away.

"Damn it," he said in a low, ragged voice.

"Windy . . . it's true?" Madigan asked. He looked and sounded like he didn't want to believe it.

"It's true." Windy grimaced and shook his head. "I rode with that bunch for six months or so, a while back. Long enough to figure out what sorry, lowdown polecats they all were." He raked his fingers through his whiskers and turned to face Madigan. "You got to understand, Jonas. Most o' my life, I've been on the right side of the law, I swear it. But there's been some hard times, too. I, uh, might've helped myself to a few cows that didn't belong to me, now and then—"

"You mean you were a rustler," Madigan cut in.

"In the eyes of the law, I reckon I was. But I only wide-looped stock from the big spreads that could afford to lose a few head. I never went after any little greasy-sack outfits. I wouldn't do that."

"Rustlin' is rustlin'," Madigan said coldly. "Did you rob banks, too?"

"I never!" Windy made a face again. "Well, there *was* that time up in the Dakota Territory—"

Madigan held up a hand to stop him. "Never mind. Are you wanted in Texas?"

"No, sir!" Windy pounded a gnarled fist into the palm of the other hand. "Now *that* I can swear to, up one way and down t'other. There ain't no paper out on me in Texas. That's why I figured I could settle down here in Salt Lick and walk the straight and narrow from now on, like I've always tried to."

Smoke asked, "How did you get mixed up with Snake Bishop?"

"I was up in Kansas, and I got a mite pie-eyed one night in a saloon and there was a fight. I got throwed in the local hoosegow with a fella name of Hackberry. Boo Hackberry, if you can believe that. We was charged with bein' drunk and disorderly, and I reckon the judge would've just give us a fine and let us go the next mornin', but Boo got spooked and didn't want to take a chance on that because, as it turns out, he *did* have paper on him in Kansas and he was wanted for murder on account of a shootin' over in Wichita where he killed a fella. Boo swore to me it was self-defense, that the other hombre reached first, but the judge was the dead fella's second cousin or somethin' like that, so he got sentenced to hang. Boo did, I mean, not the judge. But he busted out before they got around to stretchin' his neck, and he didn't want anybody in that little town where we was locked up to figure out who he really was. So I agreed to help him escape and pretended to be really sick so the deputy would come in to see what was wrong, and then Boo got his hands on the fella and knocked him out and took his keys and gun, and I figured he'd just steal a horse and get outta there, but before he left he took the deputy's gun and stove in his head with it. Killed him just outta sheer meanness, I reckon. And then he said I had to come with him, 'cause if I didn't, they'd blame me for the deputy gettin' killed, too, and would string me up." Windy nodded slowly. "At the time, it made a heap of sense."

"I can figure out what happened after that," Madigan said with a scowl. "This Boo Hackberry was part of Snake Bishop's gang, and when he went back to them, he took you with him. And by the time *you* figured out what you'd got yourself into, it was too late to do anything about it. Bishop wouldn't just let you ride off. He'd think you were too big a danger to the gang to let you do that."

Windy nodded. "That's sure the way it was, all right, Jonas. I strung along with 'em for a while, just waitin' for a chance to light a shuck without gettin' myself killed." He sighed. "I saw Snake and the others do some mighty bad things, things that haunt my dreams to this day, but I finally saw my opportunity and got away from that bad bunch.

Came down here to Texas and swore to myself I'd never break the law again." He held up a hand, as if he were swearing an oath in court. "And I never did, so help me God. I even found myself workin' for the law, helpin' you out. I never gave you cause to regret that, now did I?"

"No, you didn't," Madigan admitted. "You were a good jailer. I told Ted he ought to ask you to be deputy, but he said the town wouldn't pay for it. I don't know if he was right about that, or if he just wanted to prove he could handle everything himself. Damned shame he never really got much chance to try."

Smoke said, "So it's just coincidence that Bishop showed up in these parts, where you'd settled down?"

"Plumb coincidence," Windy declared. "I give you my word on that, Smoke. I'll swear it on as many Bibles as you want to stack up, too."

Smoke shook his head, smiled faintly, and said, "That's not necessary, Windy. I believe you. About all of it."

Windy looked a little surprised. "You do?"

"Like you said, we've fought side by side. Any man who's done that, I tend to give him the benefit of the doubt. I just wanted to get the truth out in the open, so that now I can trust you."

"You can. I've seen what Snake Bishop can do. I want to stop him as much as anybody in town!"

"I believe that, too," Smoke said.

Before any of them could say anything else, the office door opened, letting in a gust of frigid wind and an angry Miriam Dollinger, who was red-faced either from the wind, her emotional state, or both.

"I knew I would find you here, Jonas!"

He stood up quickly and held his hands out toward her. "Now, Miriam—"

"You shouldn't even be out of bed, let alone wandering

around in this terrible weather. I swear, the temperature's dropped twenty degrees in the past hour!" She tightened the shawl she wore over a short jacket. "I wasn't sure where you'd gone. I thought I might find you lying frozen in an alley somewhere."

"You just said you figured you'd find me here."

Smoke and Windy both winced. Pointing out the inconsistencies in the statements of a woman who was already mad at you wasn't the smartest thing an hombre could do.

"I think you should come on back to the house with me."

"Can't do it," Madigan replied with a shake of his head. "I didn't mean to upset you, Miriam. Reckon I should've left you a note tellin' you what I was doing. But the town needs me, and just because I've been feelin' a mite puny doesn't mean I can let folks down."

"A mite puny?" she repeated. "Jonas, you know good and well, that what ails you is worse than feeling a mite puny! You're . . . you're . . ."

She couldn't get the words out. Instead, she lifted her hands and covered her face. She didn't start crying, but it was obvious how upset she was.

Madigan moved over in front of her, gently took hold of her wrists, and eased her hands down.

"I reckon we both know what ails me," he said quietly, "and how much time I've got left. But that doesn't matter. Salt Lick is my town. The folks who live here are my friends. If there's something I can do to help them, then I got to, Miriam. I just got to. I know you can see that."

"I . . . I can see it . . . but I don't have to *like* it!"

"No, I reckon you don't," Madigan said as he put his arms around her and drew her closer to him. The two of them stood there holding each other.

Windy looked over at Smoke and said, "You reckon we

ought to go take a turn around town so we can see how things are shapin' up?"

"I think that would be a good idea," Smoke said. He still had his sheepskin coat on, so all he had to do was put on his hat and button up the coat. He and Windy left Madigan and Miriam in the office and stepped out into what had turned into a bone-chilling wind.

Maybe while they were gone, Jonas would have the sense to go ahead and ask Miriam that question he needed to ask her, Smoke thought.

It would be nice to have *something* settled, while the fate of Salt Lick still loomed so uncertainly.

And the only one who truly had the answer to *that* question was somewhere out there in the gathering storm.

CHAPTER 22

The men and horses were protected in a dry wash that twisted across the prairie. Up against the northern wall of it, they were protected from the worst of the icy wind.

Even so, the conditions were fairly miserable, and the men weren't happy. They had been upset already because the female prisoners they had taken from Thatcher's Crossing had proven not to have much stamina. All four gals were already dead, three from the rough treatment they had suffered, the fourth because she'd gotten her hands on a knife and cut her own throat.

The unexpected cash they had found in the front boot of that stagecoach had perked the boys up for a while, but then Snake Bishop had decided to wait before launching the raid on Salt Lick. Bishop had seen the blue norther coming and figured to turn the weather to their advantage.

"We'll wait until the whole town is hunkered down because of the storm," he had told them after calling a halt in this arroyo. He wasn't in the habit of explaining his decisions, but it seemed warranted in this case. "They won't be expecting a thing. We can wipe out half of them before they even know anything is going on."

"I never saw a bunch of townies put up much of a fight,

anyway," an outlaw named Clyde said, "whether they knew trouble was coming or not."

Bishop had nodded, seeming reasonable, but his hand had strayed to the thick but flexible handle of the coiled whip fastened to his gunbelt. He saw the way Clyde's face paled as he ran his palm along that handle.

"Of course, if waiting's what you want to do, Snake, then I'm sure that's the best thing," Clyde said hurriedly. "I never meant to sound like I thought otherwise. You . . . you've always known what to do."

"Never steered you boys wrong, have I?"

"No, sir, you never—"

The whip came up and lashed out, then leaped backward with a sharp crack. Clyde jumped as his eyes bugged out in terror. Then he slowly lifted a hand to his cheek, ran his fingertips along it, and then looked at them in amazement, as if he couldn't believe there was no blood on them. His rugged face was unmarked.

The rest of the outlaws looked on impassively. They knew good and well that Bishop could have put Clyde's eye out or laid his cheek open to the bone just as easily if he'd wanted to. The message was plain.

Don't question the boss's orders.

Muttering to himself, visibly spooked, Clyde had gone over to sit down with his back against the arroyo wall. The other men also settled down to wait until Bishop gave the order to move.

Unfortunately, it just got colder, and it was hard to think too much about how close Clyde had come to losing an eye when a fella's teeth were chattering and the sky was like twilight in the middle of the afternoon. More and more sullen, resentful looks were cast toward their leader as he paced back and forth, toying with the ever-present whip.

Finally, a lean-faced man with the deeply brown skin of a Mexican but the green eyes of his Irish father came over to join Bishop.

"The fellas are getting pretty restless, Snake," Paco O'Shannon said quietly. He wasn't exactly the second in command—Bishop wouldn't allow any of his men to aspire to such a position because it might make them too ambitious—but he had ridden with Bishop for longer than any of the others and could get away with things the others couldn't. "Maybe we'd better start thinking about moving on to Salt Lick."

"What if I want to wait until after dark?" Bishop snapped.

"Then we'll wait until after dark," O'Shannon replied with a shrug. "But we might have a harder time finding the place if it's started to snow by then. You've seen some of these Panhandle blizzards, Snake. A man might as well be blind if he gets caught in one of them."

O'Shannon had a good point, Bishop knew, and he had raised it without being *too* challenging about it. Bishop never let any of the men get away with defiance because he was smart enough to know that there was only one of him and more than three dozen of them. And every man there was a hardened killer in his own right. So they had to stay scared of him, always uncertain what he might do.

But no matter how scared of him they were, if he pushed them too far, they might turn on him.

"All right," he told O'Shannon with a nod. "It's time."

A grin split O'Shannon's wolfish face. He turned and called over the sound of the wind, "Mount up, boys! We're headed for Salt Lick!"

* * *

Not surprisingly, as the wind rose and the temperature dropped, the streets had cleared, for the most part. A few people still hurried here and there, bent on some last-minute errand, but now that the blue norther had arrived, most folks were staying inside.

Smoke and Windy walked from one end of the settlement to the other. Wagons barricaded the northern and southern ends of the main street. The cross streets also had been blocked by vehicles, including some buggies and buckboards, at their eastern and western ends.

That arrangement formed a defensive ring around the town that would prevent a straight ahead charge by raiders on horseback, at least in theory. Men in heavy coats, with hats tugged down and scarves wrapped around their throats, stood watch, a single man at each point who would fire a warning shot if he saw any trouble approaching. More men were on the roofs of half a dozen buildings scattered around Salt Lick, not just the bank now.

"Lookee there," Windy said, pointing up into the air ahead of them as he and Smoke walked along the main street. Several snowflakes whipped past, spit down from the clouds and moving almost horizontally because of the wind. As Smoke watched, the number of flakes increased, although they were still just flurries.

"It's here, all right," he said. "Makes yesterday seem like a lot longer ago than that, doesn't it?"

"Durned right it does. Once a blue norther hits, it's hard to even imagine when it wasn't cold and blowin' like a son of a gun."

Rufus Spencer hailed them then from the partially open door of the livery stable. When they walked over to him, the blacksmith said, "Marshal, I need you to give me a hand with something."

"Of course, Mr. Spencer," Smoke replied with a nod. "What is it?"

Spencer waved a big hand toward the slender figure standing behind him to one side in the barn. "Tell this girl of mine that if those outlaws attack, she needs to head for the bank."

"With all the women and children?" Tommy Spencer said scathingly. She snorted. "Not hardly! I can use a rifle just as good as you can, Pa. Probably better, when you get right down to it."

"That bank has nice, thick walls," her father said. "It's the safest place in town. Besides, there'll be men there to protect it and the folks who take shelter there."

"You'd think that by now, you'd realize I don't need to be protected, Pa," Tommy insisted.

"That's just it, Miss Spencer," Smoke said. "It doesn't matter how old your children are, or how capable they are, it's a parent's instinct to protect his or her young'uns. And that never changes."

"You have children, Mr. Jensen?"

Smoke felt a pang deep inside at that question. Several years had passed since his first wife Nicole and their infant son Arthur had been murdered by a gang of Smoke's enemies. He had avenged their deaths, but of course that hadn't brought them back and it hadn't really eased the grief he felt. Only time had done that . . . time, and his marriage to Sally, and the fine life they had built together on the Sugarloaf.

"I had a son," he said with a solemn smile. "He passed away . . . in part because I didn't do enough to protect him."

"Oh." Tommy's eyes widened. "I'm sorry, Marshal, I didn't mean to—"

"It's all right," Smoke broke in to tell her. "You walk down the street and see fifty different people, they'll have at least fifty different tragedies they're carrying around inside them that most folks don't know about. That's just part of the state of being human. We can't let it consume us. But that doesn't change my point that your pa is just doing what he's meant to do by looking out for you."

Tommy drew in a deep breath, frowned, and said with obvious reluctance, "All right, I guess if there's trouble, I can go to the bank with the others. But I'm takin' my rifle with me! You said there'd be men there to protect the place, Mr. Jensen, and there's nothing wrong with me helping them."

"Not a thing in the world," Smoke agreed with a nod.

Rufus Spencer said, "All right, that's settled. How are things looking out there, Marshal?"

"You mean the weather?"

"It's snowin'," Windy said, "and it's fixin' to start snowin' a lot harder pretty soon, you can mark my words on *that*!"

"Actually, I was talking more about those outlaws—" Spencer began.

If the blacksmith had been able to finish the question, Smoke would have told them there was no sign of Snake Bishop's gang yet.

But the three rifle shots that suddenly slammed through the cold air were both an interruption—and an answer!

"Three shots," Smoke snapped. "That's the signal from the men on the bank roof."

"We'd better get down there," Windy said.

"And I'm getting my rifle!" Tommy exclaimed as she turned to dash deeper into the barn.

Spencer reached over to pick up a double-barreled shotgun that was leaning against a wall. "My post is at the barricade on the southern end of town," he said. "Good luck, Marshal."

"To you, as well," Smoke told him.

"We're all liable to need it," Windy muttered.

With that, Smoke and Windy hurried out of the barn and trotted toward the bank. Instead of taking the time to climb the ladder, Smoke stood in front of the building, cupped his hands around his mouth, and shouted over the steady hum of the wind, "Hello, up there! What did you see?"

One of the lookouts appeared at the front edge of the roof and called, "Riders comin' from the south, Marshal! Looks like a dozen or more of them! They're still too far away to make out any details, but they're comin' fast!"

"That'll be Snake," Windy said grimly. "He figures we don't know he's anywhere around these parts. He plans on hittin' Salt Lick hard and fast and killin' enough folks to keep us from puttin' up a fight."

"Then he has a surprise of his own waiting for him, doesn't he?" Smoke said. He returned his attention to the men on the roof and went on, "Hold your fire up there until the shooting starts down here. We don't want to open the ball too soon!"

The lookout waved to acknowledge the order and disappeared from the edge. Smoke knew that all the riflemen hidden on the rooftops had been instructed not to open fire until someone down below did. That would probably be Sarge Shaw, who was in charge of the barricade at the southern end of the street. Apple Jack was in command of the barricade on the other end of town.

Smoke and Windy ducked into the marshal's office to grab the fully loaded Winchesters waiting there. Each man shoved a box of cartridges into a coat pocket. They would be able to fight for quite a while without running out of ammunition.

Jonas Madigan and Miriam Dollinger weren't there anymore. Smoke didn't know if Miriam had persuaded the old lawman to return to his house, but he hoped so. This weather was too raw for Madigan to be out in it . . . although, as he himself had pointed out, in the long run it wasn't going to matter much.

As they hurried out of the office, Windy said, "That fella on the bank said there was a dozen of the varmints headed this way. Snake's gang is bigger than that. Sometimes he'd split the bunch and hit a town from more than one direction at a time."

"Do you think that's what he's planning to do here?"

Windy shook his head. "There ain't no way of knowin' until he does it. But I got a hunch that might be what he has in mind."

"Then we need to warn the men on the other sides of town to be alert. Let's split up and do that."

Windy frowned at him and asked, "You trust me to do that, Smoke?"

"Why wouldn't I?"

"Because of what I told you earlier 'bout me ridin' with Bishop's gang."

"You also told me that those days were in the past and that you'd gone straight since then," Smoke reminded him. "And I don't see any reason not to believe you."

"I ain't gonna give you any reason not to believe, neither," Windy muttered. "I'm much obliged to you for this chance, Smoke."

"Let's both put it to good use."

With curt nods to each other, they split up to visit the other defensive points and warn the men posted there that Snake Bishop's gang could be attacking from different directions.

Smoke didn't know how long it would take the outlaws to arrive, but it wouldn't be very long, he was certain of that.

If the attackers to the south were already in sight, Sarge Shaw and his men would be drawing beads on them right about now. But Sarge would wait until the enemy was good and close . . .

"They're coming?" Apple Jack asked as Smoke hurried up to him at the northern end of town.

"The men on the bank spotted about a dozen riders headed this way from the south, coming hell for leather."

"Only a dozen?" Apple Jack asked. Knowing the size that the Bishop gang had been reported to be in the past, his strategic mind had leaped immediately to the same possibility Windy had voiced. "They're going to hit us from all sides."

"Could be."

Apple Jack turned his head and crisply ordered the men with him, "Get to your places and be ready." He lifted his voice to call to the defenders posted in nearby buildings, "Everybody get ready!"

High-pitched the words might be, but they contained an undeniable sound of command. Rifle barrels poked out of open windows and from behind full water barrels.

Smoke nodded to Apple Jack, satisfied with what he had seen, then turned and headed the other way. He and Windy had agreed to rendezvous at the southern end of town, at Sarge Shaw's barricade, because they knew at least some of the outlaws would strike there.

Windy hadn't arrived yet when Smoke reached the barricade, but Shaw greeted Smoke with a grim nod.

"We can see them coming through field glasses," he reported. "They're no more than half a mile away. They'll be here in a matter of minutes." The former non-com frowned worriedly. "What if they spot the wagons in the street and realize we're waiting for them? Once that happens, we've lost the element of surprise."

"If they try to break off their charge or even start to slow down, go ahead and open fire," Smoke advised. "We won't get a better chance to wipe out some of them. If Bishop goes down in the first volley, the others might give up the attack, or if he survives but loses enough men right away, he might decide that Salt Lick's not worth it."

"You really think a loco owlhoot like Snake Bishop is supposed to do something that reasonable?" Shaw asked.

"Well . . . probably not," Smoke admitted. "But there's nothing wrong with us hoping."

"Hope is a good thing," Shaw said, "as long as it's accompanied by plenty of hot lead."

Smoke couldn't argue with that. But before he could say anything else, even in agreement, shouts of alarm came from the other end of town, carried to him and Shaw by the wind from that direction. Both men turned. Shaw's breath hissed through his teeth as he drew in air in a sharp, alarmed reaction.

It took a lot to shock Smoke Jensen, but the sight that met his eyes just now accomplished that. A huge, towering, grayish-white wall loomed over Salt Lick, barreling down on the settlement with unbelievable speed. It looked almost like a gigantic wave from the ocean . . . but this moisture was in different form. It was just as unstoppable as a tidal wave, however.

Then, before anyone could do more than gasp in horror, the blizzard crashed over the town.

CHAPTER 23

Smoke had been in some terrible snowstorms on the northern plains, but this one matched any of them for sheer ferocity. The wind was so hard it felt as if it were about to knock him over, and the little pellets of snow battered and clawed at him like giant grains of sand in the world's worst sandstorm. He was blinded and could no longer see Sarge Shaw, even though the man was only a few feet from him.

The insane, banshee wail of the wind drowned out all other sounds, at least at first. Then Smoke's hearing adjusted a little, and he thought he heard someone calling his name from a great distance.

All around him was a white maelstrom. Out of that madness came a hand, groping blindly. It brushed against Smoke's arm and then closed around it in a tight grip. Smoke reached out, found what felt like a shoulder. He drew the man closer to him.

"Sarge?"

"Is that you, Smoke? Are . . . there?"

"Right here," Smoke answered the wind-whipped question.

He was able to see Shaw now, as a dark, vague shape in the thick curtains of snow.

"We need to . . . inside!"

Smoke knew Shaw was right. A man couldn't survive for very long in this storm with no shelter. The wind stole his breath, and the temperature was plummeting even more.

Smoke could barely hear himself as he shouted, "What happened to Bishop?"

"Nobody would . . . weather like this!"

Smoke understood the sentiment, even if he couldn't make out all the words. You couldn't raid a town in weather like this. Any sane man would have agreed with that, too.

The problem was that Snake Bishop wasn't necessarily sane.

Proof of that came in the shape of a dark figure on horseback that suddenly loomed over them. Flame lanced from the muzzle of a gun, visible even through the blizzard. Smoke tipped up the barrel of the Winchester he held and fired one-handed. He couldn't tell if he hit the raider, because the horse lunged on past him and Shaw, disappearing with its rider as abruptly as it had appeared.

Smoke thought he heard more shots nearby, but he couldn't be sure. A second later, Sarge Shaw sagged against him and gasped, "I'm hit!"

Smoke got his free arm around the former non-com and put his mouth close to Shaw's ear to ask, "How bad is it?"

"Don't know." The words came out through teeth gritted against the pain. "It's my right leg."

"Come on. Let's get you to the bank."

Some of Salt Lick's women and children had been gathering inside the bank already, Smoke knew. He had seen them hurrying through the street and into the sturdy brick building while he and Windy were going around town to warn the men at the various barricades. Somebody there ought to be able to tend to Shaw's wound, if Smoke could find the place in this white hell.

As he and Shaw struggled through the blowing snow

in what he hoped was the right direction, Smoke thought about what had happened and tried to figure out what to do next. The timing of the blizzard's arrival had destroyed most of his defensive plan in little more than the blink of an eye.

The only thing to be thankful for was that the terrible storm had to be as disorienting for Snake Bishop's gang as it was for Salt Lick's defenders. Nobody could see to shoot except at extremely close range, and even then, it would be a chancier proposition than usual.

There was one more thing to hope for, Smoke realized. Some of the defenders would have made it to the bank before the storm hit. Other men might head for there, knowing that it was the best place to fort up.

And Bishop would still want to loot it, too, which meant he had to show up there sooner or later.

Smoke intended to be there when that happened, ready to get Snake Bishop in his gunsights.

For now, though, he just wanted to help Sarge Shaw to safety and see about getting the man patched up.

They stumbled through the snow. With the wind blowing so hard, their progress felt like they were struggling through a giant wave such as the one the blizzard had resembled just before it struck. Smoke had a veteran frontiersman's instinct for directions, so he *believed* they were headed for the bank . . . but in this blinding white tempest, there was no way to be sure.

Suddenly they bumped into something. Keeping one arm around Sarge Shaw, he used the hand holding the Winchester to explore the obstacle. It was a hitch rail; Smoke had no doubt of that even though his fingers were starting to go numb from the cold. Keeping his right hand resting on the rail, he urged Shaw to the left. After a moment, they came to the end of it.

Now was the time for another leap of faith. The hitch rail

had been something solid to hold on to, at least. But it offered them no shelter, so they had to step out into the swirling madness again. Smoke tried to move as straight as possible toward where the boardwalk should be.

One step and then part of another, and then their shins struck something hard and immobile. The edge of the low boardwalk that ran in front of the buildings, Smoke thought. He swept his arm back and forth through the snow. Nothing blocked their path right in front of them.

"Step up!" he shouted to Shaw. "Can you manage it, Sarge?"

"I can . . . manage," Shaw replied. His voice sounded weaker, and Smoke wondered how much blood he had lost.

They made it onto the boardwalk. Snow was already starting to drift on the planks. Smoke moved forward, half-carrying Shaw now. The former non-com was no lightweight, but Smoke possessed enormous strength in his arms and broad shoulders.

Again they came up against a solid object, this time rising in front of them. Smoke felt it. Relief went through him as he realized he was touching a brick wall . . . and the bank was the only brick building he knew of in Salt Lick.

He became aware of a faint glow to their left. Light coming through the cracks around the boards in one of the bank's front windows? Had to be, Smoke decided. He felt along the way in the other direction and didn't find the doors. That meant they were on the other side of the window from the entrance.

"Move to your left," he told Shaw.

The man didn't say anything, but he shuffled his feet slowly to the left, limping heavily as he did so. Smoke had a hunch that Shaw was just about played out and might lose consciousness at any second. They needed to get inside before that happened.

The side of Smoke's right hand slid across something cold and smooth. Window glass. The light was brighter here, right in front of the window. The glow coming through the glass lit up Shaw's haggard face. Shaw's eyes were closed, but he was still moving. He hadn't passed out yet.

A few more awkward steps and they were past the window. Smoke saw another, dimmer glow. The bank's front doors had glass in their upper halves, also boarded up, he recalled, but not tightly enough to prevent any light from coming out. He had to risk leaning his rifle against the wall while he fumbled for a doorknob. Feeling the cold, brass knob, he grasped it, twisted, and shoved. He kicked the door open and Sarge Shaw practically fell through it. Smoke caught his balance and held Shaw up while his eyes struggled to adjust to the brighter light inside the bank lobby.

Three men stood there, pointing rifles at them.

No, two men and a girl, he corrected himself. One of the rifle-wielders was Tommy Spencer. She lowered her weapon and cried, "Mr. Jensen!"

"Mickey!"

That scream came from another female voice. As Smoke's vision began to clear, he saw Charlotte Shaw rushing forward from a group of people gathered toward the rear of the lobby.

One of the men with Tommy circled around Smoke and Shaw to close the door and keep the bone-chilling wind out. Smoke turned his head to say to the man over his shoulder, "My Winchester's just outside to the left. Grab it, would you?"

"Sure thing, Marshal," the man replied.

The other man who had confronted the newcomers set his rifle aside and hurried to help Smoke with the wounded Sarge Shaw. Charlotte reached them and took hold of Shaw as well, saying, "Oh, Mickey, you're hurt!" Her eyes were wide with fear for her husband.

Shaw had perked up a little at the sound of his wife's voice. He opened his eyes and said with a trace of his usual acerbic personality toward her, "I'll be all right, woman. It's just . . . a scratch."

The amount of blood soaking his trouser leg proved the wound was more than just a scratch. But the fact that Shaw was still conscious and reasonably alert, at least for the moment, was a good sign, Smoke knew.

A middle-aged man Smoke recognized as Salt Lick's doctor came up with a black medical bag in one hand. With the other, he motioned toward the bank president's desk.

"Somebody clean that off," he ordered. "Then you can put Sarge on there, Marshal."

Abner Hawkins himself rushed over to the desk where he conducted business. With a sweep of his arm, he shoved everything on the desk into the floor behind it.

"I can sort all that out later," he said. "Bring the sergeant over here, men. Quickly."

Smoke and a couple of other men lifted Shaw onto the desk. His legs hung off from the knee down. Tommy brought over a chair and propped it under Shaw's feet to support them. Charlotte sat in a chair at the other end of the desk and got her arm under his head and shoulders.

"Don't let him die, Doctor," she said.

Shaw said, "I'm not . . . gonna die. It ain't that bad . . . I tell you . . ."

No sooner had he gotten those words out than his eyes rolled up in their sockets and he lost consciousness.

The doctor said, "Tommy, you stay close here, in case I need a hand." Then he got busy using a pair of scissors he took from his medical bag to cut away the blood-soaked trouser leg.

Seeing that Shaw was in good hands, Smoke stepped back and, out of habit, unbuttoned his coat and swept it back on the right side so he could reach his gun easier. He looked around the bank lobby to see who else had made it here before the storm hit.

Several dozen women and children were in the group in the back of the room, near the massive vault door. Smoke was glad that many had reached safety here.

Of course, it might just be temporary safety, depending on what Snake Bishop did. But at least those women and young'uns were out of the storm. The bank lobby was snug and warm at the moment.

Smoke also saw the six men whose assignment it had been to come to the bank and serve as its last line of defense if the outlaws raided the town. He was glad they had made it here, as well.

Among them was Edward Warren, editor and publisher of the *Salt Lick Tribune*. Smoke had already spotted Warren's wife Evelyn and their deep-voiced son Ralph in the group of women and children.

Warren approached Smoke. He carried a shotgun and somewhat surprisingly had a gun belt strapped around his hips. A Colt .45 revolver with walnut grips rode in the attached holster. Smoke had considerable experience with such things, and he could tell that the revolver had seen a fair amount of use.

"Thank heavens you're all right, Mr. Jensen," Warren greeted him. "How badly is Sarge hurt?"

"Bad enough to knock him out of the fight, but I think there's a pretty good chance he'll survive." Smoke paused, then added, "From that injury, anyway."

Warren nodded. "I understand. None of us know what awaits us during this storm, do we? How bad is it out there?

We all heard the wind, of course. No one could miss it. And it had already started snowing a little when we got here."

"It's pretty bad," Smoke said slowly. "As bad a snowstorm as I've ever seen, or at least it could be, depending on how long it lasts. One thing about these Texas northers, sometimes they blow through pretty quickly, according to what Windy's told me. They don't just sit there and keep dumping snow for days or weeks on end. But right now . . . a fella can't see more than a foot or two in front of his face, and he'd freeze to death in a hurry if he was out in it for very long."

"What about Snake Bishop's gang? I assume it was one of them who shot poor Sarge."

Before Smoke could answer, Warren suddenly shook his head and rubbed a hand over his face in a weary gesture.

"I'm sorry, Mr. Jensen. The questions just keeping coming out of me, don't they? It's because of my training as a newspaperman, I suppose. That's a large part of the job, asking questions."

"I reckon it is," Smoke said. "And to answer your last one, Bishop's gang and that snowstorm hit the town at almost exactly the same time, one from the south and one from the north. I traded shots with one of the outlaws but don't know if I hit him. I never saw the man who wounded Sarge. The bullet just came out of the storm."

"Just a stray shot," Warren mused.

"You could call it that. Now let me ask a question." Smoke gestured toward the gun on Warren's hip. "Have you packed an iron like that in the past?"

Warren glanced down at the Colt, but before he could answer, Ralph's deep, gravelly tones came from behind him.

"Has my pa packed an iron? Marshal, haven't you ever heard of the Caprock Kid?"

Warren turned and said, "Now, Ralph, there's no need to bring that up—"

"But Pa, you were a famous gunfighter! Maybe nowhere near as famous as Mr. Jensen here, of course, but still . . ."

Even under these desperate circumstances, Smoke had to chuckle. Wasn't that just like a kid, to brag on his pa and keep him a mite humbled at the same time?

Warren looked back at Smoke and said, "I was never a famous gunfighter, Mr. Jensen. I got in a few shooting scrapes when I was young and foolish, growing up down around Sweetwater and Big Spring, but I put all that aside when Evelyn and I got married."

"A good woman can cause a man to put aside his foolishness, all right," Smoke said with a nod.

"My father was in the newspaper business, so I'd grown up with ink in my blood, as they say. That's what I started doing, and I've been at it ever since."

"But he still goes out and practices with that Colt at least once a week," Ralph said. In a quieter tone, he added, "He's gonna teach me how to shoot, too, but Ma doesn't know that yet."

"And let's keep it that way," Warren said. To Smoke, he went on, "What are we going to do now? Just wait out the storm and hope that it drives off those outlaws?"

Smoke shook his head. "They're not going to leave, even if Bishop wasn't intent on looting the town. It would be suicide for them to try to go anywhere. I'm afraid they'll be here as long as this blizzard is . . . and when it moves on, they'll pick up where they left off." Smoke glanced around the room. "Windy's not here, is he?"

"I haven't seen him."

"Or Jonas Madigan?"

"I'm afraid not."

"So those two old-timers are out there somewhere,"

Smoke said, "and there's no telling what sort of trouble they might be getting into." He put a hand on Warren's shoulder. "You're in charge here . . . What did they call you when you were the Caprock Kid? Ed? Eddie?"

"Ned."

"All right, Ned. You and the other fellas here protect the bank and the women and kids. I'm going to see if I can find out what else is going on in town."

"By yourself? I can come with you—"

"Or I can," Tommy Spencer volunteered. The girl had edged up while Smoke and Warren were talking, and she looked eager to get into the action.

"Both of you are needed here," Smoke said firmly. "As far as I know now, this is the only real stronghold left in town, and we need to hold it."

"All right," Warren said with only a faint grudging tone in his voice. "You can count on us, Mr. Jen—"

That was as far as he had gotten when the bank's double doors unlocked, letting in an icy gust of wind, a cloud of swirling and whipping snow, and three men with guns gripped in their fists.

CHAPTER 24

Smoke's hand flashed to the Colt on his hip. His astonishing reflexes and years of experience made it seem as if everything was moving in slow motion as he drew the gun and got a better look at the men who had just charged into the bank. It was possible they were some of Salt Lick's citizens who had come here to fort up and help fight off Snake Bishop's raiders.

In a mere fraction of a second, Smoke had decided that wasn't the case. These hard-bitten, unshaven men weren't any he had seen before in town. The snarls on their faces and the way they thrust their guns in front of them, ready to fire, convinced Smoke even more strongly that they belonged to Bishop's gang.

There was no time to call out a warning, only to react to the threat. As the three intruders opened fire, Smoke's Colt came up with blinding speed and roared a hot lead reply.

The man in the middle of the trio jerked back as Smoke's bullet drove into his chest. His gun went off again as his finger spasmed on the trigger, but the slug plowed into the floor not far in front of his feet, spraying splinters in the air.

Beside Smoke, Ned Warren whipped the shotgun up and touched off one barrel. The raider to the left crumpled under the onslaught of the buckshot that shredded his guts.

Even though only a split-second had passed since his first shot, Smoke had already adjusted his aim. A second shot blasted from his Colt. The third outlaw was moving, though, so the bullet caught him in the left shoulder, ripping flesh and shattering bone but not putting him out of the fight. Yelling incoherently from pain and rage, he triggered two more shots. The bullets whipped past Smoke's ear.

Calmly, he fired a third time. The wounded outlaw's head snapped back as the bullet struck him in the forehead and bored on through his brain to explode out the back of his skull. He dropped straight down, dead before he hit the floor.

Smoke bounded forward, kicked the fallen guns away from all three outlaws, and checked to make sure the other two were dead before he closed the door and shut out the howling wind. Because it had blown in so hard during the shootout, the temperature in the bank lobby had dropped noticeably.

But the wind had also dispersed the clouds of powder smoke, so the sharp tang of burned powder didn't sting the eyes and nose as much as it might have otherwise.

Smoke swung around toward the people gathered in the lobby and raised his voice to ask, "Anybody hurt?"

Ned Warren had broken open his shotgun and was sliding a fresh shell into the barrel he had fired. "I don't think anyone was hit, Mr. Jensen," he said. "Thank goodness most of the folks dropped to the floor as soon as they saw what was about to happen."

Smoke thumbed fresh cartridges into his Colt, filling all six chambers in the wheel instead of letting the hammer rest on an empty as he usually did. He might need that extra round before this was over.

"Keep guarding the door," he told Warren. He went over to Abner Hawkins' desk, where the doctor had resumed working on Sarge Shaw after ducking for cover during the outlaws' attack. "How does he look now?"

"He's still unconscious from the blood he lost," the doctor replied without looking up from what he was doing, cleaning out one of the bullet holes in Shaw's thigh. "But it looks like the slug went straight through without breaking the bone. I think he'll be fine, just laid up for a while."

"I'll take good care of him, Marshal," Charlotte said.

Smoke smiled. "I don't reckon any of us here doubted that for a second, ma'am," he told her.

Satisfied that things here at the bank were as under control as they could be, he told some of the men to drag the bodies of the dead outlaws outside, then fort up and be ready for trouble.

Then he went back out into the storm.

Windy Whittaker had just reached Salt Lick's main street after paying a visit to one of the barricades out on the western edge of town when he heard the wind kick its keening wail up to a higher notch. Windy knew what that meant. He turned, instinctively shielded his eyes with a hand even though there was no sun glare, and saw the wall of snow racing toward the settlement.

With a gulp, Windy headed toward the nearest shelter, which happened to be the hardware store belonging to Harold Lomax, one of the men who had taken turns standing guard atop the bank. Windy moved as fast as his bowed legs would carry him.

He would have preferred being wherever Smoke took cover from the storm, but a fella didn't get to choose when and where trouble came barreling toward him. As he ducked into the alcove where the hardware store's door was located, the blizzard struck. Windy glanced over his shoulder.

It was as if the other side of the street had disappeared. The only thing he could see was a wall of white being carried along by a wind that shrieked like a horde of demons.

Lomax and his wife Margaret were the only ones in the store, Windy saw as he slammed the door behind him. Some of the snow had blown in with him. The mixture of flakes and hard little pellets skittered around the floor at Windy's feet because a draft came in under the door behind him.

"Best put somethin' along the bottom o' this door to block the wind, Harold," Windy told the storekeeper. "Else you're gonna have a hard time keepin' it warm in here."

Lomax bent down behind the counter, picked up a rug from the floor, and hurried to the door to do as Windy suggested.

"What's going on out there?" he asked. "Sounds like a hell of a blow. And it's snowing so hard I can't see across the street."

"You done answered your own question," Windy told him. "That blue norther finally got here, just like I been sayin' it was gonna for days now."

"Nobody doubted you, Windy."

The old-timer managed not to snort. He knew good and well that most folks *had* doubted him. They had thought he was just running off at the mouth, the way he usually did.

Well, maybe Smoke hadn't felt that way, Windy allowed to himself. Smoke seemed able to read folks better than anyone Windy had ever met.

Smoke had sure enough seen right through *him* to his owlhoot past.

But Smoke had also been willing to overlook that past and place his faith in Windy. Windy would never forget that.

"What should we do now?" Lomax asked when he had finished stuffing the rug against the bottom of the door to block the wind. "I was supposed to take another guard shift later today if nothing had happened, but I reckon that's not likely now."

"No, anybody on top of the bank had better have gotten down by now. They stay up there, they'll freeze. And Bishop's boys were on their way in to raid the town, so we got that to worry about, too."

Margaret Lomax said, "Surely not in this weather! Even bandits can't stay out in a blizzard—"

At that moment, the hardware store's front window shattered and glass flew as bullets punched through it. Windy wheeled in that direction and dragged out the old cap-and-ball revolver holstered on his hip. He raised the heavy gun as a man on horseback leaped his mount through what was left of the window. The horse's hooves thudded loudly on the floor and its shoulder rammed a display of tools and sent the merchandise flying. The rider yelled and fired the gun in his hand as the horse's shoves skidded on the polished hardwood planks.

Margaret Lomax screamed and ducked below the counter. Her husband Harold yelled and dived behind some plows. One of the outlaw's bullets struck a plow blade and ricocheted off wickedly. The raider continued firing wildly as his gun swung in Windy's direction.

Windy was no fast draw—not even close—but he generally managed to hit what he aimed at. The old revolver boomed and spewed flame and smoke for a good foot from its muzzle. The heavy lead ball traveled at an upward angle and caught the outlaw under the chin.

The impact drove the man's head back and flipped him out of the saddle. He crashed to the floor just inside the broken window. Windy saw that the dead man's head was grotesquely misshapen from the ball that had bounced around inside his brain, lacking the velocity to blast its way on out through the skull.

The horse, terrified out of its mind from the storm, the shooting, and the leap through the broken window, lunged around wildly. Blood ran from several cuts inflicted by the sharp, broken glass. Windy had to jump out of the animal's way. He grabbed the horse's bridle and hauled down hard on it.

"Settle down, you blasted varmint," he urged the horse. "Just settle down, dang your ornery hide."

The horse did, at least to a certain extent. Windy turned his head and called, "Are you hit, Harold?"

"No, I'm all right," Lomax answered from behind the plows. "Margaret, what about you?"

"I . . . I'm not hurt. I don't think." Margaret Lomax's frightened voice came from behind the counter in the back of the store. She wailed, "Oh, Harold, what are we going to do?"

Windy didn't wait for Lomax to answer. He hung on to the horse and said, "The two of you get back in your storeroom and stay there. Take a couple of shotguns and plenty of shells with you. Better grab some blankets to wrap up in, too. With that window busted out like it is, there ain't gonna be no way to keep the place warm anymore. Stay hunkered down until somebody you trust comes to get you."

"What are you going to do, Windy?" Lomax asked.

Windy led the horse to the front door and opened it. "I got to go find Smoke. He might need my help. He's probably headed for the bank, so that's where I'll go, too."

"How will you find your way in that snowstorm?"

"I'm just gonna hope my instincts don't steer me wrong," Windy said.

* * *

Another hour, Snake Bishop thought. *Just one more hour, and Salt Lick would have been ours before that damned storm got here.*

But it hadn't worked out that way, so now he and his men would just have to make the best of it. With this blizzard going on, they couldn't make a coordinated attack on the town as they normally would have. Bishop had ordered the men still with him to spread out, find shelter, and in the process wreak as much havoc as they could.

In those last moments before the blizzard struck, Bishop had been shocked to realize that the citizens of Salt Lick had thrown up some sort of wagon barricade across the main street. He knew they hadn't had time to move those wagons into place since he and his men arrived in sight of the town, so that meant they had been expecting an attack.

That had never happened before. The gang had always taken the towns they hit by surprise. But somehow, Salt Lick had been warned.

Bishop had wondered if that had anything to do with the two scouts who had never come back, Bart Rome and Sid Atkins. Galloping toward the intended target at the head of his gang, he hadn't really had time to ponder the question, though.

But the show of defiance from those settlers was enough to make the flame of fury burn even brighter inside Bishop. He might have to wait until after the looming snowstorm to do it, but before he was finished with Salt Lick, not one building would be left standing, and every man, woman, and child in the settlement would die.

It would be as if Salt Lick, Texas, had never even existed . . .

Bishop had employed his usual strategy of splitting his force and striking from several different directions at once. That had always proven quite effective. He was in a group of Paco O'Shannon and ten other outlaws, racing toward the town, when he spotted the barricade. Instinctively, he had pulled back on the reins in surprise and slowed his horse. The other men followed suit.

Muzzle flashes erupted in the premature twilight as the defenders behind the wagons opened fire. Bullets whistled around the raiders. Bishop was about to yell an order for them to split up when the blizzard loomed up like a living creature and then smashed down over the town.

That ended the shooting from the defenders, at least as far as Bishop could see.

That was when he had bellowed the order for his men to disperse, seek shelter, and deal out as much punishment to Salt Lick as they could.

Now he was in the town with O'Shannon beside him, barely visible despite being a big figure on horseback. Bishop didn't know where any of the others were. He and O'Shannon seemed to be alone in a featureless white wasteland as the wind and snow surrounded them. Bishop knew there were buildings on either side, but he couldn't see them.

The horses were almost frantic with fear, hopping and circling under them. If they stayed in the saddles, they risked falling and being injured, maybe even trampled by the spooked mounts.

"Dismount!" Bishop shouted to O'Shannon, leaning close so the man could hear him over the roar of the storm. Even then, Bishop wasn't sure O'Shannon had heard until he saw the other man slip down from the saddle and cling desperately to his horse's reins.

Bishop did the same. His hard grip on the reins caused his horse to settle down a little.

They needed to get out of this insane maelstrom of wind

and snow, so he raised his voice again to say, "Let's see if we can find some shelter!"

"There should be a livery barn somewhere!" O'Shannon shouted back.

That was true, but finding it would be a matter of pure luck, Bishop knew. Still, all they could do was try. He held the reins with his left hand and closed his gloved right hand around the butt of his gun. He drew the revolver and held it ready. If they encountered any of Salt Lick's citizens, he was going to shoot to kill.

Bishop was pretty sure they were in the middle of the street, so they had to go either right or left. Bishop chose right. He trudged in that direction, dragging the horse with him. O'Shannon was close beside him. They couldn't see more than a couple of feet in front of them. They wouldn't know if they reached a building until they ran into it.

Calvin Bishop had long believed that fate was on his side. Something, some destiny, guided his actions and placed victims directly in his path, sheep ripe for the sheering. That same fate protected him in times of danger.

That held true now, as the wall of a building suddenly appeared right in front of them. Bishop literally almost ran into it. He stopped, holstered his gun, and rested his hand on the wall.

"Find a door!" he called to O'Shannon.

They both felt along the wall, searching for some way into the building. If they could find one, they would lead their horses inside, too. They couldn't leave the animals outside to die in the storm.

A blizzard like this was a capricious thing. The wind had been blowing at a steady pace so far, but it was capable of rising and falling. The snow might part like a curtain for a split-second, allowing a man to see farther, then slam closed again.

That was what happened just as O'Shannon called excitedly, "Here! Here's a door! I think it's a stable!" As the words came out of his mouth, they sounded louder than they would have a second earlier, because the wind suddenly eased to a mere howl instead of a roar like a giant animal.

Bishop heard a shout from his left. He jerked his head in that direction and saw a man standing there about a dozen feet away. The man had almost blundered right into them.

Instead, he stood there, eyes bulging in surprise in a weathered, whiskery face under a battered old hat held on his head by a taut chin strap. Bishop knew instantly that this was one of the citizens of Salt Lick, but a fraction of a second later, surprised recognition hit him.

He *knew* that old-timer. The name sprang into Bishop's head. The name of a traitor who had run out on the gang, something that Bishop never permitted, under penalty of death.

"Whittaker!" Bishop bellowed as he grabbed his gun from its holster and leveled it. Flame lanced from the muzzle and turned the snow around it red as Bishop hammered shot after shot at the old man.

CHAPTER 25

After leaving Lomax's hardware store, Windy kept a tight grip on the horse's reins as he led the animal down the street. The horse's big body offered some protection from the wind. Just as important, it provided Windy with an anchor to something real. Alone in the storm, he could have gotten completely disoriented in a hurry.

Of course, he and the horse could get lost, too. Having the animal with him was no guarantee that he could find the bank.

Something told Windy that was where Smoke would be. Smoke would want to make sure the folks who had taken shelter there were all right.

Once that was done, Smoke might venture out into the storm to hunt outlaws. Windy sure wouldn't put it past him. But he hoped he could catch up with Smoke first, maybe even join him in that hunt.

But first he had to find the blasted bank.

It was on the same side of the street as the hardware store. Windy used the hitch racks to guide him. But there were gaps between those racks, so whenever he came to one, all he could do was try to keep going straight and trust to luck.

The first couple of times, that worked. His reaching hand

found another of the rough wooden rails as he groped through the blowing snow.

But then, on the third try, it seemed like it was taking him an awful long time to find the next hitch rack. Could he have veered away and missed it? Was he out in the middle of the street now, without even knowing it?

Part of Windy wanted to yell for help, but he knew it wouldn't do any good. Even worse, if some of Bishop's men were wandering around in the blizzard, as seemed likely, a shout might attract their attention and draw them to him. Windy knew good and well that if any of the owlhoots spotted him, they would shoot to kill. It was always that way with Bishop's bunch. They were kill-crazy, just like the man who led them.

Windy stopped in his tracks and brought the horse to a halt as well. He stood there for a moment with the wind and snow battering him as he tried to figure out what to do next. Should he try to turn back and retrace his steps to the hardware store? At least there he would have some protection from the storm.

But that was impossible, he realized. He might wind up going around and around in a circle in the middle of the street and never even know it.

Blind or not, he had to push on.

He had taken a few more steps when he thought he heard somebody shouting not far off. He was about to yell back at them when he caught himself. He didn't know who was out there . . . but it might be somebody he didn't want to know he was here.

And it was possible he hadn't actually heard anybody. It could have been his imagination, or a trick of the storm, instead of real voices. Knowing that, Windy forced himself to take a couple more steps.

Then, in one of those flukish moments that could happen

in any blizzard, the wind let up for a moment and the blowing snow parted like the Red Sea, and there, standing twelve feet away, were two men with horses, right in front of a building Windy recognized as Rufus Spencer's livery stable.

He *had* missed the bank, overshooting it and wandering all the way over on the other side of the street. But before Windy could even think about what he ought to do next, one of the men yelled, "Whittaker!" and started shooting at him.

Windy caught a glimpse of the coiled whip fastened to the man's belt and sticking out under the bottom of his coat. That was Snake Bishop himself Windy had almost blundered into.

Bishop recognized *him*, too, and that was bad, really bad. Bishop made it a habit to kill anybody who crossed him, and that included running out on his gang.

Those thoughts flashed through Windy's mind so fast that muzzle flame had barely bloomed from Bishop's gun before the old-timer was twisting aside with the spryness of a much younger man. Even an old body was capable of a lot when survival was on the line.

Windy felt the hot breath of a bullet on his whiskered cheek. At practically the same time, he heard the slug thud into something behind him. The outlaw's horse he'd been leading screamed in pain. Windy dropped the reins and ran, turning and heading in the direction he thought the bank lay.

More gunshots crashed as Bishop fired wildly after him, but Windy didn't feel any impacts. The snow had closed back in around him. Bishop couldn't see him now and was just shooting in his general direction.

Windy couldn't see, either. Nothing but blowing snow all around him. If he missed the bank again . . . if he ran along the street and out of town, right into the teeth of the storm . . . they would find his frozen carcass somewhere out on the prairie when this was all over.

But he couldn't stay where he was, so he stumbled on into the swirling madness.

After leaving the bank, Smoke stayed on the boardwalk and worked his way slowly along to the next business. When he got there, he found the door unlocked. He twisted the knob and stepped inside, calling, "Hello! Anybody here?"

This was an apothecary, he recalled, and in the dim light that filtered in through the front window, he could make out the shelves on both walls with bottles and boxes on them containing various potions, nostrums, and pills. There was a counter in the back where the proprietor mixed medicines.

But no one was here. The owner was either next door in the bank or had taken shelter somewhere else. Smoke backed out and closed the door behind him.

The next two businesses were similarly deserted, but a light burned in the window of the one after that. When Smoke opened the door, the intense smell of leather told him immediately that he was in the saddle shop.

"Throw your hands in the air or I'll blast you, you damn owlhoot!"

The angry command came from a man who stood at the back of the shop pointing a Sharps rifle at Smoke. Lifting his hands, Smoke called, "Hold your fire, friend. I'm not part of Bishop's gang."

"Marshal Jensen? Is that you?" The man pushed a pair of spectacles higher on his sharp-pointed nose. "Dadgum it, Marshal, I nearly blew a hole in you. I thought you were an outlaw come to rob and kill me."

"No, I'm just trying to check on everybody I can," Smoke explained as he closed the door behind him to keep the storm out. He recalled the saddlemaker's name. "Are you all right, Mr. Bailey?"

"Yeah, so far," the man said. He lowered the Sharps. Smoke remembered being told that Bailey was an old cowhand who had turned to making saddles when he got too old and stove-up to sit in one all day. He did other leather work, as well.

Bailey went on, "It's blowin' and snowin' like a son of a gun out there. Did the owlhoots make it into town?"

"Some of them did," Smoke answered. "Three of them tried to bust into the bank a little while ago."

"Yeah, I thought I heard some shootin', but there's so much racket goin' on, it was hard to tell for sure. What happened to the fellas who caused the ruckus?"

"We'll bury them when it thaws out," Smoke replied. "For now, they're keeping cool in an alley."

Bailey chuckled. "Can't say as I'm surprised."

"Quite a few folks have forced up in the bank. You can join them if you want to. Stay on the boardwalk and keep a hand on the wall, and you won't get lost."

"And leave my shop undefended against that lowdown bunch?" Bailey snorted. "Not hardly, Marshal. No offense, but me and this ol' buffalo gun of mine are stayin' right here."

"It's your choice," Smoke said with a nod. "If you do decide to head for the bank later, be careful and sing out when you get there. Some of the fellas inside might be getting a little trigger-happy by now."

"I'll do that," Bailey promised.

Smoke turned back to the door and opened it. He stepped out onto the boardwalk and was about to pull the door closed behind him when a gun roared somewhere nearby. The slug smacked into the door jamb and chewed splinters from it.

Smoke crouched and swept his Colt from its holster.

Another spurt of muzzle flame lanced at him. The bullet thudded into the wall behind him. There were two guns targeting him, one straight ahead and one to the left. Smoke threw a return shot at the one in front of him and then pivoted, dropping to a knee as he fired twice in the direction of the second man.

Somebody yelled in pain and no more shots came from that side, but if Smoke had hit the would-be killer in front of him, the man wasn't wounded badly enough to knock him out of the fight. In fact, he was charging closer, the gun in his hand crashing again and again as he sent more slugs clawing at the air around Smoke.

A heavy, almost deafening boom sounded close by. That was the old saddlemaker's Sharps going off. Bailey had moved up into the doorway, taken aim at the muzzle flashes of the man launching the frontal attack, and sent a .52 caliber round rocketing at him. The thick snow muffled the echoes of the shots, so as soon as they sounded, silence followed almost instantly.

"I reckon you must've gotten him, since he's not shooting anymore," Smoke told Bailey after a moment.

"If that Big Fifty hit him anywhere, he's down and out," Bailey declared. "There ain't no such thing as a minor wound from this here buffalo gun."

Smoke knew that was right. A man struck by a round that heavy would soon bleed to death or die from the shock, if it didn't kill him instantly.

Smoke straightened to his feet and told Bailey, "Get on back inside if you're determined to stay. And you'd better reload that cannon of yours."

"That's exactly what I figure on doin'! What about you, Marshal?"

"I'm going to keep checking on everybody I can find," Smoke said.

And he had no doubt that some of those he encountered would be members of Snake Bishop's gang. But already, with help from some of the townsmen, he had started whittling down the odds . . .

Snake Bishop bit back a curse as the hammer of his gun clicked on an expended cartridge. He had emptied the gun at Windy Whittaker, but he didn't know if he had hit the treacherous old pelican or not. The storm had closed in and hidden everything more than a few feet away.

Which meant the only things Bishop could see were Paco O'Shannon, the two horses, and the wall of the livery stable. He became aware that O'Shannon was shouting at him, "What is it, Snake? What are you shooting at?"

O'Shannon had his gun drawn, ready to join in the fight if need be. Bishop motioned for him to pouch the iron and said, "It was Whittaker! Didn't you see him?"

"Who?"

"Whittaker! Windy Whittaker!"

"That old man who rode with us for a month or two before he ran off?" O'Shannon sounded as if he barely remembered the old-timer. "That was years ago!"

"It was him, all right!" Bishop said. "The traitor!"

"And he's here in Salt Lick?"

"I saw him just now, no more than a dozen feet away!"

"Well, I didn't see anything," O'Shannon said. "Did you get him?"

"I don't know. The snow got too thick again."

"What's he doing here, of all places?"

"I don't know that, either, damn it! But I saw him, I tell you!"

"Take it easy, Snake. I believe you. But whether Whittaker's around or not, we need to get out of this storm!"

Bishop couldn't argue with that. He said, "Can you get one of those doors open?"

"Let me see. Hang on to my horse . . ."

Bishop didn't care for the way O'Shannon made it sound like he was giving him an order, but under the circumstances, he ignored it. He took the reins from O'Shannon and stood there holding both horses while O'Shannon tugged at one of the big doors in the front of the livery stable. The snow had started to drift against the door already, which made opening it more difficult.

But after a couple of minutes, O'Shannon had tugged the door open enough that he was able to get his fingers in the gap, and then he dragged it out more. That let him wedge a shoulder behind the door and shove even harder. The door scraped through the snow until the gap was big enough for Bishop to lead the horses into the barn. O'Shannon hurried in after them and pulled the door closed as much as he could. Wind still whistled around it.

They were out of the full force of the storm, though, and that was a relief.

It was close to pitch dark in the barn. Only a faint glow came through the cracks around the door, along with the icy wind. Bishop was able to make out their surroundings once his eyes had adjusted. He heard horses moving around and stamping their feet in the stalls. The rich, earthy, mingled smell of hay and manure would have been enough to tell both men they were in a barn, even if they hadn't already known that.

"I don't reckon anybody's here," O'Shannon said after a moment. His voice echoed a little in the cavernous building. "This should be a good place to wait out the storm."

"Who said we were going to wait it out? There's a town waiting out there for us to loot it."

"I don't mean any disrespect, Snake—"

"Then don't give me any," Bishop snapped.

"But we can't loot anything in the middle of a blizzard like this," O'Shannon went on stubbornly. "The weather's just too bad. We have to wait until the storm blows over. Then we can tree this town like we've treed all the others."

For a second, Bishop felt a wild impulse to haul out his gun and blow O'Shannon to hell for daring to argue with him. Any show of defiance or disrespect filled Bishop with blinding, white-hot rage. It always had.

But he knew that he needed O'Shannon, so he hauled a tight rein on his temper and drew in a deep breath.

Later, when this was over, if he still felt the same way, he could have O'Shannon tied to a couple of posts and use the blacksnake whip at his waist to peel away the man's hide, bit by bloody bit. Sure, Paco O'Shannon was the closest thing Snake Bishop had to a friend in this world, but in the long run, that didn't matter.

Not nearly as much as enforcing his will.

"We'll just have to hope we have men left," Bishop said. "We may be the only ones who survive. But you're right, we can't do anything right now except wait. Let's see if we can find some empty stalls for the horses. I'm sure they could use some grain or at least some hay. But don't unsaddle them, in case we need them in a hurry."

"Sure, Snake. That makes sense. Give me the reins, and I'll take care of them."

That was more like it, Bishop thought as he handed over the reins of both horses. O'Shannon led the animals toward the row of stalls along the barn's left-hand wall.

He was passing a dimly seen door with the horses when that door suddenly flew open and a man charged out into the barn, yelling incoherently. Bishop could see him just well enough to know that he was big, had a bushy black beard, and wielded a blacksmith's hammer that was sweeping down swiftly at Paco O'Shannon's head.

CHAPTER 26

The subject of whether or not to lock the bank doors came in for considerable debate after Smoke left. Abner Hawkins suggested that they do so.

"You all saw how easily those men got in here and started shooting," the bank president said. "That could happen again at any time."

Ned Warren nodded and said, "That's true, Mr. Hawkins, but some of the townspeople, our friends and neighbors, could show up looking for shelter at any time, too. I think that's even more likely."

"Perhaps, but if they do, couldn't they knock on the door and ask to be let in?"

"Maybe, unless they were too worn out from getting here in the storm."

"Somethin' else you ain't thought of," old Shug Russell drawled. "Those owlhoots could get hold of somebody from town and force him to come up to the door and bang on it, askin' to be let in. Then when the door was unlocked, that bunch could swarm in and start slaughterin' folks. That's what Bishop and his gang are notorious for doin'."

"Shug is right," Hawkins said. "We can't take a chance on opening the door for *anyone*. It's just too dangerous. We should lock it and leave it closed. Perhaps push some of the desks over in front of it to make sure that no one can get in."

"Even if our friends need help?" Warren sounded as if he couldn't believe what he was hearing.

"It's better for the people who are already in here," Hawkins insisted. "Safer."

"I just can't turn my back on folks like that."

"Well, I can, if it means a better chance of saving the ones who are already here." Hawkins took a key from his pocket and stalked toward the door.

"Hold on there," Warren told him. "We haven't made up our minds—"

"I'm the president of this bank," Hawkins snapped. "It's my decision to make."

He thrust the key at the lock, but before he could insert it, the door flew open and banged into him, knocking him backward. Hawkins cried out in pain, surprise, and fear.

Ned Warren jerked the shotgun to his shoulder and leaped to the side so he could fire without hitting the bank president.

But he held off on the triggers, not wanting to blast an innocent person, and yelled, "Hold it right there, mister!"

The newcomer stumbled to a halt just inside the door and stuck up his hands as he bleated, "Don't shoot! It's just me, Windy!"

The old-timer was covered with snow, from his battered hat to his boots. His whiskers were even whiter than usual because of all the snow clinging to them. He shook like a wet dog, and the stuff showered off of him to fall around his feet.

Warren lowered the shotgun and said, "Windy, get on in here. Ralph, close the door before any more cold air comes in."

"Yes, Pa," the boy croaked as he scurried to obey.

Ralph had hold of the door and was about to push it shut when a hand reached in out of the storm, closed around his arm, and jerked him out into the blizzard. Ralph started to yell in alarm, but the wind whipped the sound away.

"Ralph!" Warren cried. He lunged toward the door.

Windy was closer. He whirled around and dived through the opening, right back into the storm from which he had just escaped. Warren charged out behind him, hearing his wife's screams of terror for their son coming from the group at the back of the bank lobby. He hoped someone would grab Evelyn and keep her from following him into danger.

The wind-driven snow was like a blow to the face. Warren staggered under its onslaught. He was blind and disoriented for a moment, and if he hadn't felt the boardwalk under his feet, he wouldn't have known where he was.

That feeling passed quickly, however. Warren's vision cleared somewhat. In the light that spilled through the open bank doors, he saw Windy Whittaker standing a few feet away. The old-timer had drawn his massive revolver and was pointing it at something.

"Let the boy go, you polecat, or I'll blow your damn head off!" Windy shouted over the wind.

Warren moved up alongside Windy, and now he could see what the old-timer saw. One of the outlaws, a stranger to Warren, stood on the boardwalk about ten feet away. His left arm was looped around Ralph's neck, and his right hand held a gun pressed against the boy's head.

"Back off!" the outlaw yelled. "All of you throw your guns out! I'm comin' in there, and if you don't do what I tell you, I'll kill the boy!"

Even though Warren was armed, the shotgun was useless in this situation. He couldn't risk a shot at the outlaw. The blast would hit Ralph, too. Even using the Colt on his hip instead of the scattergun was too dangerous. He hoped

Windy understood that, too, and wouldn't start blazing away with that old hogleg of his.

"Take it easy, mister," Windy said. "You know good and well we ain't throwin' down our guns. The only chance you got to survive this blizzard is to drop *your* gun and let go o' that younker. You'll be our prisoner, but at least you won't be froze to death."

"And take my chances with the law?" The man laughed harshly. "I don't think so."

"But what have you actually done so far?" Warren argued. "Ridden into town? There's no crime in that. If you let go of Ralph now and surrender, there won't be any charges against you."

"Not here, maybe," the outlaw rasped, "but what about all the other places I've been?"

Warren shook his head. "That's no concern of mine. When the storm's over, you can ride away, free and clear . . . as long as you haven't hurt the boy."

Windy licked his lips under his ice-encrusted mustache and said quietly, "I ain't sure you can promise that, Ned—"

"I'm making that promise," Warren said firmly. He raised his voice to call to the outlaw again, "Just let him go."

"No, I don't think so," the man said. Ralph whimpered a little as the outlaw pressed the gun barrel harder against his head.

Warren almost charged then. He couldn't stand seeing his son being hurt like that.

But he and Windy had been edging forward while they talked, and the outlaw had been moving back slowly, until he was in position for Ralph to take things into his own hands.

With the arm pressed against his throat, it was hard for the boy to force out words, but he managed as he unleashed a torrent of profanity in his unnaturally deep voice. The outlaw hadn't heard his prisoner speak until now and was so surprised by what he heard that he couldn't help but look down at Ralph.

Ralph pushed himself backward with his feet and legs as hard as he could. His boots slipped a little in the snow that had collected on the boardwalk, but he gained enough purchase to force his captor into stumbling a step back.

They were at the edge of the boardwalk, as Ralph must have noticed, and as he shoved the outlaw backward, the man suddenly found himself with nothing under his feet. He toppled, crashing into the snowy street on his back.

That impact jolted his grip on the boy loose. Ralph tore free and rolled desperately through the snow as he shouted, "Get him, Pa!"

Warren and Windy leaped forward. The outlaw struggled to get up as he spewed some obscenities of his own. He started to swing his gun toward Ralph, then realized he was in danger from the other direction. He tried to jerk it back toward Warren and Windy, but they both fired before he could pull the trigger.

Windy was a hair faster, so the heavy lead ball from his gun smashed into the outlaw's chest and drove in to pulp his heart just before the buckshot tore into him and left his torso a bloody mess most of the way down to his waist. The double blast hammered him back down into the street. His arms and legs flopped to the sides and didn't move again.

Ralph scrambled up and ran toward his father, but Evelyn darted around Warren first and gathered her son into her arms. Sobbing in mingled fear and relief, she held him tightly against her.

Warren wanted to embrace both of them, but instead he said, "Evelyn, Ralph, get back inside! There's no telling who else is out here in this storm!"

"Durned toot—" Windy began, but a shot cracked before

he could finish. He grunted and sagged against Warren, who dropped the shotgun to catch him.

Warren had seen the muzzle flash from the corner of his eye. He wrapped his left arm around Windy to support the old-timer, while at the same time his right hand dropped to the Colt on his hip. Maybe he wasn't as fast on the draw as he had been as a young man, but he had kept in practice enough that the revolver came out swiftly. Flame geysered from its barrel as he triggered three fast shots in the direction of the man who'd wounded Windy.

Even as he was squeezing off those rounds, Warren urged Windy toward the bank entrance. The old-timer hadn't passed out, so he was able to help a little in the desperate dash. They charged into the building, not far behind Evelyn and Ralph, and as they cleared the doors, a couple of the men inside slammed them closed.

"Doctor, Windy's been hit!" Warren called.

"Some of you men help him over here to my examining room," the physician responded wryly. Sarge Shaw had already been moved from Hawkins' desk to a pallet on the floor made of coats some of the men had donated for that purpose.

"I ain't hurt that bad," Windy objected as several men hurried to take him from Warren and carry him over to the desk. The strain in the old-timer's voice revealed the pain he was in, however.

Warren turned to his wife and son. Evelyn still had an arm around Ralph's shoulders as she hovered over him protectively.

"Ralph, are you hurt?" Warren asked.

"Gosh, no! That damned ol' owlhoot never did a thing to me!"

Evelyn was too upset to scold him for his language, and she hadn't even heard the worst of it. She glared at Warren instead and said, "You should have closed that door yourself instead of telling Ralph to do it! You could have gotten him killed!"

"Shucks, Ma, neither Pa nor me knew that outlaw was lurkin' around right outside," Ralph protested. "It's not Pa's fault."

"That's all right, Ralph," Warren said. "I should have been more careful."

"But, Pa—"

Warren summoned up a smile and said, "It's fine. Don't worry about it, son. The only important thing is that you're all right."

"No thanks to you," Evelyn said.

Warren didn't respond to that. He just squeezed Ralph's shoulder for a second and then turned to walk over to the desk where the doctor was tending to Windy Whittaker.

The old-timer was sitting up with his thick flannel coat off and his buckskin vest and flannel shirt pulled up to reveal a bloody gash in his right side. He still wore his hat and grimaced as the doctor used a wet cloth to clean away blood from the wound.

"That slug just nicked me," Windy said. "It kinda knocked the wind outta my sails for a minute, that's all."

"Hold still," the doctor told him. "I'll need to stitch this up once I get it clean. I should probably give you something for the pain."

Windy licked his lips and said, "I can think of some mighty effective medicine, Doc. In fact, I got a flask of it in my coat, if somebody'll fetch it for me."

"I was talking about . . . Oh, never mind. What you suggest will probably work as well as anything."

Warren said, "I'll get it for you, Windy," and picked up the coat to take a small silver flask from one of the pockets.

He unscrewed the cap and gave the flask to Windy, who took it with his left hand.

The old-timer swallowed a small slug of the whiskey and sighed. "Do your worst, Doc," he said. "I can take it."

Figuring it might be a good idea to distract Windy from what was going on, Warren said, "What's happening out there, Windy? Where have you been?"

"Oh, here and there. Hard to say, exactly, where-all I been, since a fella can't hardly see his hand in front of his face with all that snow blowin' around." Windy sucked in a breath as the doctor began sewing up the gash in his side. Then he went on, "But I know I was at Lomax's Hardware Store, because I killed one o' them owlhoots there when he jumped his horse in through the front window."

That revelation drew a babble of excited questions. Windy described the shoot-out with the raider, then said, "I figured I ought to get back here and join up with Smoke again." He looked around. "Smoke ain't here, though, is he?"

"He left a little while before you showed up," Warren answered. "He said he was going to go hunt outlaws."

Windy nodded. "Yep, that was just what I reckoned he'd do. I was hopin' I could join him."

"How many outlaws are in town?" a man asked.

"Is the whole Bishop gang here in Salt Lick?" another put in.

"I can't say about the whole gang," Windy replied with a shake of his head. "But I can durned sure tell you that Snake Bishop his own self is in town. I saw him just a little while ago, down by the livery stable. That no-good varmint tried to shoot me. Emptied his six-shooter at me, from the sound of it." Windy sounded a little proud as he added, "He missed, though. Reckon I was just too fast for him."

"You said Snake Bishop is at the livery stable?"

The female voice, taut with worry, made the men look

around. Tommy Spencer had approached while they were talking. Her eyes were big with fear.

"Why, uh, that's right, Miss Tommy," Windy said, although he looked like he didn't want to admit it. "Bishop and another fella who was holdin' their horses, so he had to be one o' the gang, too."

"What were they doing there?"

"I don't rightly know. They spotted me at the same time I spotted them, and uh, like I said, Bishop commenced to shootin' at me . . ."

"I'm sure they were just trying to get in out of the storm," Warren said. "Anyone with any sense would have done that. It doesn't mean your father was there, or in any danger, Miss Spencer."

"We . . . we planned to meet here, if the men at the barricade at the south end of town were forced to retreat," Tommy said. "But I know my father. He would have gone by the stable and his shop to make sure everything was all right there first." Her voice rose. "What if Snake Bishop and that other man caught him there?"

"Now, missy, your pa is a mighty smart man," Windy said. "If he was there when Bishop and that other fella came in, I'm bettin' he stayed outta sight and figured on layin' low until the storm blows over and they leave. That's bound to be what happened."

Warren said, "Or maybe he's not there at all."

Tommy leveled a glare at him. "Where is he, then?"

"Well, he . . . he could have taken shelter somewhere else, or maybe he's still trying to make his way here . . ."

"Or he's laying out there frozen to death, if those outlaws didn't murder him!"

Several of the women from town came up and tried to comfort Tommy. One of them put a hand on the girl's shoulder, but Tommy jerked away from it.

"I need to go to the stable and find out what happened to him!"

Windy and Warren both shook their heads.

"No, ma'am, that's exactly what you *don't* need to do," Windy said. "First off, you'd probably never find the place in this storm, and even if you did, those two owlhoots are likely still there. You don't want to be messin' with them."

Warren said, "Windy's right. I know you're worried, Miss Spencer . . . Tommy . . . We all are. But things are already bad enough. We don't need to make them worse by putting more people in danger."

"Who put you in charge?" Tommy challenged. "You're just the newspaper editor, not the marshal or the mayor!"

"But I'm the deputy marshal," Windy said, "and I agree with Mr. Warren; you need to stay right here where it's safe, gal."

"Safe," Tommy repeated skeptically. "For how long?"

Windy and Warren looked at each other. They couldn't answer that, and neither could anyone else here in the bank.

CHAPTER 27

Paco O'Shannon let out a startled yelp and tried to jerk out of the way of the blacksmith's hammer, which would have crushed his skull like an eggshell if it landed on his head.

O'Shannon was only partially successful at avoiding the blow. The hammer caught him on the left shoulder. He screamed in pain as he crumpled to the ground and clutched at the injured shoulder with his other hand.

Bishop struck then, lashing out with the whip he had snatched from its loop at his waist. The whip uncoiled in the gloom like the striking snake for which it was named and wrapped around the wrist of the man wielding the hammer. It left a bloody gash when Bishop snapped it back.

The bearded man cried out and dropped the hammer. He made a grab for it with his other hand, but the whip cracked again. The man jerked back instinctively, lost his balance, and fell. Blood welled from the nasty cut the whip had left on his right cheek, not far from his eye.

Bishop had intended to pluck out that eye with his second stroke, but it was a rare miss he attributed to the poor light in the livery barn. But it didn't matter; the man had no chance of reaching the hammer again. Bishop tossed the whip to his left hand and drew his gun to make sure of that.

"Stay where you are," he said coldly. "If you move, I'll kill you."

He was a little surprised at himself because he hadn't gone ahead and pulled the trigger. Most of the time, he smashed the life out of anyone who got in his way, and a part of him wanted to empty the gun into the man who'd attacked O'Shannon.

But the cunning part of Bishop's brain, the part that never stopped working, told him to wait. Maybe he could seize some sort of advantage from this unexpected encounter.

O'Shannon groaned. "Damn it, Snake, he broke my shoulder!"

"I wish it had been your head," the bearded man said. His upper lip curled in a snarl. The cut on his cheek and the bloody stripe on his wrist had to hurt, but he showed no sign of it.

"Shut up," Bishop snapped. "Can you move your arm, Paco?"

O'Shannon tried, but the effort just made him gasp. "N-no, I can't."

"You may be right about it being broken, then." To the bearded man, Bishop said, "Who the hell are you?"

"Rufus Spencer. I own this stable and the blacksmith shop next door. I don't have to ask who *you* are. You're Snake Bishop."

"That's right. And if you know who I am, you know you're lucky to be alive. Cooperate and maybe you'll stay that way for a while."

Bishop hung the whip back on his belt and kept the blacksmith covered with the gun as he went over to O'Shannon.

"Let me give you a hand up," he said. He got his left hand under O'Shannon's right arm and lifted him to his feet. O'Shannon cursed bitterly under his breath.

"I swear, I'm gonna kill that big son of a—"

"Not yet," Bishop cut in. "A man who owns a livery stable and blacksmith shop is a leading citizen in a town like this. Maybe we can make use of him, once this storm is over."

"If you reckon I'll help animals like you, you've got it all wrong," Spencer said. "Do whatever you want to me. Do your worst, I don't care."

"I'm betting at least some of the townspeople *do* care, and they'll want to keep you alive. Maybe enough to increase our chances of getting out of here." Bishop holstered his gun and went on, "Stay right where you are there, sitting on the ground, while I tend to my friend's arm. If you look like you're even thinking about moving, I'll kill you. You're not *that* important to me."

Spencer scowled but didn't say anything. He stayed where he was, with a trickle of blood running down his cheek into his beard from the cut Bishop's whip had left behind.

"This is going to hurt like hell," Bishop told O'Shannon, "but we need to fix that arm where it can't move around and do any more damage to your shoulder. Better grit your teeth."

"Just do what you can," O'Shannon said, still sounding a little breathless from the pain.

Carefully, Bishop took hold of the other outlaw's arm and moved it so that O'Shannon's hand was stuck in the waistband of his trousers. He took a coil of rope from a peg where it hung on the wall and cut a length of it with his knife. Then he wrapped that piece of rope around O'Shannon's torso and under his right arm, so that it held the left arm motionless.

While he was doing all that, he stood where he could keep an eye on Spencer the whole time.

"I'm sure it still hurts like blazes," Bishop said, "but that ought to keep it from getting even worse before we can find a doctor for you."

"Thanks, Snake," O'Shannon said through teeth he had gritted against the pain, as Bishop had suggested. "You reckon there actually is a doctor in this town?"

"In a place the size of Salt Lick, I imagine so, yeah." Bishop looked at their prisoner. "What about it? Is there a sawbones in this town?"

"Go to hell," Spencer rumbled.

"We'll find out later, from somebody who's got more sense. We can't go out in that storm right now, anyway."

The wind was still howling and the light that came through the cracks around the door was fading, showing that it was going to be an early night. While he could still see what he was doing, Bishop lit a lantern that was hanging from a nail on one of the posts supporting the hayloft. The yellow, flickering glow didn't reach all the way to every corner of the cavernous barn, but it helped.

The lantern didn't put out much heat, either, but it helped that there were at least a dozen horses stabled in here. They gave off heat. Bishop's breath fogged in front of his face, but he didn't think any of them would freeze to death before morning.

Several empty crates were stacked against the wall. Bishop put one of them where O'Shannon could use it for a seat, then kicked another over so he could sit on it. With both of them sitting there facing Spencer, who was still on the ground about twenty feet away, Bishop drew his gun again and said, "All right, I reckon now we wait. You happen to have a bottle around here, blacksmith?"

"I wouldn't give you anything to drink except maybe poison," Spencer said.

"No reason to be like that. We're stuck in here together. Might as well be civil to each other."

"Go to hell."

Bishop fingered the whip at his waist. "Or maybe we could pass the time some other way . . ."

Spencer drew in a deeper breath, obviously frightened of the whip but not wanting to show it. Bishop moved his hand away, and the blacksmith relaxed slightly.

No need to rush things, Bishop told himself. From the sound of that storm, it was going to be a long night.

The last time Smoke had seen Jonas Madigan, the former lawman, had been at the marshal's office with Miriam Dollinger. Then later, when Smoke and Windy checked at the office, Madigan and Miriam were gone. Smoke had a hunch Miriam had persuaded Madigan to return to his house.

He hoped that was the case. Madigan and Miriam could ride out the storm there safely enough. Of course, there was still Snake Bishop's gang to worry about, but the storm was the more pressing threat.

Smoke knew his mind wouldn't be at ease until he checked for himself. When he left the bank, he pushed his hat down tighter on his head and buttoned his coat, then drew his gun and stuck it and his right hand through the gap between two buttons on the heavy sheepskin garment. He wanted to keep his hand warm enough that he could use the gun accurately if he needed to.

Bending his head forward against the vicious wind, he headed toward the cross street where Jonas Madigan's house was located.

Finding it was going to be difficult in this weather, but Smoke still had faith in his instincts. Something inside him always told him which direction he was going. He stayed on a northbound course as he walked through the blowing snow. The stuff was piling up on the ground, even with the wind blowing so hard, so after a while he felt almost like he was slogging through sand.

When he thought he had gone far enough, he turned and went due west, keeping the wind on his right shoulder. He came to the boardwalk on the far side of the street. Had he gone too far? Not far enough? Using the buildings as a guide, he found that he was almost at the corner.

Madigan's house was on the other side of the cross street. Smoke cut over to that side and stepped up onto the boardwalk into the welcome protection from the wind that the buildings provided. For a few minutes, anyway, he wouldn't have the storm clawing at him quite so fiercely.

The light had grown dimmer. The hour was somewhere after the middle of the afternoon; Smoke wasn't going to the trouble of digging out his watch to check. Time didn't have much meaning in a situation like this. Everything broke down before the storm, during the storm, and after the storm.

Maybe by the next morning when the sun came up, the world would be back to normal. But Smoke wasn't going to count on that.

In the lee of the buildings like this, the wind wasn't quite as loud. Smoke lifted his head suddenly as he thought he heard something. Gunfire? Maybe the boom of a shotgun? He couldn't be sure.

Even if he *had* heard shots, he couldn't do anything about them. He had to trust that the citizens of Salt Lick would defend themselves if they were attacked. He had confidence in Windy Whittaker and Ned Warren. Apple Jack was a good man, too, and so was Rufus Spencer. Smoke couldn't be everywhere at once, couldn't do everything . . .

probably couldn't save everyone from Bishop's gang . . . but he was going to try.

He was passing the last business on this part of the street when the door opened and a man called, "Damn it, get in here! You're gonna freeze to death, wanderin' around out there."

Smoke still wanted to check on Madigan, but he supposed it wouldn't hurt anything to make sure whoever was in here was all right, too. With his head still down and his shoulders hunched against the cold, he stepped through the door. It slammed closed behind him.

The air inside the building wasn't very warm, but compared to being out in that storm, it felt downright cozy in here. Smoke lifted his head, saw that a lamp was burning on a desk. Leatherbound law books filled a set of shelves behind the desk, telling him that this was a lawyer's office.

Unfortunately, the man sitting at the desk was slumped forward, his arms stretched out and a pool of blood spreading on the blotter where his head lay. Smoke knew instantly that the man was dead, and the three men standing around in the office had killed him.

He had stepped right into a nest of owlhoots.

"Hey!" one of them yelped. "He ain't one of us!"

"Gun him!" another man shouted.

Two of the outlaws stood to Smoke's right; the third man was to his left. He hated to put a bullet hole in a perfectly good coat, but he pulled the trigger and fired a shot at the man to his left.

Even aiming through a coat, Smoke's accuracy was deadly. The man staggered back and clutched at his chest. Blood welled between his fingers.

Smoke whirled and moved to the side, his actions so swift it was hard for the eye to follow them. The Colt came out from under his coat and blasted again. Flame spurted from its muzzle and lit up the gloomy office. One of the remaining outlaws doubled over as the slug from Smoke's gun punched into his guts.

The third owlhoot got a shot off, but he rushed it and the bullet whined well wide of Smoke. Once again, Smoke's gun thundered in the office's close confines. The bullet smashed into the outlaw and flung him back against the wall behind him. He hung there for a second as the gun he held slipped from suddenly nerveless fingers and thudded at his feet. Slowly, he began to slide toward the floor, leaving a bloody smear on the wallpaper at his back.

Still moving quickly, Smoke kicked all the fallen guns into a corner, well out of reach of any of the outlaws. All three men lay crumpled and unmoving. Smoke checked them carefully. All three were dead, as he'd expected.

When time was short, it was easier to just go ahead and shoot to kill.

With the acrid tang of powder smoke biting at his nose and eyes, he checked the man sitting at the desk, too, lifting the unlucky gent's head enough to see the bullet hole in the left temple. This man was one of the citizens of Salt Lick Smoke hadn't met, but he felt the loss anyway. One more innocent cut down at the hands of ruthless outlaws and killers.

He couldn't do any more here. After replacing the spent shells he had fired with fresh cartridges, Smoke left the lawyer's office and continued his snowy trek to Jonas Madigan's house.

Once again, Smoke's instincts didn't let him down. The white picket fence in front of Madigan's house was almost impossible to see in the blowing snow and bad light, but he found it. He went up to the porch and was relieved by the sight of a yellow glow in the front window. He raised his hand and knocked on the door, not wanting to barge in.

It was never wise to surprise an old lawdog like Jonas Madigan. He might react with hot lead.

But when several moments went by and there was no response, a frown creased Smoke's forehead. He was about to try the knob and go inside anyway if it was unlocked, when the door suddenly opened in front of him.

"Oh, Marshal Jensen!" Miriam Dollinger exclaimed. "It's you."

He could tell by the look on her face that something was wrong. She stepped back so that he could come in, and as he did, he asked, "How's Jonas?"

"He . . . he's resting right now, Smoke, but it's not good." She closed the door and went on, "Right after you and Windy left the marshal's office, Jonas started feeling worse. He wanted to stay there so you could find him in case you needed his help, but I persuaded him to come back here and lie down. We . . . we barely made it here before the storm hit. He let me take his boots and gun belt off, but other than that, he won't get undressed. He says . . . he says he has to be ready for trouble."

The way her voice kept catching told Smoke how upset she was. From what he had seen of Miriam Dollinger so far, she was pretty calm and level-headed most of the time. Jonas had to be in bad shape to get her this worked up.

Nodding, Smoke said, "That sounds like him, all right. It's hard for an old war horse like Jonas to settle down if he knows something is going on."

"What's happening in town? I thought I heard some shooting earlier. Did the outlaws attack? Have they been driven off?"

"They attacked, all right," Smoke told her, "but they got here at the same time as that storm, so it wrecked their plans. They haven't been able to raid the town the way they normally would. But they're out there, all right, spread out around town ready to rob and kill as soon as they get the chance. I've run into a few of them, and from the sound of it, they've caused some trouble elsewhere in town."

"The ones you encountered . . . ?"

"They won't bother anybody else," Smoke said simply.

"Good." The vehemence in Miriam's voice surprised him. "Maybe it's not very Christian of me to be glad that they're dead, but they meant to harm my friends and neighbors. I think they got what was coming to them."

"I won't argue that point," Smoke said. "They called the tune. The only thing the rest of us can do is dance to it."

Miriam frowned. "But if those outlaws are wandering around despite the storm . . . some of them could come here."

"They could, although I suspect that most of them have already hunkered down to wait out this blizzard. I don't reckon they know this is Jonas's house, so they won't have any reason to seek it out. You probably ought to blow out all the lamps anyway. It's almost full dark now. Light will just attract attention that you probably don't want."

"That's a good idea. I'll do that."

"And I'm going to speak to Jonas for a minute," Smoke added.

Miriam didn't try to stop him as he went to the door of Madigan's bedroom. That door stood open. Smoke figured his old friend might have overheard some of the conversation between him and Miriam, but Madigan appeared to be asleep, stretched out on the bed fully dressed except for his boots and gun belt, as Miriam had said. A blanket was spread over his legs.

Madigan's eyes opened. He said, "Smoke?"

"That's right." Smoke stepped closer to the bed. "I hear you had a bad spell, Jonas."

"It was . . . nothing." The strain in Madigan's voice gave

the lie to his words. "Miriam worries, though . . . so I try to humor her."

Smoke bent and blew out the lamp on the bedside table.

"I don't know if you heard or not. Bishop's gang made it to town. They split up and attacked just as the storm hit. I've taken care of a few of them so far, but most of the bunch is still roaming around Salt Lick."

The room was dark enough that he barely saw Madigan moving as the old lawman sat up and said, "I'd better get back out there—"

Smoke put a hand on his friend's shoulder. "No, what you need to do is stay right here so you can protect Miriam. That lady's worth looking after, Jonas."

Madigan grunted. "You ain't tellin' me anything I don't already know, Smoke. But the town's my responsibility, too."

"Not any more. Windy and I are looking after it, and so are a lot of other folks. Good folks who've stepped up to battle the invaders. So you just rest and try to get to feeling better. With all the lights out, maybe the house won't draw any attention."

"Yeah. Like out on the prairie, when we had to . . . have a cold camp . . . so as not to let the Comanche or the Kiowa know . . . where we were."

"Exactly."

"Only those redskins . . . had a whole heap more honor to them . . . than Snake Bishop and his bunch."

"That's sure enough true," Smoke agreed.

"Can you . . . put my Colt there on the nightstand . . . where I can reach it easy?"

"Sure." Smoke had seen the coiled gun belt on the chair next to the bed when he came in. He slid the revolver from the holster and placed it on the nightstand as Madigan asked.

"And there's a shotgun . . . in the corner . . . Put it on the bed . . . here beside me."

"You're liable to get gun oil on the covers."

"Can't be helped. I got to be ready."

Smoke did as Madigan requested. Miriam came into the room and said, "I've checked all the doors and windows and made sure they're fastened."

"Don't you worry about a thing," Madigan told her. Smoke could hear the effort Madigan put into making his voice sound strong and confident. "We're ready if there's any trouble. Any of those blasted owlhoots show up here, we'll give 'em a mighty warm welcome, you can count on that, Miriam."

"I know. I'm not worried, Jonas . . . as long as I'm with you."

Smoke waited for a moment, then said, "I hate to leave, but—"

"No, you need to get back out there," Madigan said. "Salt Lick needs you, Smoke, and I can't tell you how grateful I am that you got my letter and came to see me."

Smoke chuckled. "It's been an eventful visit, hasn't it?"

"Just like old times," Madigan replied with a soft laugh of his own. "Good luck, Smoke. See you in the morning."

"See you in the morning," Smoke responded.

And neither mentioned the distinct possibility that one or both of them might not make it until then.

CHAPTER 28

Thomasina Spencer paced restlessly around the bank.
The worry she felt for her father wouldn't let her stay still.
Some of the women tried to comfort her and get her to sit
down, but she wasn't having any of it.

Her pa was in trouble. She was sure of that. If he hadn't
been, he would have showed up here by now. They had
agreed to meet at the bank, and it wasn't like Rufus Spencer
not to do what he said he would.

Windy came over to her and said, "Child, you're givin'
me the fantods with all this pacin' around. Why don't you
just take it easy for a spell and try to get a little rest? It's
liable to be a long night, and I don't expect any of us'll be
sleepin' much."

"You know my pa pretty well, Mr. Whittaker," she said.
"Doesn't he always keep his word?"

"Well . . . in the time I've known him, I reckon he has."

"Then the only reason he's not here is because he *can't*
be here. And nothing would stop him unless it was pretty
bad."

Windy scratched at his whiskers and made a face. "I ain't
sayin' you're wrong, missy. But even if you're right, there
ain't nothin' you can do about it."

Tommy blew out a disgusted breath and turned away. Windy let her go.

The wheels of the girl's brain were still revolving a mile a minute as she sat down with her back propped against the bank's rear wall, close to the group of women and children but not really a part of it. She had her Winchester carbine with her and placed it on the floor beside her.

The argument about whether to lock and barricade the bank's front doors had continued. Tommy watched and listened as the men finally reached a compromise. Edward Warren agreed that they could lock the doors, and Mr. Hawkins didn't insist that they shove desks in front of the entrance to block it. Those would take too much time to clear away if they needed to get the doors open in a hurry, which was a good point, Tommy thought.

The outlaws could still bust the doors down if they wanted to, but that would take long enough that the defenders could be ready for them when they broke in.

The latches on all the windows were fastened on both floors of the building, and the bar was in place on the back door. If anybody wanted to get in here, chances were they would come from the front. Loopholes had been cut in the windows there so the defenders could fire out.

The bank had a couple of pot-bellied stoves in the lobby for warmth. Both had fires going in them. A woodbox filled with chunks of firewood was located in a rear storage room. Once the doors had been closed again for a while, the lobby warmed up until it was pleasant in there.

Charlotte Shaw had brought a coffee pot and some bags of Arbuckle's when she came to the bank from the café. Since her husband was resting comfortably now, she got a pot boiling on one of the stoves and soon the aromatic smell of coffee brewing filled the room.

If it wasn't for the fact that dozens of bloodthirsty outlaws might be lurking right outside, it wouldn't seem so bad in here. That was true for most of the folks in the lobby, Tommy reflected.

Not for her, though. She couldn't rest until she knew that her pa was all right.

Which was why a plan had started forming in her mind.

Even in a blizzard, even threatened by a horde of outlaws, people had to take care of their bodily needs. Several buckets had been placed in a back room to serve that purpose, since nobody would have wanted to go out in the storm to visit the privy even if there hadn't been outlaws in Salt Lick.

Tommy waited patiently, even though the fear she felt for her pa gnawed at her guts like a hungry rat. Time passed, agonizingly slowly. She watched as every now and then a man or woman would sidle discreetly down the hallway toward that back room where the buckets were, or a woman would hold her kids' hands and take them to tend to business. After a while, nobody paid any attention to that.

Also, as the minutes crept past, weariness began to take its toll. People stretched out and rested their heads on pillows made from wadded-up coats. The lamps burned low, and nobody turned them up. Some of the men stayed awake and alert, self-appointed sentries for the others, but a good number of the folks who had taken refuge in the bank dozed off, despite what Windy had said about nobody sleeping much. Tommy heard several people snoring softly.

Other than that, and a few whispered conversations, it was quiet in the bank lobby. Nothing to do now but wait for morning and hope the storm blew over.

Judging by the way the wind was still wailing outside, it was even money whether or not that would happen.

Tommy felt her own eyes getting heavy. Her head drooped forward a little toward her chest. She jerked it up, mentally berating herself for letting weakness almost overcome her. Her pa might need her help, she reminded herself, and she had a plan that would let her provide that help.

She just had to wait a little while longer . . .

Finally, she thought it might be late enough to make her move. Nearly all the women and children were asleep now. So were most of the men. Old Windy Whittaker and Mr. Warren, the newspaperman, were talking in low tones on the other side of the lobby. Neither man so much as glanced in Tommy's direction as she got to her feet.

The next bit was tricky. She bent down and picked up the carbine, being careful not to bang the barrel or the stock against the wall. She turned so that her back was toward Windy and Warren and held the carbine straight up and down in front of her so it wouldn't be conspicuous as she started toward the hallway.

She expected to hear one of the men start after her or call to her and ask where she was going. If they noticed, however, they must not have wanted to embarrass her by asking the question with its obvious answer.

Tommy slipped into the darkened corridor, unchallenged.

She had been back there earlier, not long after coming to the bank, and she'd noticed the narrow rear staircase leading to the second floor. After casting a glance over her shoulder to make sure no one was watching her, she turned and hurried up those stairs. It was really dark in the stairwell, so she couldn't go *too* fast or she'd risk falling, which might make a racket, but she didn't waste any time, either.

She didn't know what the rooms on the bank's second floor were used for. Offices of some kind, most likely, along with storage. But nobody was up here right now, and that was all Tommy cared about. Working by feel, she fumbled her way into one of the rooms on the back side of the building. She found the window, pushed the latch to the side, and slid the pane up.

Instantly, she winced as the icy wind clawed at her face. But she forced herself to lean forward into the wind so she could look outside.

There was nothing to see except blowing snow. Tommy held the carbine outside the window and dropped it. She didn't hear it land. Whether that was because the wind was so loud or because the rifle had fallen into deep, drifted snow, she didn't know. She risked not being able to find it once she was down there, but she hadn't figured out any other way to do this.

The next step involved climbing out the window. She tugged her cap down tighter on her head so it wouldn't blow off and then lifted her right leg over the sill. She clung to the sides of the window with her gloved hands as she maneuvered herself into a sitting position. She shifted her grip to the sill and twisted around, then slid off the sill and hung from her hands. The strain of supporting her weight made her arms and shoulders protest.

That didn't last long, though, because Tommy took a deep breath, let go, and fell toward the alley below.

She knew she was taking a big risk. If she landed wrong, she could break a leg, an arm, or even her neck. If she hurt herself and couldn't get up, they probably wouldn't hear her inside the bank no matter how loudly she yelled for help. That meant she would freeze to death out here, more than likely.

But she was young and athletic and had jumped from the hayloft in the barn before without hurting herself. This wasn't any higher than that.

Even so, the couple of heartbeats it took for her to drop to the ground seemed a lot longer. Then her feet hit and she let her muscles go limp and the momentum of her fall carried her over backward. She rolled as she landed.

The snow was close to a foot deep back here. She wound up face down in the stuff and jerked her head up, feeling for a second as if she were suffocating. She shook her head, and her hair flew around her face. Her cap had come off when she landed.

Gasping from the cold, Tommy pushed herself to her feet. She walked around in circles, shuffling her legs through the deep snow. She couldn't afford to stay back here for a long time, looking for her carbine. Sooner or later, somebody inside might realize she had been gone for a while and come looking for her. The wind blowing from that open window down through the rear stairwell was bound to be noticed eventually, too. She had to find that carbine and get started on her mission . . .

Her left shin clunked against something solid.

Tommy bent, pawed through the snow, and closed her hands around the carbine's barrel. Feeling a fierce satisfaction, she straightened.

She would have liked to find her cap, too, but she thought the likelihood of doing that was a lot smaller, so she wasn't going to waste the time. Gripping the rifle in her gloved hands, she stood there for a moment getting oriented.

Then, fairly certain she was going the right way, she set out toward the livery stable, hoping she would find her father there.

And if any of those outlaws had hurt him, they were going to be damned sorry, she vowed as she disappeared into the blizzard.

Eventually, Snake Bishop figured out that he couldn't count on being able to stay awake and keep an eye on Rufus

Spencer all night. That meant he needed to do something about the blacksmith, either go ahead and kill him or figure out a way to render him harmless.

O'Shannon still cursed and complained about the pain in his left shoulder and arm, but he could use his right hand all right. Bishop told him to draw his gun and cover Spencer. O'Shannon did so, then Bishop circled around, got the rest of the rope he had used earlier to immobilize O'Shannon's wounded arm, and came up behind Spencer.

"Put your arms behind your back," he ordered.

"I told you already, I'm not going to cooperate with you."

"You can do what I tell you, or Paco will go ahead and shoot you. It's your choice. I told you before, you're not so valuable to me that I'm going to a lot of trouble to keep you alive."

Spencer growled some curses of his own, but he put his arms behind his back.

"If he tries anything, go ahead and drill him," Bishop told O'Shannon as he moved in.

"That'll be a risky shot with you so close to him, Snake."

"Then don't miss," Bishop snapped. He bent to wrap the rope around Spencer's wrists and pull it tight.

The blacksmith didn't try anything. In a few minutes, Bishop had his arms tied tightly behind his back. He pushed Spencer over, ran the rope down to his feet, and lashed them securely, too. With wrists and ankles connected that way, the rope pulled Spencer into what had to be an uncomfortable, backward-bowed shape. He lay on his side, glaring at the two outlaws as Bishop resumed his seat on the crate.

"He can't pull any tricks now," Bishop said. "We can get some rest."

"It would still be a good idea if we took turns sleeping," O'Shannon said. "You go ahead and see if you can doze off, Snake. I'm hurting too much to sleep right now, anyway."

"Are you sure?"

"Yeah. It'll be fine."

Bishop thought about it for a moment and then nodded. He stood up, went over to one of the posts that held up the hayloft, and sat down with his back against it. He tipped his hat forward and pulled it down. It wasn't long before his chest was rising and falling with a deep, regular rhythm that indicated he was asleep.

Tommy had grown up in Salt Lick and knew every inch of the town. But finding her way around under normal circumstances was nothing like the nightmare journey on which she found herself tonight.

She tried to keep a hand on one of the buildings at all times so she wouldn't become disoriented and wander off aimlessly into the storm. But that really wasn't possible, she soon realized. There were too many gaps where she had to step out with nothing around her but the howling wind and blowing snow. Even though she tried to visualize the surroundings in her head and plot her course, every time she took her hand away from a building and moved into the storm, she was afraid she would be lost forever.

Her father wouldn't have wanted her to give up, she told herself sternly. She had to conquer that fear and keep moving.

Of course, her father wouldn't have wanted her to risk her life in this storm, even if it was to save his. He would have gladly sacrificed himself to keep her safe.

Each time she ventured out with nothing to anchor her, she found another building, and she was relieved for a little while, until she had to risk it again. But she was confident that she was on the right track and making steady progress toward her destination.

Time meant nothing in circumstances such as these. She

could have been fighting the storm for hours, or it could have been only a short time since she slipped out of the bank. Tommy didn't know or care.

But it seemed like she had been at it for a long, long time before she bumped into a wall and got a whiff of a very familiar odor from the other side of it.

Even a storm like this one couldn't completely dispel the distinctive smell of hay, manure, and horseflesh. Her instincts had led her straight to the stable, as she had hoped they would.

Now she needed to figure out exactly where she was. Her objective was the rear of the stable. A small door was cut into that wall, up on the same level as the hayloft. A beam stuck out from the wall above that opening. Attached to it was a pulley arrangement that was used to lift bales of hay, which were then pulled in through the opening and stacked in the loft.

In addition to the ropes attached to the pulley, another rope hung down from the beam. This rope had knots tied into it at regular intervals. Tommy had been climbing up and down on that rope for as long as she could remember.

The door would be closed and latched in this weather, but there was a trick to opening it from outside, and Tommy knew that trick, too.

She fumbled her way through the storm until something brushed against her face that *wasn't* the wind-blown snow. She found it with her hand and could tell it was the rope she was looking for.

She took off her coat and removed the pair of suspenders she wore, then used it to rig a sling for the Winchester, which she draped around her neck once she put the coat back on. With the carbine hanging down behind her back, she gripped the rope with both hands, lifted a foot and rested it against the wall, and started to climb. With the storm causing so much racket, she hoped the small sounds she inevitably made wouldn't be heard inside.

This was the hardest climb she had ever made. Even in gloves, her hands were so numb she could barely feel them. The carbine's weight threw her a little off-balance. The hard wind caused her to sway back and forth.

She had to ignore all that and keep going. She thought about her pa, how hard he had worked and how he had devoted his life to raising her after her ma died. Maybe he *wasn't* in there. But she wasn't going to rest until she knew for sure, one way or the other.

When she reached the top, she found the little catch she had to work to open the door. It opened outward, so she had to lean far to her left and hang on with one hand while she used the other to pull the door toward her. The wind caught it and tried to whip it closed. Her grip slipped slightly, and for a second she thought she was going to fall.

Then she hung on harder and tighter, and the door cleared her. She lifted her leg and got it inside, hooked her foot against the side of the opening, and pulled herself in. It felt good to sprawl on her belly for a moment.

Then the urgency of her mission drove her to push up on hands and knees. She reached back and pulled the door closed behind her, then crawled toward the edge of the hayloft. A yellow glow rose from a lantern down below.

She paused when she was still a few feet from the edge and listened intently. She didn't hear anybody talking, but she thought she heard someone breathing. It was hard to be sure. Some of the horses were moving around in their stalls, snuffling and blowing, and it was difficult to sort out any other sounds.

She had come this far, she told herself. She couldn't stop now. She edged forward, toward the ladder that led to the loft.

She was just about to risk a look over the edge when a man's face suddenly appeared at the top of the ladder. He leered at her, and his hand shot out to grab the collar of her coat. Tommy cried out in surprise and fear as the man hauled her toward the edge. She tried to stop herself, but she was no match for his unexpected strength.

He yanked her over the edge into empty air and let go of her.

Tommy screamed as she turned over in mid-air. The cry was cut short as she crashed to the hard-packed ground on her back. As if the fall weren't bad enough already, landing on the carbine like that made extra pain lance through her. It felt like her back was broken. Whimpering, she rolled onto her side and forced her muscles to work as she tried to reach back for the weapon.

A boot toe dug into her ribs in a vicious kick. She gasped in agony and twisted in an attempt to curl up around the pain. Somebody ripped the carbine away from her. The man planted a boot against her shoulder and slammed her down so she lay on her back again.

From there, she blinked up at him through pain-blurred eyes and saw him pointing her own carbine at her face.

"We've got ourselves another visitor, Paco," the man said to somebody Tommy couldn't see. "Or maybe I should say, another hostage. If people in this town place any value on the blacksmith's head, I figure they'll value a pretty girl even higher!"

CHAPTER 29

Smoke didn't know what time it was when he got back to the bank, but judging by the emptiness in his belly and the heaviness of his legs from trudging around in the snow, he had been gone for a long time. It had to be well after the usual hour of nightfall—and supper time!—by now, although with the blizzard still roaring, that didn't mean much.

He thought there might be a few hopeful glimpses, though. It seemed like there were more lulls in the wind than there had been earlier, and when the gusts did die down, they stayed that way a little longer each time. That made it easier for him to find his way around town.

Maybe this storm was blowing itself out.

In addition to those tiny signs of improvement in the weather, Smoke regarded it as a mixed omen that he hadn't run into any more of Snake Bishop's gang as he moved around the town. Most folks would see that as a good thing, he mused. He wasn't sure about that, however. To Smoke, the lack of action meant that he hadn't been able to kill any more of the outlaws and continue whittling down the odds.

He had been gone long enough, though, that he wanted to check on the folks at the bank before he did anything else.

He was on his way there when a bulky figure loomed up

in front of him. A high-pitched, unmistakable voice rose over the wind.

"Hold it right there, mister, or I'll blast you!"

"Don't shoot, Apple Jack," Smoke called back. "It's me, Smoke Jensen."

"Smoke!" Apple Jack emerged more clearly from the waving curtains of snow. "Damned if you aren't a sight for sore eyes! I hadn't seen you since the storm hit, and I was starting to worry that Bishop's men might've done for you!"

"No such luck for them," Smoke said with a grin. "I was kind of worried about the same thing where you were concerned. Where have you been?"

"Well, at first me and a few other fellas stuck at the barricade where we were supposed to hold out. This monster of a blizzard kind of ruined that plan, though."

"It surely did," Smoke agreed.

"We traded a few shots with Bishop's bunch when they galloped into town," Apple Jack went on. "Poor Al Nelson was killed, blast it. But those outlaws just kept going, and there was nothing else to shoot at. I told the boys to head for either their homes or the bank, wherever they wanted to fort up. And ever since, I've been going around town trying to check on folks and not get lost in the storm! I never saw anything like it, Smoke."

"That's pretty much what I've been doing," Smoke said. "Have you run into any more of Bishop's gang?"

"No, I reckon I've been lucky. I know they've got to be around somewhere."

"They are," Smoke said grimly. "I've tangled with half a dozen of them."

"So I suppose that's six of the buzzards we don't have to worry about?"

Smoke grunted. "Only the burying, when it thaws out. I

think I've heard some other shots, too, so those skirmishes I was mixed up in weren't the only ones."

"Dang, I hope too many of our folks haven't been hurt or killed. What now?"

"We were both headed for the bank. Let's see if we can find it in this mess."

As they made their way through the snow, Apple Jack said, "I don't think the wind is blowing as hard now as it was a while ago."

"I agree. It's blowing almost as hard, but not quite."

"I've seen a lot of blue northers. I think the wind will lay down by morning. It might even stop snowing. But if it does . . ."

Apple Jack's voice trailed off. Smoke knew what the saloonkeeper was thinking.

If the storm eased off enough, then Snake Bishop and his men would emerge from wherever they were denned up . . . and Salt Lick would have an even more deadly danger facing it.

They reached the bank a few minutes later. As they approached the door, Smoke held out a hand to stop his companion.

"Maybe we'd better hail them before we go in," he said. "They're liable to be on edge inside, and we don't want anybody getting trigger-happy."

"No, sir, we sure don't." Apple Jack raised his voice. "Hey, there, inside the bank! Anybody hear me?" He turned his head to grin at Smoke. "If they do, they'll know who's out here. Nobody in Salt Lick's got a more distinctive voice than I do, except for maybe that newspaper fella's youngster. Just looking at the two of us, you'd think we ought to swap voiceboxes."

There was no response from inside the bank. Smoke slapped his palm against one of the doors a couple of times and called, "Hello, inside! It's Smoke Jensen and Colonel Appleton!"

He tried the door. It was locked.

From the other side, Edward Warren asked, "Are you and Apple Jack alone, Marshal?"

"That's right."

Warren must have unlocked the door. It opened slightly. He called, "Come on in, easy-like."

"They're being careful," Smoke said to Apple Jack. "That's good."

"I reckon folks learn pretty quick when there's a whole gang of killers breathing down their necks."

Smoke and Apple Jack stepped into the bank and stopped just inside the entrance. At least a dozen rifles and shotguns were pointing at them from fairly close range. Smoke closed the door behind them and smiled.

"If there had been any kind of trickery going on, I reckon you would have filled us full of lead just now," he said. "That's good."

Warren looked relieved as he lowered his shotgun and stepped forward, but his face and voice still revealed a lot of strain as he said, "We've tried to be careful." His jaw tightened. "But not careful enough."

"What's wrong?" Smoke asked, instantly alert.

Windy Whittaker stepped forward, too, and raked his fingers through his whiskers in agitation.

"That Spencer gal is gone," he said.

"You mean Bishop's men got her somehow?" Smoke asked sharply.

Warren shook his head. "No, we think she slipped out on her own after she found out that Bishop himself and one of his men are holed up at the livery stable. She thought her father was probably there and in danger."

"You'd better tell me about it," Smoke said.

They did, with Windy providing the details of his brief encounter with Snake Bishop and one of the other outlaws in front of the livery stable.

"I believed we had convinced Tommy to wait here instead of charging off and putting herself in danger," Warren said, "but then later, we realized she was gone and we found an open window on the second floor where she must have climbed out."

"If she jumped from the second floor, she could be hurt."

"That's the first thing we thought of. Some of the men formed a human chain, so no one would get lost, and we went out through the back door into the alley to look for her. I'm convinced she's not back there, Marshal, so she must have been in good enough shape to leave."

"Of course, with the wind blowin' the way it is, there wasn't no sign," Windy put in. "It had all blowed away."

Warren said, "She must have gone to the livery stable. There's no other reason she would have left like that."

"You didn't run into her pa anywhere while you were out roamin' around, did you, Smoke?" Windy asked.

Smoke shook his head. "No, I didn't see him. What about you, Apple Jack?"

"Never saw hide nor hair of him," the saloonkeeper replied.

"He could have gone to the stable, all right," Smoke mused, "and if Bishop showed up there . . . You're sure you saw Bishop, Windy?"

"Sure as can be. I got a good look at him before the varmint started shootin' at me."

"How long has Tommy been gone?"

"We don't know," Warren said. "An hour or more, at least."

"She's had time to make it to the stable . . . or to get lost. Either way, I need to go find her."

"You ain't goin' by yourself," Windy declared. "I'm comin' with you. If I hadn't come in here yammerin' about how Bishop was down at the stable, she wouldn't have got so worked up that she snuck out like that."

"I'm coming, too," Warren said.

"No, you're not," Smoke told him. "You need to stay here, Ned, and you, too, Apple Jack." He had been able to tell that the saloonkeeper was about to volunteer. "This bank will still be the main target if the gang gets back together and decides to continue the raid. I'm counting on you two and the other men here to hold the fort, so to speak. Windy and I will see if we can find Tommy and her father."

Warren and Apple Jack both looked like they wanted to argue, but neither would go against Smoke's decision.

"You're the marshal," Warren said. "You're still in charge. So we'll continue looking after things here."

"You're doing a good job so far."

Warren shook his head and said, "I don't know about that. We managed to lose a young woman."

"The gal should've had better sense than to go out in that weather and face down a couple o' owlhoots," Windy said. "I reckon she was just too worried about her pa to leave it alone."

"Maybe we'll find the two of them together," Smoke said.

The explanation of how the outlaws had known Tommy was in the loft was simple. Snake Bishop explained it in gloating fashion.

"As soon as I saw the flame in that lantern bend over and flicker, I knew there had to be more of a draft blowing through here, and that was the only place it could come from," he said as he stood in front of the two captives. "Good thing I woke up from my little nap in time to notice that."

He had found another rope and tied Tommy the same way her father was trussed up. With the other outlaw holding a gun on her pa, she had no choice except to go along with them . . . for now.

"I figured there was a door in the loft," Bishop went on. "I've seen set-ups like that before in barns. So I went up the ladder and waited for whoever it was." A grin split the boss outlaw's cruelly handsome face. "I didn't expect it to be a pretty girl, I'll admit that. I'm glad you didn't break your neck when I tossed you down from there. That would have been a damned shame . . . and a waste, too."

Tommy looked away from him. The very sight of him made her sick . . . but she was also disgusted with herself for letting him capture her so easily.

Her father looked utterly miserable as he lay there with a bandana crammed in his mouth. Bishop had used it to keep him from calling out a warning, which he would have done, even if it had caught him a bullet for his trouble.

Bishop got tired of his gloating and returned to sit on the crate next to the other outlaw.

"What are we going to do now?" the man asked. His name was O'Shannon, even though he looked Mexican. Tommy knew that because she had heard Bishop use the name.

"This business with the girl changes nothing," Bishop replied without hesitation. "We wait for morning. I think the storm will be over by then. The wind doesn't sound as bad out there now. We'll round up the rest of the boys and get what we came for, starting with that bank."

"Can't burn the town down, like we normally would," O'Shannon commented. "Not with snow all over everything."

"You'd be surprised how much will burn, even in the

snow. And anything that won't burn, we'll use dynamite to blow it to hell." A vicious grin pulled Bishop's lips back. "One way or another, I don't want one damn building left standing in Salt Lick when we get done with the place."

Smoke and Windy pressed their backs against the front wall of the livery stable. The wind still blew hard and whipped snow around them, but this was just a normal blizzard now, instead of a once-in-a-century monster of a storm. Smoke could even see faint outlines of the buildings across the street.

"There's a light in there," he said quietly to Windy, confident that the words couldn't be heard inside. "You can see it around the doors."

"Yeah, but is it Bishop and that other fella? Do they have Rufus and the gal?"

"We need to find out. If we bust in there shooting, Mr. Spencer or Tommy could get in the way of a bullet."

Windy tugged at his beard in thought, then said, "You know, I've seen 'em loadin' hay bales into the loft through a door up there in the back. There's a rope that hangs down, and Tommy shinnies up and down it like a dang monkey. I couldn't climb it, but I reckon a young fella like you might be able to, Smoke."

Smoke considered the idea and nodded. "Sounds like it might be worth a try. Let's go take a look and see if we can find it."

They slipped around the building and located the knotted, dangling rope in a matter of minutes. Smoke looked up at the little door into the hayloft. His keen brain was still working.

"It'll create a draft when I open that door," he told Windy. "If Bishop and his man are still in there, they might notice that. So we're going to have to distract them."

"I can handle that part, sure enough," the old-timer said. "I'll let you get started up the rope, then I'll hurry around front and start yellin' at Bishop. If, by some chance, the varmints are gone and it's just Rufus and Tommy in there, I reckon they'll open the door and want to know what I'm caterwaulin' about."

"If Bishop *is* in there, he's liable to start shooting at you again."

Windy chuckled. "I'm too spry for him, and the light ain't good. He won't hit me."

"You've already been wounded once tonight," Smoke pointed out.

"That little scratch on my side? Shoot, I'd plumb forgot about it already, until you done reminded me."

Smoke doubted that, but he knew the breed of man Windy Whittaker was: tough as whang leather and able to ignore any aches and pains as long as there was a job that needed to be done.

"So don't you worry," Windy went on. "I can handle the job of distractin' those two polecats."

"All right," Smoke said. He gripped the rope, using the knots tied in it for handholds. "Let me get most of the way up before you head around to the front. Then maybe shoot in the air a couple of times when you start raising a racket."

"Done and done," Windy promised.

Smoke started climbing. Even though Windy had called him a young fella, he wasn't as young as he once was. A climb like this required some effort. But Smoke was still in the prime of life, so he didn't have much trouble making the ascent. As he neared the little hatch, he glanced back down at the ground. He thought Windy was gone, but he couldn't be sure.

He reached the door and hung on to the rope with one hand, his feet braced against the wall, while he felt around for the catch. The door was pushed up, held in place by the wind, but it wasn't actually fastened, he discovered. He got his fingers in the crack and waited for Windy's signal. The arm and shoulder supporting his weight began to ache, but he knew he could hang on for as long as he needed to.

He just hoped it wasn't *too* long . . .

Windy's old revolver boomed, then boomed again, clearly audible even over the wind. Smoke heard the old-timer start yelling. He couldn't make out the words, but whatever Windy was saying, Smoke was sure it would get the attention of whoever was in the stable.

He pulled the door open, swung himself closer on the rope, and practically dived into the dark hayloft.

CHAPTER 30

Tommy's head jerked up when she heard the gunshots, close by outside. Right on the heels of those blasts, a man started shouting obscenities and challenges for Bishop to come out and fight. She recognized the leather-lunged tones of old Windy Whittaker.

Evidently, so did Snake Bishop. The boss outlaw sprang to his feet as an angry snarl twisted his mouth.

"That loco old pelican must've crawled into a bottle of whiskey and crawled back out full of courage," he said as he drew his gun. "Cover those two, Paco. I'll deal with Whittaker."

O'Shannon stood up and drew his gun, but he had a worried frown on his face as he said, "Be careful, Snake. It could be a trap."

"I'm not a damned fool," Bishop snapped. "I'll only open the door enough to plug that idiot."

He stalked toward the double doors and shoved one of them back just wide enough to thrust his gun through the gap. Shots blasted from the weapon.

Then something suddenly sailed down from the loft, and Tommy gasped in surprise.

* * *

Smoke's jump was perfect. The outlaw holding a gun on Rufus and Tommy Spencer barely had time to glance up before Smoke's boot heels smashed into his chest. The man let out a strangled scream as the impact drove him to the ground.

Over at the entrance, the other outlaw—Snake Bishop himself?—twisted around in shock, but his surprise vanished in an instant. The gun in his hand spouted flame, causing Smoke to duck as the slug whipped past his head.

That gave the man enough time to throw himself backward and ram a shoulder against the door behind him. It opened more and the outlaw darted out into the storm.

Smoke's gun rose and fell in a flash of metal, thudding against the head of the man he'd knocked down. That hombre wasn't going to be getting up for a while. He lay there senseless as Smoke threw himself to the side and rolled.

The other outlaw's gun crashed again and again as he fired back into the barn from outside. Bullets kicked up dirt from the stable's floor. Smoke came to rest on his belly and triggered twice at the partially open door. From outside came the dull roar of Windy Whittaker's old cap-and-ball pistol. For a second, the outlaw was caught in a crossfire.

The shooting stopped. Maybe they had gotten him, Smoke thought. He surged to his feet and ran to where Spencer and Tommy lay, still staring at him in surprise.

Smoke reached under his coat, drew his knife from its sheath, and slashed the ropes between their ankles and said, "Both of you get in the blacksmith shop. You'll be safer there."

He didn't take the time to free their hands.

Spencer had been tied up for so long that his legs didn't want to work. Smoke helped him up, and then Tommy, who had made it to her feet on her own, leaned against her father to support him as they stumbled toward the door into the adjoining blacksmith shop. Once they were in there, Smoke swung back toward the stable's front doors.

His gun came up as the partially open door dragged through the snow and the gap got bigger. A familiar voice called, "Hold your fire, Smoke! It's me!"

"Come on in, Windy," Smoke told the old-timer.

Windy appeared, holding the heavy revolver. "Bishop's gone," he reported. "I seen him run off into the snow and threw another shot after him, but he didn't stop."

"Did we hit him at all?"

"Don't know for sure, but I think he had a little hitch in his get-along when he run off, so we might've winged him."

Smoke nodded. "Mr. Spencer and Tommy are in the blacksmith shop. I think they're all right, but we need to check and make sure."

"I'll do that," Windy said.

"That *was* Bishop who got away? You're sure?"

Windy made a face. "Yeah. That other fella ain't him, so it had to be. The other one is— Holy cow! Dead, from the looks of it."

Smoke turned his head and saw the blood pooling around the man he had knocked down and then out. Smoke knew he hadn't shot the outlaw, so it must have been one of Snake Bishop's wild shots that had killed his own man.

Smoke wasn't going to lose any sleep over that. He moved closer to make sure and saw the man's sightlessly staring eyes. Smoke kicked the fallen gun well out of reach, just to be sure, even though the outlaw was done for, no doubt about that. The bullet that had found him had torn away most of his throat.

Windy came back to report, "I cut Rufus and Tommy loose the rest of the way. They're all right. Shaken up a mite, but they'll be fine. We can take 'em back to the bank." The old-timer grimaced. "Tommy told me that Bishop still plans to get his men together and loot the town, startin' with the bank, as soon as the storm lets up enough. He figures on burnin' things down, too, and usin' dynamite to blow up anything that won't burn. The varmint's plumb loco, Smoke. He always was, I reckon, but he's worse'n ever now. He wants to destroy the whole settlement."

Smoke nodded as he listened to the wind outside. "It'll probably be dawn, or close to it, before the storm really settles down. I hope Bishop does come for the bank first."

"You do?"

"That's right," Smoke said, "because that's where we're going to be waiting for him."

Everyone at the bank was excited to see Rufus and Tommy Spencer when they arrived there with Smoke and Windy a short time later. After greeting them warmly, though, Edward Warren frowned at Tommy and said, "You worried us half to death, young lady."

"Well, I was worried about my pa," Tommy answered with a defiant jut of her chin. "And I was right to be, too, because he was in a heap of trouble."

"I would have been all right," Spencer insisted. "And even if I hadn't been, it wasn't worth your life to try to rescue me, Tommy. You think I'd ever forgive myself if anything happened to you because of me?"

She shrugged. "I don't reckon I thought about that. I just wanted to help you if I could."

He put a brawny arm around her shoulders and said, "I know that, girl. And I appreciate it." He looked at Smoke and Windy. "Just like I appreciate the two of you risking your necks to save us."

"I just wish we'd been able to corral that durned Bishop,"

Windy said. "Or ventilate him, one or the other! If he was out of the way, the rest of that bunch might decide the best thing for them to do is light a shuck outta here, as soon as the weather cooperates enough."

Smoke said, "With Bishop still on the loose, though, they won't do that, will they?"

Windy shook his head. "I reckon they're more afraid of him than anything else. If he wants to destroy the town, they'll do their best to accommodate him."

"Destroy the town?" Warren echoed as his eyes widened in concern.

To the men who had gathered around, Smoke explained what Spencer and Tommy had overheard Snake Bishop saying to the other outlaw, whose name, evidently, had been Paco O'Shannon. That explanation turned into an informal council of war as the men began to discuss how they should meet this threat. Tommy wanted to stay and take part, but her father told her to go sit with the women and children.

"That didn't work out so well last time, did it?" she retorted.

Spencer glared, but she wouldn't budge. Finally, he relented and jerked his bushy-bearded head in a nod.

"She's a good shot with that carbine of hers," he told the other men. "Reckon we can probably use her help in holding off those outlaws, even though I don't like it."

Warren asked Smoke, "Should we go out and try to recruit some other defenders before dawn, Marshal? Even with the men he's lost, Bishop's gang probably outnumbers those of us in here."

"Probably," Smoke agreed, "but we've risked enough. We can't afford to lose anyone, so I think the smart thing to do is wait here and let Bishop come to us. This is a good strong building, and I think we can hold it."

"What if he decides to attack somewhere else in town first?" Apple Jack asked.

"Then we'll have to go out and stop him," Smoke replied with a grim cast to his features.

"He won't," Windy declared. "He's mad now, and when Snake Bishop gets mad, he goes plumb loco and pizen-mean. He's got his sights set on this bank, and he won't let nothin' stop him from tryin' to take it."

Apple Jack frowned and said, "You almost make it sound like you know this Bishop fella, Windy."

The old-timer glanced at Smoke, the only other person here who knew the truth about his background. Windy took a deep breath and blew it out, causing his mustache to flutter a little.

"I do know him," he declared. He looked around at the other men. "I reckon it's time you fellas knew the truth. There was a time when I rode with Snake Bishop and his bunch. Not for long, mind you, and not from any choice o' my own. I kinda blundered into the deal and then didn't have a good way out right away. But I never took part in any of his raids, and I got away from that dadgum sidewinder as soon as I got the chance." Windy regarded them solemnly and pushed his lips in and out for a second before he went on, "If you want me to leave, just say the word."

"We're not going to banish you into that storm, Windy," Warren said. "You've never been anything but trustworthy since I've known you."

"Yeah, I feel the same way," Apple Jack put in. "I believe you, Windy. Shoot, you've already shed blood fighting Bishop tonight."

Murmurs of agreement came from the others.

Smoke put a hand on Windy's shoulder and said, "It's settled, then. You're one of us, Windy, and nothing more needs to be said about it."

"That's right," a new voice put in. They all looked around to see Sarge Shaw standing there, leaning on a chair he was using as a makeshift crutch to keep the weight off his bandaged leg.

"Should you be up and about, Sarge?" Apple Jack asked.

"I'm feelin' better now," Shaw replied. "And if there's going to be a fight, just try keeping me out of it!"

His wife came up behind him and said, "You'll be wasting your time if you argue with him. This man's head is harder than any rock I've ever seen!"

That drew several chuckles, even in this perilous situation. Smoke was glad to see that the men could still laugh. That relieved the tension a little.

"Right now the storm is still too bad for Bishop to make a move," he said, "and once it lets up, if it does, he'll still need some time to gather his men and get them ready to attack. I don't think anything is likely to happen until dawn. So most of you might as well get some rest while you can."

"Because things are liable to get a mite busy after a while," Windy added.

Snake Bishop tried not to limp as he led the group of men along the street. After one of the bullets thrown at him had creased the outside of his right thigh, he had broken into an empty store, cut up a shirt to make bandages, and wrapped the bindings tightly around his leg. That was enough to stop the bleeding and brace his leg so he could still use it.

He had spent the next several hours roaming around Salt Lick, finding his men in the various places they had taken shelter from the storm. Some were in businesses, others in houses that had been abandoned by their occupants. Bishop didn't know where those townies had gone, but he didn't care as long as they didn't get in his way.

As the gang regrouped, Bishop sent other men out to hunt for the outlaws he hadn't come across yet. He and the rest of the bunch went back to the livery stable. Bishop was ready to fight if the blacksmith, the girl, that old reprobate Windy Whittaker, and whoever Whittaker's ally had been were still there, but the place was empty except for Paco O'Shannon's body.

"Look at that," Bishop had growled to his men. "They murdered poor Paco in cold blood! You can see why I want to leave this town in nothing but ruins when we ride away."

In reality, he knew there was a good chance it was one of *his* bullets that had ripped O'Shannon's throat out, but he didn't see any need to go into that. He wanted to get his men stoked up into a killing frenzy, and O'Shannon's death helped serve that purpose.

The rest of the gang answered Bishop's summons and filtered in during the night, until he had thirty-two men gathered in the barn. He assumed that the ones who hadn't shown up yet wouldn't be coming. The skirmishes during the previous evening had claimed more men than Bishop thought, but he believed he still had more than enough guns to wipe out the town.

The men were hungry, cold, and wanted whiskey and women. They could take care of all of that . . . once they had wiped out Salt Lick's defenders.

Bishop stepped over to the barn's doors and opened one of them enough to peer out into the street. The gray light of approaching dawn filled the air. The wind had dropped down to little more than a breeze. Snow still fell, but only in soft flurries. The white stuff was piled up close to a foot deep in the street and deeper than that where it had drifted. It wasn't enough to cause them any trouble, though.

After studying the street for several minutes, Bishop had decided it was time to make his move. He was too filled with rage to wait any longer. He led the men out of the barn, and now they moved up the street toward the bank.

Before they got too close, however, Bishop ordered, "Split up and spread out. It's possible some of those townies may have forted up in there. We don't want to give them one big target. No more than two or three men in a group. Stay behind cover as much as you can."

For a gang of outlaws, they were actually fairly well-disciplined. They did as Bishop said, breaking up into small groups that advanced up both sides of the street toward the bank, darting from place to place, using parked wagons, water barrels, and building alcoves for cover.

Bishop advanced alone, gun in his right hand and whip in his left. The whip writhed and coiled and left serpentine patterns in the snow.

With the gray light strong enough now to reveal him as he strode along, he knew he was making a target of himself, but he didn't care. He didn't think any of the settlers would have the guts to shoot him. If some of them were holed up inside the bank, they were probably thinking about the best way to beg for mercy . . . mercy that he would never deliver to the likes of them.

He was about half a block away when one of the bank's double doors abruptly opened and a lone man stepped out. Bishop expected him to throw his hands in the air, surrender, and plead for his life.

Instead, the man stood there, tall and broad-shouldered and giving off an almost visible air of calm strength. Bishop stopped short and glared at him, figuring he would cow the man with his fierce expression.

But as if he were just asking an idle question, the man drawled, "I reckon you're Snake Bishop?"

Taken aback by the man's casual attitude, Bishop's scowl became even darker.

"That's right," he said. "Who the hell are you?"

Even at this distance, Bishop could see the faint smile that curved the man's lips.

"I'm Smoke Jensen," he said.

CHAPTER 31

Smoke saw Snake Bishop stiffen in apparent shock as the outlaw realized who he faced. Smoke didn't expect that revelation to make Bishop back down; not for a second did he think that. But he did feel a certain satisfaction in knowing that Bishop was aware of who he faced.

Then Bishop growled, "I don't give a damn," and the hand with the gun in it flashed up. Muzzle flame split the overcast dawn gloom.

Even though Bishop's gun was already drawn, Smoke almost beat him to the shot. The Colt that had leaped into Smoke's hand as if by magic crashed so closely on the heels of Bishop's that the two reports blended into one.

Neither shot found its mark, however. Bishop's bullet was a clean miss that flew past Smoke and chipped brick from the bank's front wall. Smoke's slug tore through the right side of Bishop's coat and narrowly missed his body. Still firing, Bishop broke into a run to his left. As he triggered, he yelled to his men, "Get in there! Kill him! Kill anybody you find!"

Guns roared from both sides of the street. With that storm of lead clawing at the air around him, Smoke had to duck back into the bank and slam the door behind him.

"Here they come," he called to the defenders. "Give them a warm welcome!"

Men with rifles crouched at the loopholes, ready to open fire. Glass shattered as bullets struck the windows from outside, but the thick planks stopped the slugs from penetrating into the lobby. When that first volley from Bishop's gang was over, the men inside the bank returned the fire, spraying lead along the boardwalks on both sides of the street.

At the same time, riflemen in the rooms on the bank's second floor opened the windows there and joined the battle. Tommy Spencer was up there with her carbine, among others.

Smoke had a loaded Winchester waiting for him. He picked it up and joined Windy Whittaker at one of the windows. The old-timer cackled as he blasted shot after shot at the outlaws through a loophole.

"Look at the varmints hop!" he crowed. "They look like horned toads who wandered onto a hot skillet!"

Nearby, Edward Warren and Apple Jack did their part, as well. Beyond them, Sarge Shaw manned one of the shooting positions, sitting on a tall stool from the tellers' cages so he could fire through one of the openings.

The women and children had withdrawn into the vault. The door wasn't completely closed, but it was pushed up enough that a bullet couldn't go through the gap. Ralph Warren hadn't wanted to go, but his parents had insisted and the deep-voiced youngster had complied grudgingly.

For long minutes, the bullets went back and forth so thickly in the street that a bee couldn't have buzzed through them without being hit. Some of the outlaws' shots either found a loophole or punched through the boards over the windows. Inside the bank, a couple of the defenders cried out and fell backward as they were wounded.

Outside, the outlaws didn't have enough good cover, so

the barrage from the bank took a heavier toll. Men toppled off the boardwalk with blood welling from the bullet holes that had sprouted in them. Other outlaws collapsed where they were to twitch away what little was left of their ill-spent lives.

All the bank's windows were broken now, so the cold, early morning wind blew through the lobby, carrying with it a shouted command from Snake Bishop.

"Everybody at them! Now!"

Even though Smoke and the other defenders had inflicted a lot of damage on the gang, there were still plenty of outlaws eager to spill their blood. If they managed to reach the bank itself and poured bullets through the loopholes, the ricochets alone might make the lobby a killing ground.

"We have to stop them!" Smoke called to his new-found friends.

But even as the remaining members of Bishop's gang leaped from cover and charged toward the bank with their guns blazing insanely and spouting flame and lead, an unexpected volley raked them from behind. Several of them stumbled and fell as slugs ripped through them. Smoke raised his eyes from his rifle's sights and peered through the clouds of powder smoke to see a new group of Salt Lick's citizens attacking the outlaws from the rear, catching the gang in a crossfire that was tearing it apart with every second that ticked past.

And leading that second band of citizens, Smoke saw as his spirits leaped, was Jonas Madigan.

"Come on, boys!" Madigan roared to the men with him. "Give 'em hell!"

The gun in Madigan's fist slammed out shot after shot as he and his allies cut down the outlaws. With the gang disoriented, Smoke knew this was the time for the finishing stroke.

"Follow me!" he shouted to the other men in the bank as he leaped to the entrance and slammed the doors aside. He came out shooting, swiveling left to right and back again as he cranked rounds from the Winchester. Every time the rifle cracked, another outlaw fell, drilled cleanly.

A few members of the gang acted like they wanted to throw their guns down and surrender, but then they continued fighting, no doubt realizing that nothing was waiting for them but a hangrope. One by one they fell . . .

Until the only member of Snake Bishop's gang still on his feet was Snake Bishop himself. As the shooting died away, Bishop found himself standing alone with the bloody corpses of his men scattered around him. Either they had protected him inadvertently, or some bizarre providence had, because Bishop appeared to be unwounded as he stood there, gazing around in shock.

Smoke handed his empty Winchester to Windy and strode forward.

"Drop your gun, Bishop," he said. "It's over."

"You . . . you . . . you're Jensen," Bishop snarled.

"That's right."

"Famous gunfighter. Well, you're not faster than my whip—!"

With his left hand, Bishop lashed the whip at Smoke's face, trying to make him flinch. At the same time, Bishop jerked up the gun in his right hand.

Smoke never moved, except to drop his hand to his Colt, pull the iron with smooth, blinding speed, and squeeze the trigger as the barrel came level with Bishop's chest. The roar of Smoke's shot and the crack of the whip blended together.

Smoke lifted his left hand, touched the tip of his index

finger to his cheek. It came away with a tiny spot of crimson on it.

That was as close as Snake Bishop had come.

Bishop staggered, dropped the whip and his gun, and pressed his left hand to his chest. Blood leaked between the splayed fingers. He stared at Smoke for a moment, eyes wide with shock and pain.

Then those eyes glazed over in death and he pitched forward, face down in the bloody snow.

"We done it!" Windy said. "It's over!"

It was, Smoke thought as he slid his Colt back into leather.

He turned to Jonas Madigan, who walked toward him with a big smile on his leathery face.

"You did it, son," he said. "You saved Salt Lick."

"No," Smoke said, "the people of Salt Lick saved the town, Jonas, including you."

"And it felt mighty good, too. Mighty good."

With that, Madigan broke stride and his gun suddenly slipped from his hand. His coat swung aside enough to reveal the dark red stain on his shirt. Smoke sprang forward to catch his old friend as Madigan started to fall.

"Yes, sir," Madigan whispered. "Mighty good . . ."

"I won't go through with this if there's gonna be a bunch of cryin'."

"Yes, you will go through with it," Smoke said firmly, "and if anybody cries, especially Miriam, well, I reckon she's earned the right."

Jonas Madigan chuckled and said, "Yeah, I guess so, for puttin' up with me, anyway."

Windy Whittaker said, "There durned well *better* be a weddin', after I done got myself all slicked up to be the best man." He licked his gnarled old fingers and wiped them over his unruly white hair. The brown tweed suit he wore was dusty and a little moth-eaten, but Windy thought he looked downright spiffy and Smoke wasn't going to contradict him.

"Never heard of a weddin' where the groom got hitched while layin' in bed," Madigan grumbled. "Somebody help me up so we can go out to the parlor. It'll be crowded enough in there."

Smoke glanced at the doctor, who nodded his approval. Madigan's wound had looked bad, but it wasn't fatal, and he still had some time left, according to the physician. Maybe not a whole lot . . . but some.

Enough to make Miriam Dollinger his wife.

Smoke and Windy helped Madigan into the parlor. The former lawman was right: it *was* crowded. Edward Warren was there, along with his son; Tommy Spencer and her father; Apple Jack; Sarge and Charlotte Shaw, Sarge using an actual crutch now; and of course, Smoke and Windy, the doctor, and the pastor of the local Baptist church, who would be presiding over the funerals of the half-dozen citizens killed in the gang's occupation of the town and the ensuing battle. The preacher had a joyous task to carry out, though, before attending to those grim chores.

"Are we ready?" the minister asked.

"Ready as we'll ever be, I reckon," Madigan said. He stood between Smoke and Windy, both of whom were ready to prop him up if need be. Madigan seemed to have found some new strength, however, and he stood tall and straight as he turned toward the parlor door and watched the entrance from the hall leading to the back of the house.

Miriam Dollinger appeared there, wearing a beautiful blue dress, her hair put up, as lovely as could be as she smiled at the man she was about to marry.

She made Smoke think about Sally, and how happy he would be to return home to his own wife. That would have to wait for a spell, because he knew he would need to stay on here until arrangements for a permanent marshal could be made.

One thing had already been decided: whoever took the job would have to be all right with the deputy who came with it.

Windy Whittaker had earned that badge.

And as Miriam stepped up beside Madigan and took his hand, the clouds finally began to break up outside. A ray of sunlight slanted through, and in its glow, a few final snowflakes danced as they settled to the earth.

Visit our website at
KensingtonBooks.com
to sign up for our newsletters, read
more from your favorite authors, see
books by series, view reading group
guides, and more!

BOOK CLUB
BETWEEN THE CHAPTERS

Become a Part of Our
Between the Chapters Book Club
Community and Join the Conversation

Betweenthechapters.net